ALSO BY

V. S. Santoni

I'm a Gay Wizard

IN

THE CITY OF THE NIGHTMARE KING

I'm a Gay Wizard

IN
THE CITY OF THE
NIGHTMARE
KING

V. S. SANTONI

wattpad books

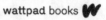

wattpad books

Published in Canada by Wattpad Books, a division of Wattpad Corp.
36 Wellington Street E., Toronto, ON M5E 1C7

www.wattpad.com

First Wattpad Books edition: October 2020
ISBN 978-1-98936-536-6 (Trade Paper original)
ISBN 978-1-98936-544-1 (eBook edition)

Library and Archives Canada Cataloguing in Publication information is available upon request.

Printed and bound in Canada

1 3 5 7 9 10 8 6 4 2

Cover design by Laura Mensinga
Images © grandfailure via Adobe Stock
Typesetting by Sarah Salomon

Author's Note

Dear Reader,

Two terms that featured prominently in the first book have been changed: *Asura*, are now *Void-spawn*, and *Devas* are now *Creators*.

This one's for all my gay wizards

Excerpt from the Diary of an Unknown Wizard

There's an old story that wizards tell around the Institute. Some say they first heard it in the Night Market, that place where all dream creatures slither around. It goes something like this:

> *In the beginning, there was the Void. Darkness. But not nothing. No. Nothing is the absence of something, but this darkness wasn't an absence. It was alive. Maybe the Void was one consciousness, or maybe there's no such thing as oneness in the Void—either way, some of the Void split away and became the immortal Void-spawns.*
>
> *Some Void-spawns were content to exist in the endless nothing, but others longed for more than the Void's cold embrace. They longed for love. They dreamed of it, despite having never*

known such a feeling. Some say their dreams took on a life of their own and became Everywhen—the dreamworld. Those Void-spawns fled into Everywhen, and absent of the Void's influence became the Creators.

The Void grew jealous, sending its loyal Void-spawns to destroy the world the Creators had built; however, the Creators had planned for such treachery and built another world— ours. Using clockwork that they'd forged in Everywhen, they built this world and gave it meaning, purpose. And so, before the Void-spawns could wipe them out, the Creators fled into our world, continuing their quest to build a place of infinite love.

But the Void's loyal servants wouldn't let the Creators go in peace. They chased them, fought them, hunted them down. The war lasted eons. Some say the Void-spawns eventually succeeded in their tireless quest to annihilate the Creators, but in doing so lost their way back to the Void and became trapped in the maze of Everywhen. As the story goes, the Void-spawns came to know our world, their new prison, as a cursed land that damned their bodies to an endless cycle of death and rebirth.

Many in the Night Market insist that a shadow war continues between the Creators and the Void-spawns, and that wizards are their descendants.

When We Last Met Johnny and Alison . . .

After outcasts Alison and Johnny barely survived a run-in with a gang of bullies, Alison encountered a pale woman in black who offered a book that promised her revenge. She convinced Johnny to help her, and they cast a haywire spell, causing an earthquake in their hometown, and making the Marduk Institute—a secret organization that claimed to train wizards—aware of their existence. The Institute kidnapped Alison and Johnny, whisking them away to a walled-in facility in the Ozarks. The Institute's head scientist, Melchior, explained that Alison and Johnny's power allowed them to manifest psychic phenomena in inexplicable forms. Melchior also told them that their old lives had been erased. The Institute was no magic school—it was a prison.

Inside, they met fellow prisoners Blake and Linh. Blake told them wizard society was divided into two castes: wizards born into long-running magical bloodlines, called Lineages; and those who weren't, non-Lineages. Legacies, magical fraternities that conferred great privilege and power to their inductees, helped Lineage children maintain their family's generational wealth and power. But the Legacies also allowed some non-Lineage wizards to join their ranks in exchange for loyalty—for helping to protect wizard society's old hierarchal power structures.

When Johnny started classes, he met fellow non-Lineage wizard Hunter, and their fates became inextricably entwined. Over the coming months, a vicious monster Johnny called *the Sandman* plagued his dreams. Johnny and Alison delved into uncovering the Institute's secrets and came across a mysterious man in white who led them to a clockwork manual. Johnny initially dismissed the manual as useless. After Johnny discovered a Defector conspiracy within the Institute, the mysterious man in white manipulated Johnny into escaping, convincing the boy that only he could help Johnny defeat the Sandman. Linh helped Johnny and his friends break out, but Johnny didn't follow the Defectors to Sanctuary. Instead, he chose to find the elusive man in white, Gaspar, a long-defected former Institute scientist.

At Gaspar's hideout, Johnny and Alison came across the woman who gave them the earthquake spell book. Gaspar and the woman, a black cat Mara, deceived Johnny and Alison to conjure a cintamani—a legendary wishing stone. Summoning the stone also unleashed the Sandman, a powerful being sworn to annihilate any who sought the cintamani. Gaspar revealed that the Institute cursed all non-Lineage wizards to death, and he intended to use the cintamani to destroy the Institute and liberate wizardkind. The black cat Mara, however, solely desired to send herself back to the Void.

Johnny and Hunter ventured into Everywhen to retrieve the stone, but when they finally found it, it merged with Hunter's soul and he *became* the cintamani. The black cat Mara, the only one who knew how to activate the cintamani, used its power to return to the Void. Before Gaspar could use the rest of the stone's power to destroy the Institute, Hunter used it to banish himself and the Sandman to the Void, saving Johnny from the undefeatable creature.

The Institute felled Gaspar and recaptured Johnny and his friends. Melchior scanned their thoughts and gathered everything they knew about the Defectors. Later, Johnny discovered the clockwork manual he'd earlier dismissed and realized that it belonged to Gaspar. In the book, Johnny found a spell called *unwinding*, that allowed him to retrieve things from the Void. Using the spell, Johnny reached into the Void and pulled Hunter back out, rescuing him.

Chapter 1

Joey Ramone's voice came blaring through the radio, hiccupping Dad's favorite old punk song. The racket jolted my nervous system, like being hit with an electrical wire only more nasally. A tropical air freshener hung from a vent flap. Dad's favorite scent—Hawaiian Breeze. Hadn't smelled that since the Institute kidnapped me. Next to me, Dad drummed on his steering wheel and mouthed lyrics. Outside, trees rushed by in a warm green blur. *Wait—where the hell am I?* I thought. *What the hell's Dad doing sitting next to me?*

He took his eyes off his road long enough to give me a funny look. "You all right, Juanito?" Dad didn't have an accent. When he said my name in Spanish it always sounded a little funny. His familiar voice almost hypnotized me.

My last memory put me at the Marduk Institute. But now I found myself in Dad's Camry while he drove down a backroad.

"You . . . remember me?" I asked, confused. The Institute claimed it had purged us from our loved ones' memories.

"Juanito, did you bump your head?"

White flowers bloomed on the catalpa trees roadside—springtime. Dad's touchscreen dashboard read *March 29, 2020*. The last three months floated around like bits and pieces in my head, but I didn't remember anything specific about them. Dad turned left down an exit with a beat-up road sign that read *Misthaven*. Misthaven, the northern Missouri town outside the Institute. Melchior had warned us that it was under heavy surveillance. An unlikely coincidence. But my memories leading up to this moment didn't make sense. Sometime in December I'd gone looking for Gaspar. After the Institute recaptured us, everything got blurry. "Dad, what's going on?"

"Juanito, are you okay?" Dad tested my head for a fever. I flinched when he touched me. His hands felt real. Real as the seat I was sitting on, or the trees flying by outside, or the air blowing through the vents. This couldn't be a dream.

"Dad, what's going on?"

"Weeeeell, we're on our way to a town called Misthaven. I got a job at a newspaper there, remember?"

No. I didn't. Or maybe I did. Memories poured in like grains of sand. Mom and Dad finalized their divorce last fall, then Dad fell into a deep depression and struggled to find meaningful work for a few months. Alison's mom had died in December. The *Misthaven Inquirer* offered Dad a job in . . . February—maybe early March?—so we picked up and left Chicago.

This had to be a spell. More Institute magic. Or, what if it wasn't? What if the Institute and all my experiences—meeting Hunter and Blake and Linh, fighting all those monsters, breaking out—had never happened? My memories blanked out after Gaspar's. Besides, if all that had really happened, why did I also remember Dad getting the job in Misthaven? Even the night before the big drive stayed fresh in my mind: Dad had told me to tape up all the boxes, and I whined because movers were coming to do it in the morning anyway. *Remember what Tia Frances always says, Juanito*, Dad had told me, *si lo puedes hacer tu mismo, lo haces*. Aunt Frances' Spanish idiom meant, "If you can do it yourself, you do it."

Then there was Alison. My last night in Chicago, she visited me and told me her grandma wanted to move to Florida.

She lamented on my bed about the bare walls stripped of band posters. "Where's that signed *Black Parade* poster you had?" she asked. She loved that one. I won it in an online giveaway. I'd stashed it away to give to her before I left. When I handed it to her, all rolled up and cinched with rubber bands, she looked like she wanted to slap it out of my hands. But she didn't. She just cried. I did too.

Melchior's words in the white room at the Institute, where they took me after extraction, rang sharply: "Imagine the world around you as a ticking clock"—then epiphany struck. One last test, to make sure this was real. Eyes closed, I pictured the vivit apparatus, the magical clockwork that governed our reality. When wizards moved the cogs and wheels—whether with their minds or their hands—it caused unexplainable phenomena: magic. To see the clockwork, wizards need only imagine it in their mind's eye. The machinery's orange-gold color shimmered with a brightness that even shone past closed eyelids.

"Juanito, what're you doing? You're acting strange?"

Nothing—no glowing clockwork. The magical foundation no longer ticked and tocked behind reality. Maybe it never existed at all.

"Are you okay, Johnny?"

"Yeah, Dad. I'm . . . I'm fine."

We drove along Main Street, past the *Welcome to Misthaven* sign and a long-abandoned fairground, both on my right. It all looked familiar. Town hall stood at a fork where Clanden Road and Main Street intersected. Dad veered right at the crossroad, eventually passing the Misthaven Fire Department, and drove until he reached Pine Street, where he headed left. The road led up to an idyllic subdivision past a wooden sign that read *The Pines*. White colonials lined the street on both sides, and elm trees swathed the lane in broken shadows. Each house came outfitted with its own little portico and a miniature American flag in brackets near the front door. No denying it: I knew this place. I rolled down my window. Barbecue soaked the air with a delicious smell, and children played loudly. I first visited Misthaven with Hunter. We rode in from the Institute on a small bus, and Hunter spent the whole day showing me around. Nothing had changed. How was that possible if my memories weren't real?

Dad parked in our new driveway and stepped outside, knotting his fingers behind his back and stretching with a grunt. Our house dripped with the same pastoral energy as every other aluminum-sided *Better Homes and Gardens* photo op in the neighborhood. Places like this—bucolic little towns where people still left their doors unlocked and everyone knew each other—always grabbed me as urban myths.

"Isn't this place beautiful," Dad said excitedly. He never gave me the impression he wanted to live somewhere like this. He still wore cut-off shirts because he liked showing off his sleeve tattoo, which he got during his drummer-in-a-screamo-band days. How would the PTA moms here respond to a tattooed single dad and his kid with the stretched earlobes? I walked to the driveway's edge to scope things out.

Across the street, an old man in a bucket hat watered his primrose bush with a garden hose. He noticed me staring and waved. I did the same, awkwardly. Dad opened the front door and walked in, and I abandoned my investigation and followed. Light flowed in through the many windows, showering the inside. The entryway parted the living room on the left and the dining room on the right. A sunroom bridged the den and the back porch, and a stairwell to the second floor divided the kitchen and the dining room.

A moving truck pulled up to the mailbox. Dad stepped outside to give them a hand. I ambled into the sunroom. The previous owner left behind a coat rack, and a fire poker in a metal stand on the hearth. Our freshly trimmed backyard offered no clues, so I headed back inside to search for cameras hidden under the vent covers. The front door swung open and a mover staggered in with his back to me, struggling to squeeze our couch through the opening. Dad wedged himself through the doorway and tried to help them, but the mover dropped the couch. I caught it before it smashed Dad's toe, though. He thanked me and walked into the kitchen, allowing the movers to finish their job without his meddling.

Having turned up nothing downstairs, I headed to the second floor and crept into the master bedroom. I checked the bathroom, opening the medicine cabinet and all the drawers, looking for anything that might lead me back to the Institute. My search proved fruitless.

I thought about using magic even though I didn't excel at it—it had taken me months to learn how to cast a light sword (a dangerous spell if you didn't know the physics behind it). I imagined heat gathering in my palm, light rays coalescing into a glowing ball. The next step required courage and caution. If I cast aside those pre-requisites, I chanced the spell going haywire and turning into a fire-ball and blowing me up. My magic really shined in Everywhen, the dreamworld, because I'd spent the most time there harnessing my abilities against the Sandman. The unpredictable risks involved in using magic in the real world turned me off to the idea altogether. Besides, I hadn't even managed the first step.

The Marduk Institute's website, I thought. It turned up once before, during my initial investigations into the Institute. A quick phone search could answer many questions. Unfortunately, it wasn't in my pockets. I headed downstairs and into the kitchen, where Dad kept a watchful eye on the movers.

"It's a new start for us, kiddo," Dad said when he saw me. "No more dirty city with all that smog and all those rude people." A mover dropped a box labeled *Books*. "Hey, careful! There's some good stuff in there."

"Dad, do you have my phone?"

He felt his pockets and pulled it out. "You left it in the car."

A search for "Marduk Institute" didn't uncover anything. No suspicious webpages detailing an elite microcommunity with a private school for gifted children. It didn't matter what search engine I used, the results never changed. The Marduk Institute simply didn't exist. And if the Institute didn't exist, I didn't dream this place up, either. Even if Misthaven appeared familiar, it must've been a coincidence. A very, *very* strange coincidence.

The movers carried and hauled and lifted and pushed and pulled until they'd gotten everything inside. After they'd left, Dad hauled me into the living room, where boxes lay stacked shoulder to shoulder.

"Let's clear out some of the boxes in here before dinner time, okay?"

Dad handed me a box cutter and pointed to the stack in the bay window. I eased the top one down, then dropped to one knee and sliced it open. Junk bundled in Bubble Wrap filled the inside. A picture frame with a family photo sat near the top. Even after the divorce, Dad's sentimental nature prevented him from throwing away all these old photos. This one was from one of our many excursions to North Avenue Beach. Mom stood to my right, in a wide-brimmed hat and a floral-print sarong over a striped bathing suit. Dad wore blue swim trunks and a ratty white shirt, and flashed a peace sign with a cheesy grin. I jutted out between them with a silly look on my face, wearing an outfit that made me look like Dad's Mini-Me. Mom and Dad had met at North Avenue Beach, where they'd communed over their creative interests. We'd gone there at least once a year.

"Do you ever . . . miss our family—me, you, and Mom?" I asked.

Dad stopped rummaging. "It takes a lot more than a piece of paper to make a family, Juanito. A family isn't something you're born into, or two people taking wedding vows. A family is something deeper, and a real family can endure anything." Dad always said stuff like that—more for himself than for me. He turned back to the box. "Oh wow," he said, taking out an old handheld radio. "I haven't seen this thing in years."

"What is it?"

"A shortwave AM radio. I used it when I was a kid to look for number stations."

"Number stations?"

"They're like top-secret spy broadcasts. Well, they might be. They might be aliens, for all we know." He checked the radio for batteries and out clunked two Duracells. They'd probably been gathering dust in there since the '90s. "Let me go find some batteries." Dad headed upstairs to check his electronics box. The family photo drew me back in. We looked really happy in it. I wanted to feel that way again: part of a family—a whole family, not something people dismissed as "broken."

Dad walked back in with new batteries, slid them into the radio, then flipped it on. Fuzzy static poured out of the speakers. "All right!" Dad said. Now that the old thing lived again, he set about fiddling with the tuner. A boy's garbled voice mumbled something through the speaker.

"Wait—" Dad put his ear to it "—I think we have something."

He fingered the dial until the voice came through clearly: "You are trapped in a dream! You are trapped in a dream!"

Dad raised an eyebrow, unable to comprehend the boy's words, but the message turned my blood to ice. The frequency dropped, and I quickly snatched the radio and started turning the knob, searching for the signal, but the speaker only pumped out static.

"Juanito, you okay?" Dad asked.

Dad had always said I was pale for a kid born to a pair of islanders. I'm sure I looked even ghastlier than usual right then. It took me a few beats to collect myself. "Yeah, I'm fine."

He studied me a second longer, not sure why my skin had suddenly gone pale. Then he rested his hands on my shoulders. "Let's take a break and get something to eat." He walked into the kitchen to look for his phone, but I stayed in the living room, staring at the radio, thinking about the ominous message. The more I thought about it, though, the more I doubted myself. After spending the whole day psyching myself out, my mind was playing tricks on me.

"Johnny, do you want some pizza?" Dad asked.

Pizza, the panacea for my concerns. Worrying served no purpose. Our little family thrived again. Far from perfect, but it was mine. This demanded celebration, not suspicion. No more harrowing descents into Everywhen; no more epic clashes with the Institute.

Chapter 2

Dad and I settled around the dining room table. He had ordered a pizza from the local Italian place, Maria's. It had pineapple and jalapeno on it, my favorite (I don't trust people who don't like pineapple on their pizza). Dad always said you didn't know a place until you had the local pizza. If the sauce was too bitter, then the place probably wasn't very friendly. Too many toppings? Too many problems. Too few toppings? Too little money. Maria's pizza sauce was too sweet. But I didn't care. The Institute was fading like a bad dream, and for the first time in months, I felt happy.

"What're you so happy about?" Dad teased.

I walked around the table and wrapped my arms around his shoulders, and I stayed there for a good long minute. Dad put his hands on my forearms and squeezed, but my sudden affectionate burst confused him. "Come on, Juanito. You never act like this. What's up?"

"I'm just glad to see you happy, Dad."

"You want to watch *The Nightmare Before Christmas* after dinner?"

It was our favorite movie. I settled back down. "Sure."

The doorbell rang. Dad and I gave each other a curious glance. We didn't know anyone in Misthaven. Hopefully the neighbors hadn't decided to come over and drop off a welcoming casserole. Our neighbors in Chicago never did stuff like that, thankfully. Dad headed for the door, and I followed.

"I'm coming!" Dad shouted.

Dad opened the door to Alison on the other side, standing there with her grandma, Hilda. Hilda wore a teal, flamingo-print muu-muu, with her braided ponytail slung over her shoulder. Alison was draped in all black as usual. Something about Alison struck me. Not her looks or anything superficial like that. The feeling reso-nated deeper. She *felt* more real than everything else around her.

"Good evening, Ernesto," Hilda said.

"Hilda, Alison, why don't you two come in," Dad said. He didn't sound surprised to see them. My shock at seeing Alison froze me in place, so Dad nudged me out of their way. They slipped off their shoes and set them near the door, then Dad gestured to the dining room. "We've got some pizza if you two would like some?"

"How kind," Hilda said. Alison and Hilda headed in first, and I waited for everyone to sit before I joined. With no appetite in sight, I studied Alison's hair, her eyes, the way she placed her body.

She shifted uncomfortably and flipped her hair over her shoul-ders. "Nice to you see you too, J."

"I, uh—hey, sorry. I was . . . thinking . . . about something." The jarring situation left me forgetting to act normal. Alison leaned forward and examined me. Something about that glint in her eye, like she trying to figure out if I were real or not. Dad and Hilda's presence there kept me from popping off about the Institute.

Dad reached across the table and set a plate in front of her. He did the same for Hilda, but she waved it off. "I'll just have a cool drink," she said. German immigrants had raised Hilda in Chicago. Her accent fell somewhere between Midwestern and European. Dad walked into the kitchen and brought back a water pitcher and poured her a glass. She took a gentle sip then set the glass on the table and placed her hands in her lap. Stiff as ever. It was like sitting with royalty. That haughtiness had rubbed off on Alison.

Alison's pizza lay untouched on her plate. Did she remember the Institute too? That would explain the strange behavior. Her attention shifted to my dad, then to the room.

"You're not hungry," my dad said delicately to Alison.

"Hmm?" She caught herself. "Oh no, I'm not that hungry."

Hilda's patience for Alison's manners had dried up years ago, which she conveyed with a sharp look.

"Johnny," Dad looked pointedly at my food. The greasy pizza stained the paper plate with a big orange spot. Maria's pizza looked good at first, but really it was trash. "You aren't hungry either?"

No. My hunger had evaporated upon seeing Alison. But I nervously lifted the pizza and took a bite anyway. My actions pressured Alison to do the same. "Mmm, yum," she said in a way both awkward and curt. Alison's emotions always rested on the surface, making her extremely easy to read. Her discomfort mirrored my own. Was her mind like mine, a jumble of fragmented memories?

Hilda cleared her throat and clacked her nails against the table. The quiet unsettled my dad too. They wanted Alison and me to carry on like we always did, but we were too busy psychologically profiling each other.

"When do you start your new job?" Hilda said, her words cutting the tension.

Dad kept his focus on me. "Tomorrow."

"This is quite the departure from Chicago, Johnny. Do you think you'll like it?" the old woman asked.

My head wasn't in the right place to field questions. The whole predicament weirded me out. "I—yeah, sure. I'll get used to it."

"That's a good mentality for you to have." She sounded happy with my answer. "I know things were difficult for you two in Chicago, but here you get a *fresh new start*. I hope you won't try to stand out too much again." That meant she hoped we'd go back into the closet. As she saw it, Alison and I going back into the closet guaranteed us a smooth return to "normalcy." Typically, Alison responded to Hilda's passive-aggressive bullshit with her own searing candor. Her choice to let Hilda's words slide spoke volumes.

"Johnny, you've been acting weird all day," Dad said, checking my head again for a fever. "You sure you're doing all right?"

"What's going on?" I asked suddenly. "Are you two just visiting, or what?"

"Well," Dad said, "the school year's almost over, so Alison is coming to stay with us for the summer. If she wants to finish school here, I told Hilda that I'd keep her." Dad waited for Alison and me to squeal, but when we didn't he looked disappointed. "Isn't that . . . exciting?"

"Yes!" Alison said, with such thunder in her voice that it shocked me. "We are very excited!" Her jubilation rang hollow. She was acting. Back in Chicago, she'd forced me to join theater club. The teacher always criticized her for overacting. At the time the criticism pissed her off, but she never lost that tendency.

"Yeah!" I backed her with a big, fake, toothy smile. "This is awesome. I can't believe you guys did this." Maybe I overdid things a little too.

"And behind our backs too," Alison said. "You two sure are some sneaky emm-effs."

"Alison!" Hilda said.

Alison corrected herself: "Uh, sneaky *rascals*."

"Will you be staying the night?" Dad asked Hilda.

"No. Our family is expecting me by tomorrow afternoon. I'll be driving the rest of the evening." Hilda scooted her seat back and rose. "Thank you for inviting me in, Ernesto. Alison, walk me out, dear."

"I'll come with you," I said, eager to continue my analysis.

We walked Hilda outside. Alison and Hilda didn't speak on the way to Hilda's old station wagon. Their already-awkward relationship had grown tense after Ali came out. Verbal sparring matches between Alison's mom, Cecilia, and Hilda occurred with some frequency at their house. They didn't even say goodbye before Hilda got in the car, revved the engine, and left. Alison watched the car until it vanished in the distance.

Finally alone, I felt safe asking Alison what she remembered. If she didn't know anything, she'd tell me. "Hey, Ali, what did you do in February?"

My question rattled her. It could've meant anything, but the ghostly look on her face said a lot about what she was thinking. She concocted several answers but never spoke a single one. "I don't . . . remember. Weirdly."

Her memories didn't match up either. The three months before we found ourselves entering Misthaven remained blurry. "Alison, do you remember . . . *anything*?"

"What do you mean?"

"Do you remember . . . the Marduk Institute?"

Her ghostly look turned to dread. "Yes."

"What exactly do you remember?"

"I don't know. It's kind of—"

"Patchy?"

"Yeah."

"Like you remember some things but not everything?"

"What's going on?"

"I don't know."

Dad came to the front door. "Hey, you two. Are you just going to stand in the driveway all night?"

There was no way we'd had the same dream. If she remembered the Institute, then she had to remember Blake and Hunter and Linh. But why couldn't we remember everything?

Chapter 3

With a great many questions lingering, I told Dad I wanted to show Alison my new room and dragged her upstairs. She ambled about in there and absorbed her new surroundings. It didn't look that different from my old room in Chicago. A vanity with a mirror sat near the door, and my bed lay pressed up against a wall because I slept like an overly defensive dog. Not much else in there but piled, unopened boxes.

"Ali," I said, "do you remember Blake, Hunter, Linh—the Defectors?"

"Yeah."

"What about being extracted into the white room? The vivit apparatus?"

"I . . . It's like I remember some stuff, and it seems totally real, but other stuff—like you moving and everything—that seems real too."

"Like you have two totally different sets of memories?"

"Just like that. Hey, hold on," she said, suspicion rising, "how do I know you're really you?"

"What?"

"How do I know you're really Johnny?"

"How do I know you're really Alison?"

She looked perplexed. "You still kind of . . . *feel* like Johnny?"

Magic coursed through all life, and its spark enveloped almost everything except for ordinary humans in mystical energy called an aura. Wizards sensed auras in two ways. The wizard sight allowed them to physically see, or *hard-read*, the aura as a golden halo shining around the subject. Hard-reading also gave the wizard the power to visualize the vivit apparatus. I knew from earlier I couldn't use my wizard sight's hard-reading aspect. The second method wizards used to detect auras was more subtle, passive. Wizards could emotionally feel auras. They manifested as a wave of smells and sounds and emotions. Alison's aura sounded like an aisle of electronic Halloween decorations coming to life all at once. The noises were faint, but they were still there. This told me that our wizard senses, although substantially dulled, hadn't vanished completely.

Alison looked uncomfortable with the realization that our wizard senses still worked. "Something weird is going on. Creepy too. You think this is all some Institute trick?"

"How do we find out?"

"Have you tried any other magic-y stuff?"

"Yeah, none of it worked."

"Well, if we're here, Blake's got to be here too."

"And Hunter?"

"Yeah, J, Hunter too."

Dad knocked. I opened the door. He stood there, still chewing pizza, greasy sauce staining his lips. "Hey, Alison, I know it's been a long day for you. If you're not hungry, you can just go take a bath. I've got towels and everything. Johnny, I know you're excited to see her, but why don't you let her settle in and come finish dinner?"

"I'm not hungry," I said. Dad was being weirdly helicopter-y. Or maybe he found our behavior a little strange. Either way, his parental oversight irritated me.

Alison patted me on the shoulder and headed for the door. "We'll talk more tomorrow, J. I need a shower, or I'm going to stink like that mothball-ridden car." She stopped next to Dad. "All right, Mr. D, lead me to my *boudoir*."

How she managed such a nonchalant attitude at a time like this didn't make sense. Regardless, she got Dad off our asses.

Before heading to bed, I thought about Everywhen, the dream-world all humans shared that only wizards held the power to control. Wizards' abilities flourished in the dreamworld. If magic still coursed in my veins, it assured me easy command over my dreams. I thought to test that theory. That night I dreamt, but no magic granted me power over it. I attended the dream as an observer:

I lay in my Veles Hall dorm, poring over Gaspar's notes. His secrets were disguised in a handwritten clock-building manual. He spent his time at the Institute researching the Void, tossing random things into it—lamps, car parts, cutlery—then fishing them back out to study the effects. The book contained the spell he used to fetch things back out—he called it *unwinding* because the spell "unwound the Void's threads from around a subject." Reportedly, things usually returned in one piece without any strange consequences. The Void didn't destroy anything caught in its cold vastness. It merely held them in a sort of stasis. Hunter, having become the cintamani, exhausted its power to banish the Sandman to the Void and sent him along with it, but according to Gaspar's notes, that meant Hunter hadn't really died—at least, I hoped not. Theoretically, the Void kept Hunter's soul in a torpid state, but it didn't whittle it away or kill it. Using the manual, I reached into the vivit apparatus and conjured a glowing machine that shone with a weak, pulsing red. I tampered with the engine until it whirled to life, then I waited for Hunter to materialize before me. But he never came. So, I stormed through Veles Hall looking for him. My investigation led back to my dorm, where Hunter tumbled out of my standup closet and sent us both crashing to the floor with him naked on top of me.

He smiled in my face and said hey and kissed me, and then shivered as a draft filled the room. He looked down then and realized he was naked as a cat, and jumped off me and covered himself with his hands. "Johnny!" he said, searching for something to cover up with. He pulled off my sheet and wrapped it around himself. "What the hell's going on?"

"You used the cintamani to get rid of the Sandman, but it sent you both to the Void."

"Weirdly enough, I kind of remember that."

"So . . . you were trapped in the Void?"

He flipped his straight brown hair out of his eyes. Cute boyfriend was very cute. "I guess. I—I was somewhere really dark. Then all this light shined all around me and I ended up"—Hunter scanned my room—"here."

Two Smiths, one with blond hair and the other black, kicked

in my door. The black-haired Smith grappled me into a corner. Hunter swiftly kicked the blond in the stomach and ran for the door, but the Smith caught Hunter's sheet and pulled him back. Then the blond Smith sprayed Hunter in the face with *eirineftis*.

Eirineftis stunk like rotten raspberries. At low doses it neutralized our powers, but at higher doses it worked as a full-on knockout gas. We didn't know where it came from or how the Institute made it, but if you heard a Smith rattling a canister inside their blazer, you had better steer clear.

The Smith holding me back reached into his blazer, fumbled out his own can, and sprayed me too. That dreadful odor brought tears to my eyes. They burned. Then came a cough, a hack, a deep wheeze.

And I woke up and rolled off my bed and hit the floor.

Daylight filtered in through the window behind my desk. The dream left my heart racing. But in my chest there was also yearning— for Hunter. I missed his big cute grin and his squinty green eyes. My Institute memories didn't seem all that believable considering I lacked the power to control dreams, but the dream itself said otherwise.

I dashed into Alison's room and shook her awake. "Alison, wake up. I had a really weird dream."

She got up and yawned. "Probably not as weird as the one where I'm married to Ross Lynch, and Harry Styles is our baby."

"What?"

"Nothing. You were saying something?"

"I had this book, it was a notebook—Gaspar's notebook—and it had this spell inside that I used to pull Hunter out of the Void, and he was naked—"

"Gross, J, I don't want to hear about your weird sex dreams."

"Ali, do you remember? Hunter used that cintamani thing to stop the Sandman. Remember?"

Quiet revelation crept across her face. "I'm not sure. Kind of?"

"What do you mean?"

She searched her thoughts for a proper response. "I don't know how to put it—it's like . . . when you have a word on the tip of your tongue, but you can't remember it."

"So, it feels familiar?"

"Mmhmm, but nothing comes to mind."

Dad knocked on the door frame. "Hey, kiddos," he said, kicking into a strange jig in the hallway. "You two ready for school?" We stared until he felt awkward about the weird dance. Embarrassed, he straightened up and cleared his throat. "You better get ready. Don't want to be late."

We waited until he'd left to keep talking. "We've got to find Blake and Hunter. If they remember, too, then this place must be a trick," I said.

"Definitely. Now let's hurry and get ready before your dad has a stroke."

Dad wrangled Alison and me into the car. Alison chewed on her thumbnail and stared out the window in the backseat. I didn't plan on staying in school all day, not when there was an important investigation to undertake.

"Now I know you two think I'm some musty old boomer, but I'm actually Gen X—" Dad rambled. His voice sent shivers up my spine. Alison still *felt* like Alison, but something about him was off. He didn't give me a feeling at all. It's like he was empty.

If this place wasn't real like the voice on the radio had said, who was the guy sitting next to me, and how was he able to mimic my dad so well?

"You okay, kiddo?" he asked me.

"I'm fine," I said, hastily deflecting his question.

Misthaven High School was just outside the Pines, not far from Dad's new house. Parents dropped their kids off at a sidewalk around a traffic circle out in front. Dad pulled up behind a gray Scion and parked along the curb. He reached over and handed me a jingly pair of keys. "One's for you and the other's for Alison. Do you both have your phones?"

"Sure do," Alison said, already heading out the door.

"I love you, kiddo," Dad said to me.

A brown boy with curly hair hopped out of the gray Scion and climbed some steps to a lightly packed concourse before the main building. He stopped near four other kids gathered around a bench under an oak tree. A girl with blond hair hugged him and he laughed and greeted the others—friends obviously. I didn't know why the scene riveted me. Thunder groused in the cottony slate-colored sky.

Dad's words finally reached me. "Love you too, Dad." He was still staring at me when I opened the door and chased after Alison.

"That guy isn't my dad," I said as we walked onto the concourse. Alison didn't respond. She kept extra guarded around new people. Her looks already attracted a lot of attention, but her height drew especially curious eyes. I decided against making her any more uneasy, given our situation. We didn't get too many looks on our way into the main building, though.

A chipped and faded black dragon mural with the words *Misthaven Drakes* encircling it hung over the main office's entrance. A musty smell filled the cramped office, making me want to gag.

Alison turtled her hand into her sleeve and used it to pinch her nose. A middle-aged secretary handed us our schedules and locker tickets. I stored the schedule in my back pocket. We hurried outside and up a staircase, leaving the main building via a skywalk that connected to the second one. Alison and I slowed down and studied our surroundings. The high school was a piffling three buildings, each two stories tall, but the scant number of students made it feel bigger. We found our locker in an alcove. Unlike our school in Chicago, each student only got a half locker. I didn't hate that because Spencer Pruitt, the bully at our old school, used to stuff me into the full-sized ones so much they made me anxious. Alison got the top locker.

"I'm on bottom," I said.

"All your life," she said.

I stored my backpack and checked the schedule. English at 7:20. Math at 8:15. The blandness made me miss the Institute. That felt a little messed up. I found myself craving a nasty Styrofoam-tasting bagel from the break room in Veles Hall. Alison analyzed her locker like she didn't know what to do with it. Her old one in Chicago primarily housed My Chemical Romance posters.

"What're you thinking about?" I asked, not because I didn't already know but because I wanted her to prove me right.

"I'm trying to figure out what to do with this locker." Called it.

A familiar chuckle drew my attention. Shock washed over me in tingly waves when I saw Hunter standing near some lockers close to ours, laughing and joking with three other guys, all of them wearing Drake's letterman jackets.

"Alison, look," I said, tugging her shirt.

Alison narrowed her eyes at first then leaned forward. "Is that—"

"It's Hunter. Let's go talk to him." Alison didn't look too sure about going over there and striking up a conversation with those guys, but we needed to find out if Hunter recognized us.

We approached Hunter and his friends. They stopped talking as we neared, two of them ogling Alison. She gave me a funny look then fired them a dismissive smile.

"Hey, man, I like your shirt," Hunter said, staring at my Twenty-One Pilots T-shirt. "I love that band!"

Our eyes met, but there was no connection. I waited for him to recognize us, but when he didn't, I briefly balled up my hands, nails digging into my palms. Unlike my dad, some unexplainable instinct told me this *was* Hunter. Alison bumped me with her elbow. We didn't have all day for me to build the courage to ask him if he remembered us.

"Thanks," I said, cracking a grin. "Do you . . . remember us?"

The question took him by surprise. He uneasily stole a look at his friends, gauging their reactions, but they looked just as confused. "No?" he said sweetly. That one declaration crushed all my hopes. I refused to believe I'd dreamt him up, though. As great as Hunter was, he was no figment. There had to be some reason he didn't remember us.

I fought back a dour expression and smiled. "Sorry, I must have you confused with someone else."

"My name's Hunter, what's yours?"

Oh, the angst. I wanted to punch myself until I had no teeth. "Johnny."

One of Hunter's friends checked out Alison and said, "And your friend's?"

"This is Alison."

"Hey, Alison," Hunter's friend said to her. "Mine's Scott."

Alison scanned him: He had a thick, meaty neck, sparkly blue eyes, and black hair. But she didn't feel like flirting with cute jocks. "Hey, Scott."

"You're like a sexy vampire." Did he really think that sounded like a compliment?

"Lucky for you I don't bite virgins."

Hunter suddenly raised a hand to his head, briefly losing balance. Scott eased an arm around Hunter's back and steadied him. "You all right, bro?"

"Yeah," Hunter said, regaining composure. "Just one of my headaches." The first bell rang. "Hey, maybe I'll see you around," Hunter said, softly patting me on the arm before walking away with his friends. I watched him until Alison nudged me.

"He doesn't remember us," I said.

"Maybe he's like Sleeping Beauty and needs true love's kiss to help snap him out of it."

"What do we do?"

"I don't know. Were those guys checking me out?"

I was taken aback. "What're you talking about, Ali?"

"Those guys with Hunter. Were they checking me out?"

"What—I don't know!"

"Fine, whatever. Maybe we'll bump into Blake."

Alison and I parted ways because we didn't have homeroom together. I walked to the third building and into Room 203. Science tables divided in two rows filled the stuffy lab. Students occupied almost every seat, except for one near the back. Hunter sat there talking to a brown-haired girl at the table in front of his. He noticed me browsing for an empty seat and waved me over. Our homeroom teacher, who stayed behind her desk checking her teeth for lipstick stains, didn't even see me walk in. *Good*, I thought. I settled next to Hunter as the last bell rang. The teacher took roll and, finally spotting me, made me introduce myself. Then the announcements came on, and some soulless sounding girl rambled about PTA meetings and lunch programs.

Hunter folded his arms on the desk and lay his head down, looking up at me while the announcements droned. "Why'd you move here at the end of the school year?"

"My dad got a job and we had to move."

"Where'd he get a job at?"

"The *Misthaven Inquirer.*"

Hunter straightened up. "Your dad works at the newspaper? That's cool. My parents are farmers." That didn't surprise me. This Hunter mirrored my real boyfriend in almost every way. "Where do you live?"

"The Pines."

"I live out in the country."

The brown-haired girl spun around to us. "Hey, Hunter's new friend."

"This is Tiffany," Hunter said.

With her long, wavy brown hair, bright-eyed expression, and sharp, angular features, Tiffany looked sixteen going on twenty-five. She probably smoked a pack a day and drank a bottle of Evan Williams before every football game.

"Hey," I said, and the two of them went on discussing some drama I was not privy to.

I needed to meet up with Alison after class, to continue our investigation. I texted her to meet me outside after homeroom.

"You should join the football team next year," Hunter said while I was midtext.

"Huh?"

Hunter rose to his feet and every light in the room dimmed. A mirror ball descended from the ceiling, scattering white dots every-where. Hunter reached for my hand, yanked me off the stool, and pressed our bodies together. "*Johnny*," he sang, "*You should join the football team with me. We could be magic together.*"

Back in Chicago, Alison had made me listen to *Hamilton* on repeat whenever we studied. That left me hating musicals. Instead of singing back, I just said, "I don't think that'd be a good idea."

"*Why not?*" he kept singing.

"Because we'd end up making out while everyone else played."

The classroom split in two and both sides slid in opposite direc-tions, leaving us standing in the middle of the football field, both in uniform. "*But this is every gay boy's high school fantasy,*" he sang.

"Not mine."

"*Why not, Johnny?*"

The ground rumbled. Football players, dressed in blue, charged across the field toward us. This was why I couldn't join the football team: the idea of getting squished under these guys terrified me. Hunter squeezed me against his chest and whisper-sang, "*Will you follow me into the dark?*"

I stared up at his shining green eyes. The stampede neared. "I'll follow you anywhere."

Bam.

They crushed us.

Nothing but darkness.

The bell rang, and I nearly jumped off the stool. Hunter and Tiffany laughed, but I didn't stick around to feel embarrassed. I flew out the door and walked outside, to a bus stop near the traffic circle.

Fifteen minutes later, Alison texted me and said she planned on staying behind to search for Blake. That sounded like a good idea. I left the bus stop to explore Misthaven alone.

Chapter 4

Misthaven's public library was along Pine Street, south from the high school. The familiar building implored me to investigate, but I risked the librarian catching me and reporting me to the school. A few blocks down, Willow Avenue bisected Pine Street and crooked southwest, winding around Lake Misty all the way to the water bottling company.

The sun tortured everything in Misthaven today. It boiled the lake and turned the valley into a steam bath. Even the birds refused to step outside. I kept to the shade and followed the shoulder for a while until I found a sign that read *Dreadthistle* and below that *2 miles*. I knew little about the neighboring town. The Institute bus didn't go there, and Hunter had never talked about it. All the mystery, and its short distance from Misthaven, made me curious to visit. I walked for ten minutes until I came upon a sign that read *Thank you for visiting lovely Misthaven*. I continued toward

Dreadthistle until I came across another sign that read *Now entering beautiful Misthaven*. Confusion struck. The empty wooded road behind me betrayed no secrets. I turned and walked the other way, trying to leave Misthaven, and again found the same sign: *Now entering beautiful Misthaven*.

My dulled wizard sense warned me of strange magic thickening the air. However, without proof, my feelings amounted to little more than paranoia. A crack that stretched from the roadside formed an *S* in the asphalt. If I walked toward Dreadthistle and found the same crack, in the same spot, that would confirm my suspicions—unknown magic had warped space around me. I started down the road again, desperately wanting to believe I wasn't trapped here, but again, I passed the *Now entering Misthaven* sign, with the crack shaped like an *S* in the same spot as before.

Panicking, I thought about using the forest to reach Dreadthistle, but I didn't feel like going in there alone. Hell, I didn't feel like going in there with other people. Too dangerous. Nothing around me inspired new ideas, so I kicked the sign and gave it the finger. My big toe hurt all the way back to Misthaven.

The bizarre experience had confirmed my fears: Misthaven wasn't real, and some strange magic was keeping us here.

I went home and sunk into the living room couch. My phone buzzed—a text from Dad: How's your first day going, Juanito?

A sickening feeling hit me. I lurched forward and wrapped my arms around my waist. If this place wasn't real, that wasn't Dad texting me. It was something else.

A cream-colored Lexus pulled up around three thirty. Tiffany applied some eyeliner in the driver's seat, with Alison sitting next to her. I wanted to know why Tiffany decided to take Alison home—Alison never hung out with girls like her—but the day's events dominated my thoughts. Alison got out of the passenger side, but Tiffany kept putting on makeup, too busy to leave just yet.

Alison walked in and immediately noticed the look on my face. "J, what happened?"

"I went walking earlier and I tried to leave town . . . but I couldn't."

"What do you mean?"

"I couldn't leave town. I walked all the way to the Misthaven sign, and I went past it, then something looped me around and I ended up right back here."

We heard Tiffany drive off. "Are you . . . sure?" Alison asked.

"Yes, Ali. I walked past the sign and marched right back into Misthaven. We can't leave this place."

"But we . . . drove in. How could we have gotten here if we can't leave?"

"Do you think I'm messing with you?"

"Don't get defensive, J. I'm just trying to make sense of all this."

"I'm guessing you didn't find Blake?"

Alison looked dismayed.

Dad rushed in then and gave me a stern look. "Where the hell have you been?" Alison stepped aside as he stormed into the living room. "Your school called me and told me you weren't in any of your classes." Creepy. He looked like my dad, even sounded like him, but I knew nothing about what, if anything, inhabited that body.

"Juanito, answer me," he said loudly. I didn't respond; he continued: "I get a job somewhere new and *this* is the stunt you pull your first day of class? I had to leave work early. Do you know how that makes me look, Juanito?" My silence further frustrated him. "Is this because of your mom, or me? We can only do our best. You and me and Alison, okay? We came here for another chance, Juanito. If you're going to ruin this for both of us, then I at least deserve an explanation."

Dad kneeled before the couch and put his arms around me. "We've got to make this work. Please, this is our second chance. You've got to promise me we'll make this work."

Dad bought a rotisserie chicken for dinner and served it with instant mashed potatoes and canned peas. Then he dumped butter all over everything. For him, a culinary home run, but for Alison, our resident vegan, it was completely inedible. Dad drove back out to the store and got her something different. When we finally settled around the table, he asked about our day, but neither of us said much. My thoughts stayed on that stretch of road between Misthaven and Dreadthistle.

We washed up and headed for bed after dinner, but I didn't intend on falling asleep any time soon. I waited by my window for midnight. When warmed under the glowing sun, Misthaven pulsed with life, but at night, Misthaven stood still as a cemetery, her dormant streets sleeping comfortably beneath a starlit veil. Even travelers thought twice before venturing out, for every Misthavener knew not to wander out past twelve. When midnight came, so too did the eerie mist billow out into the empty streets. Its silent tendrils crept over everything like a fiendish ivy—crawled into every mailbox, slipped under every car, slithered between every gutter. Its dull gray rose, drowning all warm, earthly colors in undead whiteness. And when daytime's memory vanished from the world and only ghoulish shadows remained, a gurgling sound pierced my ears, turned my skin to ice. It sounded like a ravenous stomach's twisting pleas. But its growl resonated low and deep, like a wolf, greedy with hunger. And strange whispers rode on that unsettling sound, so indistinct as to be completely unintelligible.

Beyond my neighbors' rooftops, trees shook violently. The ravens sleeping on their limbs took off into the night. Giant shadows moved through the forest, wordlessly declaring dominion over Misthaven. My first trip here with Hunter, I said, "This place is weird."

"Yeah, it is," he'd said, "Kids at the Institute call it the witch's cauldron because late at night, the mist from the lake rises and swallows everything in the valley. Weird thing about the mist is, it never comes over the Institute's walls. Supposedly, if you look real hard, you can see giant shadows roaming in it. Like Void-spawns the Institute's forced into servitude."

Those ominous words echoed in my mind. And if the strangeness at the road between Misthaven and Dreadthistle proved anything, powerful magic was afoot.

Chapter 5

My thoughts swung between staying in class the following day or continuing to look for Blake. I didn't know where to start, and I didn't want to risk getting caught again and having Dad wedge himself into our investigation. But we needed to find Blake and escape. After I got in the car, Alison came out looking completely different from her usual self, her mess of fishnets and ripped-up clothes replaced with a Hello Kitty shirt and some skinny jeans. She'd even traded out her signature combat boots for Vans slippers.

Dad gawked at her when she got in the car. "You look . . . *different* today."

She looked uncomfortable with him acknowledging the change. "Just trying something new."

Dad dropped us off at school and we headed for our lockers. "Are we going to keep looking for Blake today?" I asked her.

"Maybe that's not such a great idea," she said, sounding unsure of herself.

"What're you talking about?"

We reached our locker and she opened hers. "J, you heard what your dad said. Plus, what if we're wrong? We're going to look totally crazy."

"Ali, after all that weird stuff I told you about, you think I'm making this up?"

"No, it's just—Johnny, if Blake were here, we would've already seen him at school."

"He could be in trouble."

"Where are you going to look for him, J?" Her words hushed me. Even I knew we didn't have a starting point. "All I'm saying is we need to lie low for a while and gather more information. We don't want to get in over our heads."

We'd been in Misthaven for nearly a week when Dad gathered us around the dinner table on Thursday and grilled us about our new lives. Alison's budding friendship with Tiffany Young, a popular cheerleader, proved Alison's nonpareil flexibility in strange, new situations. Not surprising considering she'd also adjusted to the Institute faster than I had. I, on the other hand, acclimated to our new surroundings like a brick through glass. Fitting in at the high school didn't matter to me, though. Finding Blake and getting out of this creepy place demanded more attention. I had started to think Alison didn't believe Blake was even here. Maybe she only faked being normal to hide her own investigation, but something about the spring in her step told me she enjoyed all this. That scared me. I felt alone.

Dad sliced into the vegan meatloaf Alison had forced him to make. He picked up a sopping piece and placed it on my plate. "So, how's your first week going, kiddo?"

"Great," I mumbled, scraping my fork loudly against the plate.

Dad looked more annoyed with me than concerned. He cut Alison a chunk too. "What about you, Alison?"

"Great! Me and this girl Tiffany have been hanging out—"

"Is that the sweet girl that's been giving you and Johnny rides home every afternoon?" Dad interrupted.

"Yeah. She's rad. Supersmart too. She speaks fluent Mandarin because her dad makes her visit her grandparents in Xiamen every spring. But she keeps trying to get me to do a make-over, and I don't know—anyway, we were talking about sum-mer vacation"—I'd never heard Alison prattle this much in my life—"and we decided that we were going to spend all summer on the beach here in Misthaven. One of her friends, this guy Scott—Johnny's met him—his folks own a lake house. We're probably going to hang out there all summer."

Every syllable she spoke twinkled with excitement. She loved it here. The whole thing pissed me off. I impersonated Tiffany: "And you can totally, like, jam out to Shawn Mendes all summer!" My sarcasm left Alison wrinkling her nose at me. "Jeez, Ali, I never thought you'd be into all this normie bullshit—"

"Johnny," Dad said, cutting into his meatloaf. "That's enough. Maybe you should follow Alison's lead and try to fit in better. You said all the kids at the high school are nice to you."

"It's fine, Mr. D," Alison said. "Johnny here's just pissed his crush barely even talks to him." She wagged her head at me like a snake. I exhaled through my nose. Hunter sat next to me in nearly every class, and even though I didn't really care about school, I hated that my mind stayed permanently fixated on kissing him. I longed for him to remember how we once were. But Hunter wanted me to join the football team, not make out with him behind the bleachers.

Later that night, a loud staticky burst woke me up. I threw off my covers, walked to the door, and cracked it open. It sounded like Dad's radio screeching downstairs. No one else stirred, so I went to turn it off. The hallway distorted the sputtering static, slowly giving it form, and as I came to the stairs, the noise took shape—a muffled voice. It repeated something too quietly for me to understand. I hurried downstairs and found the shortwave on an end table, a boy's voice coming through: "My name is Mikey. You are trapped in the Dreamhaven." I snatched the radio and, even though I knew it wouldn't work, yelled back, "Can you hear me? Can you hear me?"

The boy's voice vanished and the staticky noise turned to silence. Dad's door squeaked open, so I snuck into the kitchen, got a glass of water, and promptly returned to my room. If Mikey was the same boy I'd heard on the radio the first time, that meant we were trapped in a dream, stuck somewhere in Everywhen, without our magic. That explained why I hadn't been able to escape. The whole picture grew clearer: After bringing Hunter back from the Void, the Institute had taken us under the Heka Building and imprisoned us in this dream prison. Wizards were most powerful in Everywhen. Somehow the Institute had locked our abilities. That complicated things—how could I escape a dream prison without magic?

I wanted to wake Alison and tell her, but I didn't need Dad's impostor eavesdropping. If he caught me, who knew what he would do.

I stayed up all night thinking about Mikey. Not knowing his identity made me question his reasons for telling me about the

Dreamhaven. He could've easily been tricking us. When morning bird songs sounded outside my window, I rushed into Alison's room.

"I'm starting to miss being an only child," she grumbled as she got up.

"Yeah, yeah, good morning. Listen: Dad's shortwave radio came on last night and woke me. I went downstairs to see what was going on, and there was some boy named Mikey talking on it. He said this place was a *dream prison*, and that we were trapped here."

"Do you stay up all night so you can wake me in the morning and tell me weird stuff?"

"Alison, I'm serious."

"So am I. Johnny, we've been here for a week. You can't honestly believe we're trapped in a . . . *dream prison* all because you heard some kid say that on the radio. It could've been a podcast, or a dream."

"Then how do you explain our memories?"

"I don't. I was reading an article on Buzzfeed about how really close friends sometimes have shared dreams."

"Alison, I literally couldn't leave this place."

"J, you're imaging things—"

"I'll take you out there myself—"

She went on, talking over me. "Maybe all the stress from moving set you off or something—I don't know. Point is, there's nothing weird going on. And if we're wizards, why can't we use magic?"

"There could be an anti-magic field, like that one at Gaspar's."

"Or maybe you're terrified that our lives are really boring so you're making things up. You're scaring your dad, and you're making me nervous, too, J. Can you please try to forget about all this stuff?"

Dad walked past the door. "Hey, you two, better get ready for school."

Alison gave me her menacing "worried sister" look, and it made me feel ten inches tall. "I need to get ready, J." I walked out into the hallway and she closed the door behind me. She wasn't going to listen. But I wasn't wrong: the Institute had trapped us in a dreamworld, and they'd stripped us of our powers too.

During homeroom, Hunter noticed how spaced out I looked and nudged me with his elbow. "Hey, bro, what's wrong?"

"Nothing. Just had some strange dreams."

Tiffany turned in her seat and rested her arms across the backing. "Alison says he's really into weird stuff. You should take him to the *verge* sometime, Hunter."

Alison says he's really into weird stuff? What else had Alison been saying about me behind my back? I decided against obsessing over Tiffany and Alison's conversations. "What's the verge?" I asked Hunter.

"It's nothing."

"You two might even find that magic wishing pond, or the unicorn," Tiffany teased.

"Magic wishing pond? Unicorn?"

"None of that stuff's real. Stop messing with him."

"I bet Old Man Johnson thinks it is," Tiffany said.

I looked to Hunter. "Old Man Johnson?"

"Brian Johnson. Some old conspiracy theorist that lives out in Misthaven Housing community, the trailer park near—"

"Says this whole place is a dreamworld," Tiffany interjected.

"He even tried to get some folks to go with him to the verge one time. *Creeeeepy.*"

Tiffany inadvertently sparked new life into my investigation. "Do you know where he lives?" I asked.

Hunter and Tiffany looked confounded. Not many people bought into Johnson's ramblings. "Why do you want to know where he lives?" Tiffany asked.

"Just curious."

She sneered at me and called to a girl sitting an aisle over. "Hey, do you know where Old Man Johnson lives? Like, we know he lives in the trailer park, but where specifically? Johnny's *curious.*"

The girl lowered her bad boy romance novel. "He doesn't even live in a regular trailer. He lives in a tiny camper with this huge canopy out in front. I heard it's far away from all the other trailers too. He's a hermit."

"How do I get there—to the trailer park?" I asked.

"That little bus that goes around town all day. It passes by in front of the trailer park."

"Is there a stop nearby?"

"There's one out in front of the school."

Before the bell rang, I texted Alison and told her to meet me at our locker before first period. Maybe Old Man Johnson knew Mikey—maybe he *was* Mikey; either way, he was another puzzle piece bringing us one step closer to understanding the situation. The bell rang and I darted to our locker. Alison showed up shortly after.

"What is it, J?" she asked, sounding exhausted with me.

"Have you been talking about me with Tiffany?"

"What?"

I readjusted my priorities. "Never mind. I'm headed to Misthaven Housing Community to look for Brian Johnson."

"Who's Brian Johnson?"

"He's a conspiracy theorist. According to Tiffany, he thinks this place is a dreamworld."

"Like that Mikey kid on the radio?" Her tone was sarcastic.

"Exactly."

"Johnny, if you skip class, you're going to get in trouble again, and your dad's going to be pissed."

"Alison, this is our chance. Stop acting like all of this is normal. You know there's something weird going on."

"You're the only weird thing going on, Johnny. I've got to get to class."

She tossed away my concerns without a second thought. Her sudden attitude shift left me dizzied. Either this place had corrupted her mind or she had bought wholesale into the fantasy: Here, she wasn't just accepted; she was popular. The Dreamhaven's promise, popularity and acceptance, proved a seductive lure, especially for those who'd never known either, but it remained a wild-eyed serpent, a menacing lie, the illusion's every piece twisted and crooked in some way.

Chapter 6

An old rusty sign guarded a lonely bus stop down the road from the traffic circle in front of the school. With nowhere to sit, I paced, still pissed at how weird Alison had been acting. No one had followed me, so I waited there for the bus. The blustery storm clouds overhead looked like tarnished silver, fading from gray to black. Earlier, a light rain had dappled the streets with turbid, brown puddles. The bus pulled up to the curb and I got on.

The bus headed south along Pine Street until the suburban homes lining both sides turned into abandoned brick buildings, the road becoming old and pocked. Eventually, Pine Street turned into River Road and curved southwest. Misthaven Housing Community came before the bend in the road, marked by a moldering wooden sign with the property's name on it. Dry rot had eaten the wood, leaving it chipped, fractured, and crumbling. The bus stopped in front of Hill Street, a broad gravel path that looped into Darkwood forest and stretched for less than half a mile before retreating to the main road. I got off the bus and crunched across the pebbles, making my way into the trailer park.

Misthaven Housing Community lay hidden deep enough in Darkwood Forest that sunlight barely reached it through the canopy. The cheap living attracted good and honest people working too hard for low wages, but society often ignored places like this, making it a perfect place for crooks to conduct their shady dealings. Single- and double-wide trailers greeted me along the lane, some in shambles with yellowed and rusting aluminum siding while tidier ones kept well-groomed cinderblock flowerbeds out front. I searched for Old Man Johnson's camper—and spotted Blake, crouched, and looking for something under a trailer's lattice skirting. My faint wizard sense confirmed it was really him. Blake's aura sounded like a skateboard rolling across pavement, and if you closed your eyes you felt a windy blast weaving through your clothes as you sped down a hill. A deep plunge into Blake's aura uncovered loneliness and guilt situated at the heart around which those denser sensations orbited.

"Blake," I called.

He looked over his shoulder. "Johnny!"

Hearing him say my name assuaged my fears that he'd lost his memories, like Hunter. We almost hugged, but we stopped and silently debated whether to man up and shake hands instead. He gave me a big, chuckling hug anyway.

"You recognize me?" I said.

"Huh?"

"Never mind. What're you doing here? How did you get here?"

"No clue. I woke up in this trailer, with a new foster parent and everything. I still had some of my memories from the Institute too."

"Do you remember anything from between January and now?"

Blake considered the question briefly then shook his head. "Not clearly, no." Three months gone in a blur, just like Alison and me. "Have you seen Alison or Hunter?"

Every weird event and coincidence spilled from my lips like a waterfall. Blake gave me a curious look when I mentioned Mikey.

"Why haven't you been at school? What were you doing?" I asked.

"I've been skipping, so I could check this place out."

"Why were you looking under that trailer?"

"I was looking for hidden cameras."

"Let me text Alison and tell her I've found you."

I sent Alison the message, and a minute later she dinged me back: Are you serious?

I texted, Dead serious.

Does he remember anything.

His memories are patchy. Like ours. Are you going to sneak out and come meet up with us?

It took her a while to respond: I don't think that's a good idea. One of us has to hold down the fort.

Don't you want to see Blake?

Of course, I do, and I will, but one of us needs to stay behind just in case.

In case what?

Just go on without me. I'll meet up with you at home later. Tell Blake I miss him.

I lowered my phone, irritated but hardly surprised. "She says she misses you."

"Is she going to meet up with us?"

"No, she said she wanted to stay behind just in case."

"In case what?"

"Exactly. She's been acting weird."

"She'll come along when she's ready. Let's go find this conspiracy nut you were talking about."

We set out together, searching for Brian's camper. Blustery, rain-scented winds howled through the swaying pines. While I worried about getting caught in one of Misthaven's downpours, Blake kept a pensive look on his face, eyes fixed to the ground.

"What's wrong?" I asked.

"You said the kid on the radio called himself Mikey?"

"Yeah, why?"

"Nothing. Just curious." Blake's somber dodge sold him out. Blake hated talking about certain things, his past chief among them. We used to sit together for lunch every day at the Institute. Blake loved telling us everything he knew about Legacies, Defectors, Void-spawns, anything magical, but when the questions put him in focus—his extraction or his life before the Institute—he always fell silent. Somehow, that name twigged something in him, but I wasn't going to force him to explain.

Twenty minutes later, we found an old camper sitting on weathered cinderblocks. Its tightly sealed and blacked-out windows kept out any light. A portable awning partially attached to the entrance—its other half partway posted into the ground—shielded the front. It began to pour. We rushed under the tarp and knocked on the shaky door. The kids at school painted Old Man Johnson as a loose cannon. For all I knew he'd greet us with a shotgun blast to the face. Or maybe he'd scream and throw mangy cats at us. The cats scared me only slightly less than being shot. Slightly. The door flew open and revealed a burly old man in thick flannel. He scanned Blake and me through some foggy spectacles. "What do you want?" he grumbled through a wiry beard.

"Are you Brian Johnson?" I asked.

"What's it to you?"

"My name's Johnny. I'm looking for Brian Johnson. I need to talk to him."

"Who sent you? Are you with the feds?"

"N-No I'm not with the feds. I go to school at Misthaven High."

He waited at his door, examining us. Then, a familiar sensation: eyes on my nape. The feeling triggered a memory—whenever a wizard infiltrated your thoughts, your magical senses registered the intrusion. Your instincts also revealed the intruder's identity. My weak wizard sense pointed to Brian Johnson. To block out a nosy wizard, you needed to envision a barrier in your mind. I didn't know if the trick still worked, but I promptly imagined a brick wall. He studied me a little longer before his face grew softer, more confident. The uncomfortable feeling lifted.

"*You*," he said with certainty. Old Man Johnson stepped outside and peered around the canopy. He regarded our environs suspiciously. "Hurry inside. Quickly!"

Blake and I scurried into the trailer without hesitation. The small camper stretched back about ten feet before terminating at a bunk under an aluminum foil-covered window. Clear plastic containers filled with dirt, water, and leaves sat on a dinette to our right. Baked beans steamed in a saucepan on a stove nearby, filling the air with a sugary scent. The old man rushed in after us and slammed the door. "We've met before."

"We . . . have?"

"I'm Luther Dorian. The librarian from Misthaven." I remembered then why the library had seemed familiar—Linh had taken me there to meet Luther Dorian. He worked with the Defectors, a rebel group that helped wizards escape the Institute. That this batshit crazy old guy knew my name, or anything about Luther Dorian, lent credence to his bizarre claim. If this was Luther Dorian, then he'd used magic to disguise himself. And if that were true, then he couldn't be a prisoner here like we were. It also suggested he knew a way in and out of the Dreamhaven.

"Why do you look like that?" I asked. Though the flannel mountain didn't resemble Luther—Luther, as I remembered him, measured five feet, four inches, wore sweater vests, walked stiffly on one foot, and spoke with a high-pitched whine—he still conveyed Luther's idiosyncrasies.

"First: Who led you to me?"

I told Luther about the strange radio broadcasts, Mikey, and the rumors swirling around the high school.

"Do you know this Mikey?" he asked.

"We think it may be another one of the Institute's prisoners."

"Speaking to you through a shortwave radio? I've been here a long time and that's a new one."

"Do you think it could be a Mara, or the Institute?"

"No telling. If it were the Institute, they would've sent copies instead of bothering with another prisoner."

"Copies?"

"Some of the people out there are real," Luther said, "and the rest are just copies made to look like real people. As that Mikey fellow said, you are in a prison the Institute calls 'the Dreamhaven.' It was built in Everywhen to contain difficult prisoners. The Institute scans wizards' memories then constructs a semi-idyllic life for them in the Dreamhaven. They populate this semi-idyllic life with copies of people from the wizards' memories. As an added warning: the Institute can also control those copies. The purpose of all this is to pacify the wizard, so they don't go digging into Misthaven's *peculiarities*. I believe integrating a new wizard into the Dreamhaven takes some time, though. You may have experienced a time-loss."

That explained the missing three months. The Institute had used that time to scrape out our memories, then harnessed that information to recreate a new life for us.

Our families, Misthaven, the high school—all parts in a pernicious dollhouse the Institute had fabricated to mollify us. But my friends felt different from everything else. Their realness triumphed over all the illusions. Luther didn't scan our thoughts earlier merely to uncover secrets; his intrusion had helped him determine our authenticity. Still, I wondered why Hunter's memories had vanished completely while ours survived only partially affected.

"Are you going to tell us why you look like that?" Blake asked.

"I'm using a spell to disguise my appearance. The Institute ransacked Misthaven looking for Defectors. Although they didn't capture me, I worried that they'd identify me if I didn't don some other form." His words loosened another memory: Melchior had scoured our thoughts after recapturing us at Gaspar's hideout. His investigation undraped Luther's entire operation in Misthaven. Guilt pinched my conscience, but my mental shield didn't hold a candle to Melchior's boundless magic.

"Can you help us get out?" I asked.

"Maybe," Luther said, "but if we're to leave, we'll need to do it quickly."

"When?"

"This evening."

"This evening?" I said, shocked at Luther's declaration. "We'll have to go get our friends."

"There're more of you in here?"

"Two more."

Luther rubbed his face pensively. "Then you'll have to fetch them quickly. I can't give you any more time. The Cave of Miracles only appears once a month. Tonight is our only chance to escape for a long while."

"Cave of Miracles?" Blake asked.

Luther stared at the trees outside through the small window in the front door. The rain had slowed to a sleepy drizzle. "The residents of Misthaven aren't completely unaware of the strangeness surrounding them. Local legends speak of a cave in Darkwood Forest that leads to other worlds. The locals call this place the Cave of Miracles."

"Are the legends true?" I asked.

"Yes, but the cave is not quite a cave, per se." Luther checked my face to confirm I understood. "It's a passage, a world between worlds, leading from one to another. I use the passage to reach the Dreamhaven so I can study it. Hence all the samples." He waved his hand at the table.

When I first met Luther, his duties included conducting research in Everywhen. I never imagined he physically journeyed there using a tunnel between worlds. Until now, I'd believed dream travel provided the only path into Everywhen. That magic gave us the ability to transform our corporeal bodies into dream stuff then back again didn't surprise me, though—Maras used that trick all the time. The Cave of Miracles boasted the power to rejoin our minds and bodies, and move them from under the Heka Building to wherever the cave led.

"I've tried to convince others to escape, but you're the first prisoners I've encountered who are self-aware," Luther said.

"So, you're not even sure this will work?" Blake asked.

"Would you rather stay here?"

"Do we need to bring anything?" I asked.

"No. You'll need to travel light." Luther ushered us out the door. "Now, quickly, go get your friends and return before the mist rises."

The bus ran for another few hours, until about six. That gave me plenty of time to grab Alison. But I didn't know what to do about Hunter. Somehow, we'd have to convince him to come with us, memories or not. I hid that detail from Luther because I didn't want a lecture on time constraints.

Blake stepped outside first. "Where are you going?"

I joined him and we walked. "I'm going to get Alison."

"What're we going to do about Hunter?"

"We've got to get him to come with us."

"What about his memories?"

"We can figure out all that once we're out of here."

"I can't leave—I convinced my foster parent I'm sick. That's why he's let me stay home all week. But I'll go with you to the bus stop."

On our way to the bus stop, I watched rivulets run between the rocks in the gravel, making them shift and churn underfoot. Thunder growled in the skies overhead. My chest ached—this place had proven itself a lie after all.

The rain died, and the air got so muggy it felt like a soggy towel wrapped around my head. "Blake, does Alison know how you were extracted?"

Blake didn't show any feelings. His stoic nature made him tough as hell to read. Going from home to home for years left him justifiably stiff in the emotions department. He seemed well-adjusted, charming, but sometimes his eyes revealed the pain bubbling just under the surface.

"Never mind," I said.

"No, it's fine. She doesn't know about my extraction. I don't really like talking about it."

We reached the bus stop. The heat vaporized the moisture on the empty road. I didn't expect the bus back any time soon. "We don't have to, then."

"We're friends, right?" Blake asked.

"Friends?" I laughed. "I pretty much idolize you."

He scanned the turbulent clouds. Blue patches emerged through the gray, at first only a few, but as the storm moved on, the sky went cerulean. "I'll tell you how I was extracted," he said. "I'm going to warn you, though: it's kind of a messed-up story."

Blake started his story in Chico, California, where he and his best friend, Gerald, fashioned themselves leaders over six foster kids, all living in the same double-wide trailer. One kid, Mikey, kept to himself mostly, but his snowy-white hair inspired morbid curiosity among the others. Their caregiver, a boozy fortysomething, collected children for the middling state checks she used to buy liquor. Her trailer was occluded off a country road, with a sizeable backyard and a forest behind it. She divided the children's rooms into one for boys and one for girls. Although she let the kids play in the backyard, she demanded they stay away from the forest because she said monsters lurked there. They didn't really—she just wanted to keep them off missing-child posters at Walmart. The first time Blake's wizard senses kicked in, a dreadful feeling—like a cold, dead thing tip-toeing up his spine—led him into the girl's room. There he found a slight girl with pigtails lying on her bottom bunk and crying.

"Hey, what's wrong?" he asked, approaching slowly.

The girl buried her face in a pillow, to hide it from Blake. As Blake neared, he spied a meshwork of cuts crawling up her arm. "Hey!" Blake yanked the girl up by her arm and forced her to look at him. "What happened to your arms? Are you cutting yourself?"

"You wouldn't believe me!"

Blake demanded she explain the cuts. She pointed to a rag doll sitting on a rocking chair in the corner. The ratty old thing rose to a little under two feet and wore a faded pink floral dress. Two graying pigtails fell around its lifeless face. Their foster parent said the doll had belonged to her family for generations and warned the children not to mess with it. Blake found the tale ridiculous and demanded she stop hurting herself, but the girl stuck to her story and told Blake she knew not to trust him. A short time later, their foster parent discovered the girl's cuts and called Child Protective Services to take her away.

The uneasy feeling plaguing Blake didn't go away, though, and a few weeks later, he came across another kid, a boy with short brown hair in a rattail, covered in what resembled self-inflicted cuts. Blake confronted him about it, and they got into a heated argument before the boy stormed off. Later, Blake told Gerald about the boy and asked him to help keep an eye out.

After their foster parent fell asleep that night, Blake caught the boy with the rattail sneaking into the backyard with the creepy doll. Blake and Gerald followed him into the woods and watched as the boy set the doll on a tree stump and brandished a butcher knife. They watched in horror as the boy begged the doll to leave him alone before he sliced into his arm. Gerald ran to stop the boy, but Blake's wizard senses detected a disturbing presence that drew his attention. He tracked the feeling to behind a nearby oak tree where he found Mikey, a sinister smile stretched across his face and glowing red eyes. Blake's instincts told him that, somehow, like a puppeteer, Mikey was making the rattailed boy cut himself.

Gerald wrestled the knife from the boy's hand. The boy cried and raved that the doll made him do it, so Gerald burned the doll.

He then cobbled together a story about the doll going missing. Blake thought about confronting Mikey, but he needed to interrogate him privately.

Blake paused briefly before continuing his story. Just like Blake, the heavens rumbled but shed no tears. I waited breathlessly for him to start talking again, and when he did, he told me the day after he caught the rattailed boy in the woods, he set out to find and confront Mikey. Blake searched all over the house and found Mikey lurking in the backyard. Mikey gave Blake a menacing look before he disappeared behind the tree line. Blake followed him through the forest until he popped out on the other side, near an old road. There, he spotted the boy with the rattail standing in the street as a freight truck barreled for him. Blake ran to save the boy, but Gerald popped up and pushed the boy off the road first. For Blake, time slithered as he watched Gerald stand helplessly in the road without enough time to dodge the speeding vehicle.

Blake blamed himself for Gerald's death and vowed to never fail anyone like that again. That's why he protected us. I wanted to allay his concerns, remind him that the forces we faced loomed over us like unstoppable giants. But I didn't want to trivialize his feelings. He had made his pain into a prison, its walls higher and sturdier than the Institute's.

Blake continued: He found Mikey lurking near the crash site, the same horrifying delight spread across his face; the same red glow in his eyes. Mikey retreated into the forest. Blake gave chase, cornering Mikey at a riverbank. The unsettling tingle that ran through Blake's body as he approached made his stomach tight. Something twisted occupied Mikey's body, joyously using him to bring suffering into the world.

"I'm not letting you hurt anybody else," Blake said.

In a deep, inhuman voice, Mikey said, "What will you do to stop me?" He moved forward. Frightened, Blake took a few steps back and stumbled over a rock. Blake's fear excited the strange creature inside Mikey.

"Stop!" Blake said, inching back as Mikey came closer. Mikey paused midstep, like an unseen force had frozen him. Blake didn't know it then, but that's when his magic emerged. With will alone, he paralyzed Mikey.

"This body is stronger than yours," Mikey said.

"What's wrong with you, Mikey? What's going on?"

A searing pain burned in Blake's head. He dropped to his knees and covered his ears as the agony sharpened. That terrible creature residing in Mikey's body burrowed deep into Blake's mind. It sought to control his body. Blake grabbed his head, fell on his side, and curled into a ball as everything went black.

"And when I opened my eyes," Blake said to me, "I was in the white room with Melchior."

The bus turned down Pine Street, heading toward us. "What happened?" I asked, confused by the ending to Blake's story.

"Mikey was a somnambulist, and apparently, some psycho Mara had taken over his body. Even though Mikey was stronger, it wanted my body because I was older. Right when it tried to possess me, the agents came in and extracted me."

"Where'd they take Mikey?"

"Under the Heka Building, like they do with all somnambulists."

"You think the Mikey that spoke to me over the radio is the same person?"

"I don't know. Luther *did* say this place was for the Institute's highest security risks. My only question is: Why haven't we seen him in here? Why did he have to speak to you through a radio?"

"You think it's a Mara trying to trick us?" I asked.

"I don't know, but if it's the same Mikey, I doubt the Institute would've left him possessed. And even if it is Mikey and he's still possessed, he just told us we were trapped here. He didn't tell you about Luther or anything."

"What if he's manipulating us. Like the black cat Mara did with Gaspar?"

"We don't have many choices, Johnny. We either stay here, or trust Mikey and Luther."

The bus pulled up then. I said goodbye to Blake and boarded. I didn't doubt that the Mikey from Blake's story and the Mikey who spoke to me over the radio might be the same person, but if that was the case, where was he and why was he helping us?

Chapter 7

The bus stopped between the high school and the library. I didn't need to get caught, so I hurried to my house and stole inside before anyone saw me. Dad's copy skulking around, waiting to eavesdrop, threatened to complicate things. "Dad," I called as I walked in. No one said anything back, so I decided to wait for Alison. Not even one text dinged my phone all day. Even the copy spared me the obligatory, "Hey, son, how are you?" Alison's silence made me nervous, though. I messaged her: Where are you?

Alison texted back, I'll be there in a while.

Probably out with Tiffany again, I thought. After everything we'd talked about, Alison still just wanted to play pretend, a willing prisoner in a jail of enticing lies. The living room's drawn curtain cast everything in darkness. I parted it a bit and checked outside. Cottony gray clouds still dressed the sky, but the rain had ceased some time ago. Hopefully, the weather stayed that way. Looking for

Luther's cave during a downpour sounded like a nightmare. Two neighbors—a burly man with white hair and a bald spot, and a middle-aged woman with a red bob and a minidress—talked near a mailbox across the street. Their conversation didn't look too lively. The man sorted through the mail in his hands while the woman spoke. Paranoia arose in me. In any other circumstance these innocuous neighbors didn't warrant a second glance, but here they could be wizards or copies. They turned and stared simultaneously, and I shut the curtains. I stretched across the couch and waited for Alison to show up.

I woke with a shock at the slamming of the front door. An unfamiliar silhouette waited in the entryway. Alison flipped on the lights. She didn't look like herself. Her gently flat-ironed hair fell into curls, and she wore a soft pink eye shadow, almost the same color as her skin. Alison normally used foundation to further pale her already ghostly complexion, but now her skin looked radiant. She hung her backpack on the rack near the door and approached warily. "Well? What do you think?"

"About what?"

"The makeover? Tiffany finally convinced me to get one. Is it stupid? Do I look bad?"

"Makeover? Alison, what're you talking about?" It galled me that she wanted to talk about makeovers at a time like this. I pulled out my phone and checked the time. It read 8:45. "Ali, do you have any idea what time it is?"

"I went to Tiffany's house—it was huge; she's freaking gross rich—anyway, some of the other girls from school were there too.

They were all cheerleaders. They said they wanted to do my makeup because I was pretty."

"Okay?" I said, waiting for her to explain further.

"J . . . what if this place isn't all that bad?"

"What're you talking about, Ali? This place is a prison."

"How do you know?"

"What do you mean how do I know? I went and talked to Brian Johnson and found out he's really Luther Dorian in disguise. He told me this place is a prison the Institute built in Everywhen. It's called the Dreamhaven." Alison's skin took on a sickly color. "He said the people in this place aren't real either—he called them *copies*. He can get us out of here too. There's a gateway in Darkwood Forest that leads back to our world. But it only opens on a full moon. We have to leave tonight, or we won't get another chance for a month."

"How do you know he isn't lying?" Alison asked, her voice weak.

"Because he knew who I was, Ali. He recounted everything that happened at the Institute. How could some random old guy I've never met before know all that?"

"How do you know I'm not one of those . . . things? A *copy*?"

"Because I'm not convinced our wizard senses are totally gone, and I just know it's you. And that boy at school that looks like Hunter, that's really him too."

"Why're our memories patchy?"

"Luther said the Institute mind-wipes everyone they throw in here, but for some reason it didn't work on us . . . not all the way, at least."

"It worked on Hunter."

"I don't know why."

"What if I don't want to go?"

"Why wouldn't you want to go? Nothing here is real, Ali."

"It seems pretty real to me."

"It's not, okay? It's all bullshit."

"Maybe I want it to be real. Maybe I'm sick and tired of the 'real world' and I just want to stay here."

"You can't keep running from reality! You already did this once." Ali got quiet. Back at the Institute, her obsession with living out fantasies in Everywhen got her lost in the dreamworld, forcing me to magically join minds with our friends—called a *dream rave*—to save her.

"I told those girls I was trans."

"And?"

"They didn't care. They just kept talking about how pretty I was. They invited me to Scott's party tonight."

"Ali, they're trying to trick you. They're trying to keep you here."

"You have no idea what it's like."

"Come on—"

"I'm not doing the four hundred–meter sprint at the Oppression Olympics, J. I'm just saying, you don't know what it's like to get clocked by some random jerk who thinks you're trying to *trick* people. Everyone constantly acts like I'm some oddity to be debated about in a *discourse*. I'm sick of people treating me like I'm a fucking concept.

"I was at school all day and no one said anything mean to me. Everyone was nice, and told me how pretty I was, and they all wanted to be my friend. No one acted like me being there prompted a very special episode of *Misthaven High*. Maybe I'd rather live in some shitty dreamworld. It's better than the other one. Everyone accepts us here. There's no Institute. No bullies."

"Ali, we're *in* the Institute. This is all a bunch of bunk. The bullies are still out there, they're just manipulating us into thinking there's nothing going on. This is what bullies do: they make you think you're crazy, that their version of the world is better, but it's not. You can put on all the makeup you want, buy new clothes, join the cheerleading team, and go to the homecoming dance with all your new friends, but it'll never change the fact that we're living in a lie."

Alison's face went completely expressionless. Shutting down was second nature to her—as much as Alison played tough, she hated arguing, and she hated it even more when I was right.

She headed to the stairwell. "I'm going to my room."

"We need to get out of here and go meet up with Blake and Luther."

"I need a sec, okay?" Her voice shook, like she wanted to cry. She didn't want to leave this place. Much as I longed for that to confuse me, it didn't. I craved this happy ever after—a school that accepted us, people who liked us. But no matter what I wished for, Dreamhaven remained a lie. We can only shut our eyes to the fire burning all around for so long before we start to sweat.

We risked Dad's impostor coming home any minute, but Alison needed time to let everything go. I gave her some space, and walked upstairs to my bedroom and waited in the doorway, staring at all the sealed boxes there. Even if nothing here really existed, the Institute had molded it after my memories. The tape peeled from one box atop a stack near the door. The PS4 and VR headset Dad got me last year rested on newspapers inside. One time I forced him to play it, and it scared the hell out of him. He cracked me up ranting and raving about how realistic it seemed. I wanted to set it up and play another game with him, just to watch him freak out, but my real dad forgot about me months ago. Everything about this cruel place only served to remind me that my old life no longer existed. No family. No future. Nothing.

The front door creaked open and deep, heavy thumps echoed in the stairwell. Dad's copy, no doubt. He must've been headed to bed. Hopefully he didn't come in and start talking to me. My elementary school yearbook was hidden under the PS4. I pulled it out and looked inside. Alison's picture was next to mine, both of us looking goofy. Nothing seemed as scary back then as it did now. Children fret about imaginary things, but make-believe monsters get very real with time.

Another plodding footstep—the oddly labored movements unsettled me. My calm attempts to continue perusing the yearbook evaporated when another thundery step announced he'd made it to the top of the stairs. The door was nudged open then, Dad's copy looming there, watching me like a menacing shade.

"Juanito," he said, voice twisted into a shrill croak.

I backed deeper into the room, searching for a weapon, but nothing caught my attention.

"Juanito!" he screamed, frightening and erratic.

"Dad?" I said sheepishly, hoping to trick the copy into believing that I didn't know anything.

"Juanitooooooo." He chuckled. "Juanitooooooooooo, Juanitooooooo, Juanitooooooooooo."

"You okay, Dad?" I asked, still feigning innocence.

"You can't guard your thoughts from me," the copy said. "Whatever you know, I know." The impostor stepped into the room, and when the moonlight hit him, I glimpsed another man's face beneath Dad's—a younger man, late twenties, with brown curtained hair and blue eyes. No doubt remained: a Smith was driving Dad's copy.

"I got a call from your school while I was at work," he said. "They said you didn't show up for any of your classes. Again. Did you skip school *again*, Juanito?" I kept quiet. "I thought we talked about this. I've always trusted you, but lately . . . lately things have been different." The copy lowered his head. "You know, first it was your mom—" He dragged his feet across the carpet, lumbering toward me.

"What do you mean?"

The copy's eyes grew large, wild. "You know what I mean, Juanito. It's the whole 'gay' thing. You know your mom didn't know how to handle that."

"What're you talking about?"

He spoke lowly. "I'm talking about the divorce, Juanito. I'm trying to talk to you like an adult. I've always given you a lot of freedom because I trusted you. It's time you pay back some of that trust. Behave like an adult. Speak to me like an adult."

His manipulative vitriol got to me. I dropped the act. "You're not my dad. Stop fucking with me."

Suddenly, the weirdness vanished from his voice and he spoke plainly. "It's your fault our marriage fell apart. Why did you think we put you in that boarding school, that *Christian* boarding school?" he said, hissing the *S* in *Christian*.

"I said knock it off!"

Dad's copy approached the vanity near the door. He wobbled the frame back and forth. It squeaked on its hinges. A giggle escaped his lips. Then he rammed his head into the mirror and cracked it, and he stayed there, pressed against the impact, blood trickling down the glass. Slowly, he twisted his forehead into the cracks, and the sound of ripping flesh and crunching glass filled the air. Bloody shards fell to the floor.

"You're trying to ruin my life, aren't you?" The copy removed his bloody face from the glass and gritted his teeth. "This is all *your* fault!" he pointed a long finger at me. "Everything is *your* fault." He came closer, still pointing an accusatory finger at me. "This is all your fault. Our lives have been ruined because of you. Your mother and I were happy until you came along."

My bedroom door suddenly slammed shut of its own accord, trapping me with the copy. "Don't you feel like you owe me?" The copy closed the space between us, backing me against the writing desk under the window. Its voice warped, becoming imp-like. I briefly considered prying open the window to escape. Even if I hurt myself jumping out, at least I'd get away from this damn thing. The copy giggled again, then covered his face with his hands. "I don't know why you're so scared." He uncovered his face and revealed one like mine, though its milky eyes lacked pupils. Something flat and solid pressed up against my back. I glanced quickly—the desk behind me had been turned into a rock wall. Under me, the carpet melted into quicksand. I struggled to free my feet, but the muck gripped them like cement. The copy was using magic. He approached me, a sinister grin on his face.

"Alison!" I shouted. The copy snatched my neck and drove his thumbs into my throat. I pressed down on his wrists and yanked, but his daunting strength enfeebled me, my struggling only provoking a tighter grip.

"Shut your mouth!" he yelled, viciously wrenching my throat until the air fled from my lungs. The pressure welling in my head brought tears to my eyes. I fought to suck in a breath as everything around me grew blurry.

Crash!

The copy hit the floor at my feet, blue ceramic shards tumbling to the carpet. I fell on my knees wheezing painfully. Alison looked down at the copy in horror. She had smashed the lamp on my night-stand over its head. Blood matted the copy's hair, but his chest still rose and fell. Strangely enough, even though the Smiths bore the power to control the copies, the copies themselves were still subject to this world's laws, meaning that things could, indeed, die in the Dreamhaven. And that included us.

Under me, the quicksand had reverted to floor, and the wall behind me had also disappeared. Alison pulled me to the door. "Come on," she said, "let's get out of here." I staggered after her, still clutching my throat and coughing.

We raced downstairs. The front door was gone, in its place another wall. We ran into the sunroom, but another barrier had replaced the French doors that led to the lanai. "You two had bet-ter respect adults!" The copy yelled from upstairs. A few jarring thumps in the stairwell signaled his descent.

"Johnny," Alison said, "what the hell is going on? Why's your dad trying to kill you?"

"I told you, Ali, that isn't my dad. It's some copy of my dad. I think there's a Smith controlling him."

"That thing coming after us is a Smith?"

Before I could answer, the murky-eyed doppelgänger peeked his head through the archway between the sunroom and kitchen. "You two have been very naughty." He came into the room, unsteadily pointing a butcher knife he'd taken in the kitchen. "You should listen to adults when they tell you what to do."

"Sorry about the whole lamp thing," Alison said nervously as we backed into a wall. "I kind of overreact when someone's strangling my best friend." We still hadn't thrown away the last owner's coat rack, so I snuck behind Alison and headed for it. "Where'd you get that lamp anyway? Pier 1? It was kind of fancy. I'll get you a new one if you want, Mr. D." Her skittish joking bought me enough time to reach the coat rack. I lifted it, shouldered her aside, and swung the base, but the doppelgänger caught the pole.

"That wasn't very nice," the copy said. He snapped the coat rack with unimaginable force, sending wood shards everywhere. Then he snatched my shirt with one hand and flung me across the room. My back hit the wall and I crumpled to the floor, breathless.

Still waving its knife at Alison, the copy corralled her into a corner. "Can you believe he did that?" he asked. "My own son. I should slit his throat. But I think I'll slit yours first!" He stabbed at Alison, but she screamed and sidestepped the attack, and he buried his blade into the wall. Enraged, he jerked the weapon back out and took another swipe, but she dodged that one too.

Unbelievable pain shot through my back and legs, but I shored up the strength to stand. The broken rack's pointy end lay on the floor near me. I nabbed the makeshift stake and headed for the copy. He reeled back with his knife, but I drove the stake through his shoulder before he could take another strike at Alison. The copy spun around, screaming and reaching for the stake sticking out of his back. The coat rack's base waited nearby. He finally pulled the stake from his back right as I smashed the base across his face. But he kept standing. He swung left and right, slashing wildly. Alison snatched the poker from the holder near the fireplace and drove the hook into his head. For a second, the copy didn't even know what had happened. Blood dribbled from the wound and the copy stopped moving. Then, slowly, it turned to Alison, blood trickling from his eyes and mouth, and collapsed. The copy briefly reverted into a Smith with brown hair and blue eyes. On his blazer's lapel, a nametag that read *Žižek*.

In a blink, the Smith's body vanished.

"Come on, we're getting out of this place," I said, pulling Alison to the door with me. We needed to hurry back to the trailer park, find Blake, then go find Hunter. Not knowing Hunter's location made things harder, but we were running out of time.

Chapter 8

Dad didn't need his car anymore, so I took his keys off the hook in the kitchen and handed them to Alison. "Are you serious?" she said.

"We don't have enough time to walk."

"This may be a dreamworld, J, but if we get pulled over, that's it. Game over. Fin."

Her point gave me a sobering pause. We didn't possess the magic to dream up licenses, and if we drove out like this, we risked getting caught and having our plans waylaid, if not destroyed.

"Hope you're ready for a walk."

The road between the Pines and Misthaven Housing Community was four miles long, and although a straight shot, it still took an hour and a half to walk. Even worse, nighttime turned the broiling summer heat into a sopping humidity that soaked our clothes. Alison didn't say anything the whole way but folded over, panting, when we reached the trailer park. "If I have to walk anymore, my feet are going to start a union and argue for better pay and safer working conditions."

"We need to find Blake before the mist comes. Come on."

Our feet wrecked, we got to Blake's foster home. I stepped on the cinderblock porch and knocked loudly on the screen door. It shook the whole trailer. Alison leaned against the side and rubbed her feet through her shoes. Blake opened and saw me standing there, then he looked around the corner and spotted Alison.

"Hey, boyfriend," Alison said.

Blake darted outside, slid his arms around her, and leaned in for a kiss, but Alison stopped him and pointed at her lips. "Lips . . . chapped . . . need . . . water."

Realizing that Alison teetered dangerously close to passing out, Blake brought us inside. The trailer smelled like patchouli and lemongrass, and a window unit pumped cold air into the room from behind an entertainment center. Blake's foster brother, a pale boy with a blond buzz cut and a scar that split his brow, relaxed on a sectional, watching a noisy TV show. He gave us a look that bordered between nasty and curious. I recognized him from school although we hadn't spoken. His tough-kid, chronic bitchface belied the fussy book stack near him with nothing but gay romance novels.

"Hey, Ben," Blake said, "these're my friends, Alison and Johnny."

"You've been home all week. Where did you meet them?"

"I . . . met them on the internet."

"You invited strangers from the internet here?"

"We've been talking for—a while."

Uneasy after our run-in with Dad's copy, I feared Ben served as another vessel for the Institute's agents. But his presence itched my wizard sense. The Dreamhaven confined him, too, but he didn't yet know it.

"What's that?" Ben asked, pointing at a smattering of blood on Alison's jeans. Imperceptible in the darkness, the bright red popped under fluorescent lights. A clammy horror overcame me. Our whole plan was about to unwind.

Alison spied the stain and fretted. "I . . . was working on a costume for Halloween."

"It's April."

"I celebrate Halloween year-round. It's"—she searched the room until she found a hanging calendar with a picture of Jesus—"a religious thing."

Ben looked askance, his chocolate-brown eyes making a case for the implausible. He didn't buy the story, but he didn't press it, either. Blake walked into the kitchen, opened the refrigerator, and pulled out a water jug. He got Alison a plastic cup from an adjacent cabinet over the microwave and poured her a glass, which she greedily drank. Blake came into the living room and handed me a cup, too, and I drank until my throat no longer felt like a scratchy deathtrap.

Alison poured herself another glass and drank some more. Satisfied, she set down the glass and let out a powerful grunt. "We almost died getting here."

"Ben, we need to talk in private. Can we use your room real quick?" Blake said.

Ben shrugged. Blake nodded to the hallway that led from the kitchen to the trailer's rear. We followed the narrow passage into Ben's room. A huge bed swallowed most of the space, with a tattered patchwork quilt atop a mattress. Schoolbooks were piled high on his dresser. Unlike the rest of the house, Ben's room smelled cute, like bubblegum. Alison squeezed between the bed and the dresser and checked Ben's wardrobe.

"He seems nice," she said, sifting through twenty differently colored polos.

"I like the new look," Blake said.

Alison turned and saw Blake flashing her a playful grin. She put her arms around his neck. "I'm rebranding."

"Really?"

"No." And with that, she pecked him sweetly on the lips. Blake reeled her in for a second kiss. A smile spread across her face.

The digital clock on Ben's dresser read *11:30*. "You guys," I said, waving. "We're running out of time. And we still need to get Hunter."

"He might be at Scott's party. And if not, someone there will know where he is."

"We're going over there covered in blood?" I asked.

"Why *are* you two covered in blood anyway?" Blake asked.

"We had to kill J's dad," Alison said.

"It wasn't really my dad. It was one of those copy things Luther mentioned. The Smiths can take over their bodies."

"That's creepy," Blake said, looking unsettled as he left the room.

"That boy out there is a wizard," I said to Alison.

"And?"

"Shouldn't we get him out too?"

"Yeah right, J. He wouldn't even believe us." A soft agony filled her face. "I didn't even believe you at first."

Blake returned with two black shirts. He handed one to Alison and the other to me. Alison took the shirt and walked into the hallway bathroom. Blake's sturdy shoulders stretched broader than mine, so the big shirt swallowed me. Alison came back in with the shirt hanging off one shoulder because it was too big for her too.

"How are we getting to that party?" I asked Alison.

Alison searched her pockets and pulled out a paper slip with someone's phone number scribbled on it. She stared at the digits painfully, like their presence alone chewed her up inside. "Tiffany gave me her number, in case I needed a ride. I don't have my phone, though."

Blake left the room, and came back with Ben's phone and handed it to Alison. After a short exchange, Alison hung up, but she didn't return the phone. She held it like she didn't want to let it go—to let any of this go, not even after Dad's copy tried to kill us.

"She said she'd come get us." Alison handed back the phone. "We need to wait outside, though. She's not going to know which trailer we're in."

Blake noticed Alison's sadness but didn't say anything. She didn't like people pushing her to talk about her feelings. She'd tell us when it suited her.

Blake returned Ben's phone as we headed out the door. "Where're you going?" Ben asked.

"A party."

"Can I come?"

Alison led Blake away. "Sorry, invite only."

We headed outside and waited fifteen minutes before Tiffany's Lexus pulled up. Alison slid into the passenger seat next to Tiffany, and Blake and I hopped in the back.

Tiffany turned and studied Blake. "Who's he," she asked Alison.

"My boyfriend."

"He's cute." Tiffany sized up Alison's outfit. "What are you wearing?"

"I didn't get to change. I had to borrow one of Blake's shirts."

"I've got some stuff in the trunk. We'll look through and find you something when we get to Scott's."

Hearing Alison talk like that reminded me of when she joined the football team back in middle school, to impress her longtime crush: Todd Pilkerton. He used to rave about the Chicago Bears, so Alison had spent hours on Wikipedia, teaching herself about the sport. Football research bored her, though, and they grew apart when Todd realized they didn't share any of the same interests. To me, Alison usually talked about punk bands and obscure cult horror movies, but with Tiffany she changed into someone else. Which was the real Alison? The one I knew, or the one sitting and babbling about makeup gurus?

North Misthaven's sprawling mansions, with their slate rock walls and fields that ran for miles, rested deep in the country. Tiffany abandoned the main road for a rutted driveway that led to a log house perched on stilts along Lake Misty's shores. Cars filled the driveway, but a gravel lot out front provided additional parking space. Tiffany wedged her car between two jeeps then got out and headed for the trunk with Alison. Alison borrowed a fuzzy pink jacket and some heels but kept her jeans. We walked to Scott's house and climbed a staircase to a deck that encircled the home like a hula-hoop. A tall guy in a letterman jacket puked over a rail near the front door. His teammate patted him on the back.

Rap music blared through the cracked front door. We ducked our heads as we walked in right as the mist crawled out from the forest and started snaking through the parking lot, slowly covering everything. Although the entrance lacked refinement—just an alcove with an end table and a fallen-over coat rack—the A-frame parlor faced the lake. A smoky fog bank covered nearly all the water, though. Drunk teenagers packed the room from corner to corner, jabbering loudly and sipping from red plastic solo cups. I scanned the crowd but didn't spot Hunter.

"Come on, let me get you a drink," Tiffany said. She waved for us to follow then burrowed into the throng. Lacking party experience, Blake lit up upon seeing the festivities in full. Either the AC was broken, or the crammed bodies produced heat at atomic levels. Colognes, perfumes, and raging hormones combined into a heady mixture that smothered me like a horny teenager's Burberry-scented pillow. In short: I wanted to die. Thankfully, Tiffany quickly led us through the living room and into the kitchen, where the claustrophobic mob thinned out to a few clusters huddled together. In the middle of the kitchen, the island overflowed with half-drunken liquor bottles and opened plastic cup sleeves. Hunter was leaning against a wall at the entrance to a hallway. His verdant eyes fixed on me when I walked in. He clamped his teeth on his cup's rim, like he'd stopped drinking to stare at me. Scott and two other guys talked to him, but he didn't look too invested in the conversation.

"What are y'all feeling," Tiffany said, gesturing to the drinks.

Alison bumped me with her elbow. "Go get him," she whispered while pointing Tiffany toward a bottle. But I couldn't just go over there and kidnap him. I needed to jog his memory, but going off on a tangent about our old lives as wizard boyfriends didn't sound too sober—he'd laugh and think I was high. I needed more time, but we didn't have any. What *was* time in this place? Too much going on. People surrounded us and the heat choked me. Panic set in and I felt blood rushing to my head.

"I have to get out of here."

I bolted out of the kitchen, down the hallway past Hunter and his friends. Six kids in a line blocked access to the downstairs bathroom, so I ran upstairs and walked into the master bedroom, then into the lavatory and slammed the door. I ran some water at the sink and splashed my face before taking a few deep breaths. Blasting off into full-blown panic didn't help anything, but parties always did this to me. The racket downstairs compromised my ability to think, and right now, I really needed that intact. I had to get back in there and convince him to follow us. Somehow.

I went to leave and turned the knob, but the door didn't open. It was jammed. I thought about kicking it down, but I didn't want to draw attention. The Institute didn't currently know our where-abouts in the Dreamhaven. That much was clear; otherwise, at least a few partygoers would've turned into agents and tried to kill us. My earlier suspicion the Institute's powers had serious limitations in the Dreamhaven proved true so far. If we didn't hurry, we risked the Cave of Miracles closing before we got there. Then the Institute would have plenty of time to hunt us down. Right then, the door opened and Hunter walked in. My heart stopped. I raised a hand, wordlessly warning him not to shut the door, but he did anyway.

"Sorry," Hunter said, "I didn't know anyone was in here."

"The door's busted."

Hunter turned the knob. "Shit. You're serious."

"It's not really the kind of thing you make up."

He left the door alone and headed for me, awkwardly stopping just short. "I've got to pee."

I was in his way. Embarrassed, I stepped aside and faced the door so he wouldn't think I was looking.

Now what? I couldn't just stand there. If the direct approach failed—telling him the truth—few options remained. Kidnapping him sounded good. It wouldn't be that hard either. He stood a little shorter than me, and I'd won every bed-wrestling match he'd chal-lenged me to (although he usually just giggled and let me pin him). But I didn't need him screaming and alerting his friends. They might turn into agents and kill us. A much simpler idea sparked in my mind. I searched the bathroom for something heavy. I'd knock him out and drag him outside like a caveman, and call Alison and Blake to help me toss him in Tiffany's car. Okay, bad idea.

Hunter flushed the toilet and washed his hands in the sink. He leaned against the counter after drying them off and patted the space next to him. "This is pretty funny," he said. I sidled up beside him. "We could kick in the door." His words slurred.

"Do you have your phone?"

He searched his pockets. "Man, I left it with the guys." Even if I restored Hunter's memories and we escaped the bathroom, it was well past midnight. Braving the mist to reach the cave wouldn't be easy—assuming Luther was still waiting for us. Hunter bobbed his head drunkenly. He stunk like every liquor bottle in that kitchen. But he also had on this cute athletic cologne, a mix of bergamot and mint that made me want to bury my face in his shirt. "Where'd you go today after homeroom?"

"I skipped."

"Why?"

"I didn't want to be there."

"Can I tell you something weird?" he said. "I feel like I know you. I know we just met, but I feel like I've known you for a long time. Like I can just tell you anything. I'm being weird, huh?"

"No."

"Am I talking too much?"

"I like hearing you talk." *I could listen to you talk all night. If I could only hear one thing for the rest of my life, it would be your voice.*

Hunter spun toward me. "Do you like me?"

No point in lying. "Yeah."

"Can I kiss you?"

A pleasant surprise. We barely knew each other in this world, but even here you couldn't keep us apart. We were like two speeding trains on a collision course. "Yeah."

Hunter pinned me against the counter and brought his whiskey-tasting lips to mine. His sloppy drunk kiss didn't tower as history's most perfect embrace, but it still hushed the noisy world, made us feel like two fools lost in a daydream. Our passions flared. He pushed me up against the sink until I was sitting on it, then he ran his fingers up my shirt and I cupped his face in my hands. Something sparked between us then, like a supernova exploding between our lips.

Gently, he pulled away, his face warped with confusion. "Johnny? Where are we? Is this the Institute?"

"Hunter? You remember the Institute?"

He groaned and didn't say anything back, but I could tell: his memories had returned. All that true love's kiss bullshit wasn't so silly after all. Hunter grabbed my knees and strained. I thought he might kiss me again, but instead he threw up on my shirt.

Chapter 9

Hunter lay at my feet, passed out on the bathroom floor. Drinking himself into a slobbering coma suited Hunter's brand. I still needed to get that door down. I thrust my foot at it—it shook but remained in place. Damn thing was sturdier than a redwood.

Hunter groggily got up halfway and leaned against the cabinet below the sink. He put a hand to his head and squinted painfully. "Johnny?"

"I'm going to get us out of here, Hunt," I said. My foot landed against the door with another futile thud. Frustrated, I reeled back and swung at it one last time, but the door flew open, and I smashed some guy in the shin. A couple had been kissing on the other side.

"Ow! What the fu—" said the guy.

"What's your problem?" his girlfriend yelled at me.

"Door's busted, sorry! We needed to get out," I explained. I slung Hunter's arm around my shoulder and hoisted him. He wobbled up and stabilized himself.

"What's going on, Johnny? Why do I feel sick?"

"We don't have time, Hunt."

I rushed back downstairs with Hunter. Scott gave me a funny look when I walked in shouldering him. "What's wrong with Hunter?" he asked.

"Who's that guy?" Hunter muttered.

"He's really drunk," I said.

Scott sighed and shook his head like this was nothing new for Hunter. "One of us'll get him home."

"He wants to come with me."

"I want to go with Johnny," Hunter said.

Alison chattered with some girls near the island. Blake lounged bored on a stool nearby, munching on some chips from a big bowl.

"That palette's horrible. So chalky and gross. I found one at Ulta for, like, twelve bucks—"

"Alison," I said.

She turned and saw Hunter hanging off me like he was about to sink to the floor, and excused herself and pulled us aside with Blake. "J, you didn't drug him, did you?" she asked quietly.

"No, Ali, he's drunk."

"Let's hurry back to Luther's," Blake said.

"What're y'all talking about?" Hunter said. "Is anyone going to tell me what's going on?"

"All in good time, country boy," Alison said. We headed back into the crowded living room. Alison spotted Tiffany talking to some people. "Hey, Tiffany, we have to go."

"With Hunter?" Tiffany asked.

"Yeah, he's supersick and wants us to take him home."

Tiffany held up a cup. "I've been drinking. And it's misty outside."

"I've got a truck . . . I've got a truck?" Hunter said. He was like me when I first woke up in the Dreamhaven. His real memories struggled against the fake ones the Institute had implanted. At least this Hunter came equipped with a vehicle.

"I'm driving us in Hunter's truck," Blake said. "I'm the designated driver, anyway."

Alison gave Tiffany one more clumsy goodbye and we left. Outside, the mist had chased everyone who'd been on the deck earlier inside. Scott's noisy rager drowned the strange sounds bubbling in the mist, but the farther we moved from the house the clearer the noises grew: hums, hisses, shrieks, and yelps sang a haunting medley. It made me want to move faster.

Hunter pointed to a new-ish red pickup truck with hardened mud covering the undercarriage. "That's mine."

We walked to it, and Hunter prodded his pants until he found a key. Blake grabbed it and headed for the driver's side. "Load him into the back."

I helped Hunter into the back seat, and he plunked face forward with a groan. He pulled himself together, slowly sitting up. I slid in after him. Alison jumped into the passenger seat and looked back at us. "Are his memories back?"

Hunter dropped his head in my lap. "Yeah," I said as Blake slipped the key into the ignition. The engine rumbled to life, and he backed out and we speedily drove away.

"What're you guys talking about?" Hunter said.

"Hey, gay cowboy, who are we?"

"What?"

"Just answer the question, Romeo."

"You're that goth chick that never shuts up, and I'm lying on Johnny, and I think Blake's driving."

"Your milquetoast boyfriend is charming as ever. How did he get his memory back?"

"I don't know. I kissed him and . . . bam."

Alison gave me a ludicrous look then mouthed the word "okay" and turned around.

"We're going to have to sober him up," Blake said. "We don't know how dangerous the journey to Luther's cave is going to be. We need him close to a hundred."

Shrouded in the mist's oppressive blanket, the normally inviting Misthaven had become a disorienting oubliette, forcing Blake to drive slowly. Alison's face remained stiff, and as she watched the ghostly mist sweep by outside her mind wandered. She probably wanted to be back at that party, debating how to make Jell-O shots with Tiffany.

We came to a red light at a four-way intersection with a gas station to our right. The time on the dashboard radio read *12:30*. A loud crash frightened everyone in the car and Blake almost bashed his head against the roof. A raccoon scurried across the road, and it quickly became apparent the creature had knocked over a trash can while rummaging for food. Alison snickered at us for acting silly, but I'm certain she jumped almost as high as Blake. The light remained the same bright red. Longest red light ever. I rubbed Hunter's hair to calm myself, and he smiled peacefully.

A loud *clack* split the air. And another. And another. *Clack, clack, clack.* It sounded like tap shoes. I slowly turned and looked. Hidden in the fog, a shadowy figure danced under a lamppost, creeping across the street toward us. Whoever that was, they were freaking me out. I rapped my knee against Alison's seat to get her attention. She turned and I pointed, and she saw the figure dancing under the bleary, orange streetlight.

"What the crap is that?" she asked.

The dancing shadow stamped on the asphalt, inching toward us with every spasmodic jerk and twitch—sometimes a ballerina, sometimes a tap dancer, always on beat with some unseen, unheard symphony.

"The mist is messing with us," Hunter said, "All the kids at the Institute say to ignore it." But ignoring it didn't make it go away. It continued its strange, hypnotic motions, coming closer and closer.

"Forget that," Blake said as he stomped on the gas and ran the red light. The shadow kept dancing until it vanished in the mist behind us. Blake didn't make any other stops after that; he sped all the way back to Luther's camper. Hunter feebly lifted himself off my lap, still holding his aching head as we exited the car.

Blake opened my door. "You good?" he asked Hunter.

"I feel like crap."

"Good enough. Let's go."

I slid out and waited for Hunter to follow. His white Nikes hit the pavement and I moved behind him, staying nearby in case he needed help.

"You going to tell me what's going on?" Hunter asked, putting his arm around me for balance.

"Do you remember using the cintamani and everything that happened?"

"Of course," he said. "What's going on?"

I told Hunter everything in the time it took us to reach Luther's door. He didn't have much to say in response. By the look of it, he was speeding toward an early hangover.

Luther cracked the door and eyed us through the opening. "What took you? It's nearly one in the morning. Do you have any idea the kind of misery we're going to experience trying to find the cave?"

Luther grew even more wary when he noticed Alison and Hunter. He gave them a quick scan, surely checking to see if they were copies before he let us in. Hunter pushed passed everyone and fell face-first on Luther's bed.

"You brought a drunk teenager with you?" Luther said, annoyed.

"He'll be fine. I'll make sure of it," I said.

"Johnny'll keep me safe," Hunter said into a pillow.

"Are you ever going to tell us what's going on?"

"We don't have time. We must leave immediately and venture into Darkwood Forest, or we'll lose our opportunity and the cave will disappear."

"What about that fog?" Blake asked. "We need to know more about what we're up against."

"From what I've gathered, the mist is sentient," Luther said. "And extremely hostile. If it thinks we're trying to escape, it will use its powers to confuse and even attack us. I haven't determined whether there are several Void-spawns that exist in the mist or if these are merely manifestations of the mist's power. The mist itself may be a Void-spawn for all I know. The best thing we can do is stick together and quickly find the cave." So, the Institute's powers to track us grew significantly if we traveled in the mist. That explained why no agents came after us at Scott's—we got there and ran inside before the mist got to us. But if what Luther said was true, that meant the Institute knew our current whereabouts. And that compromised his operation in the Dreamhaven. No wonder we had to leave quickly.

"Don't you already know where it is?" Alison asked.

"The cave is rarely in the same location."

"You mean it moves?"

"Yes. We can find the cave in a grove of aspen trees the locals call 'the verge.'"

"Where does the Cave of Miracles lead to?" Alison asked.

"The City at the End of the World."

"The what?"

"We don't have time. Just stay close to me and I'll tell you more when we get there."

The City at the End of the World? Luther's elusiveness around our questions made me uncomfortable. The old man drew out a brass pocket watch engraved with two dragons, one lightly tinted and the other dark, locked in fire-breathing combat inside a heptagram. He popped it open and checked the time before stuffing it back into his raincoat. "I'll drive as far as I can."

Luther's escort brought me little comfort, and seeing Hunter too drunk to stand made things even worse. Reaching the cave required directly confronting the mist without our powers. The malevolent force hiding in the mist let us sample its twisted magic on our way to Luther's. Now it didn't need to hold back. Blake followed Luther without pause, but Alison hung back, shrinking inward, making herself small—something she did when gripped with terrible fear. Hunter woozily slumped off the bed and nearly fell, so I steadied him with my arm around his back. With great bravado and one eye shut, Hunter puffed out his chest, put on a brave face, and marched to the door with me. Alison apprehensively joined us.

Luther stored his beat-up, mustard-yellow station wagon beside the camper, hidden behind a bush. He packed us like sardines inside the old clunker and drove out of town, heading south along Pine Street. The lonely country roads that spiderwebbed around Misthaven were so dark Luther's flimsy headlights could barely pierce the gloom. Thick fog clouds rushed past the window like a smoke screen. Even the robust pine trees that dominated this region, lush and full in the spring, lurked spectrally in the mist.

Hunter leaned on my shoulder, still fighting the half hangover set upon him.

Heading east, Pine Street turned to River Road. Luther passed the dam and the water bottling company on the left, going around Lake Misty and deep into Darkwood Forest—toward Thelema Hills, the mountain range around Misthaven. The tense mood in the car hung thick. Blake put a hand on Alison's knee, and it scared her so bad she nearly screamed. He chuckled and slid his arm around her shoulder, settling her down, but they remained terrified. Uncertainty marked even Luther's old, craggy face.

Luther's old car wobbled to one side, then a loud boom came from behind us. The vehicle tilted to the right, forcing Luther to struggle against the wheel for stability. But it kept veering, so he parked on the shoulder. With that, our short ride met an unceremonious end. Luther turned the crank on his squeaky window and rolled it down, then he hung his head outside and looked back. After a speedy study, Luther brought his head back in and faced us. "I've lost a tire. The mist isn't going to make this easy. Let's get out and head into the forest. We need to hurry and find the verge—the mist won't go there."

The old man got out of the car and rumbled through his trunk until he found a big flashlight. He flicked it on and started for the tree line. We all got out and huddled close around him, following his shaky beam through the brush. A breeze howled through the spindly pine branches, and an owl uttered a few restless hoots, but below the forest's scant noises, the mist's frightening sounds hummed on the air. A powerful and strange aura pervaded the mist—it felt ancient, older than anything on Earth. Reading deeper into the aura, images of the Void filled my mind, its demonic influence leaving an indelible impression upon the mist. It hungered, the mist, and nothing could sate its lust for violence and misery. Because my time directly in the mist had been limited, I never noticed that it stunk like eirineftis. A strange observation I kept to myself. To redirect my thoughts I focused on Luther's flashlight, but the middling ray only managed a dull spot on the opaque fog wall.

Branches snapped and cracked loudly, a cacophony resonating through the forest. A hooting owl departed its perch and flew overhead. Then silence. We stopped moving and looked underfoot, but the noise didn't come from us. Luther swept his flashlight across the blackness, but the light bounced too much for a clear investigation. We suffered some relief when we thought the clamor was over, but the horrifying sounds rose again, stretching furiously into the night.

"What is that?" Alison asked.

Luther hushed her and kept waving around the flashlight, hoping to find what prowled behind the noise. We clustered even more tightly around him as he focused on steadying the beam. The light fell precariously on one spot, but Luther's shaky hands failed to keep it still. More limbs broke, the disturbance coming nearer. A tremble shook the forest floor. Something massive pounded the ground in the distance—it sounded like a giant foot. Blake pointed westward, where an invisible force shattered a few flimsy pines. Another *thwomp* resounded through the forest.

"We need to run," Luther said, turning and taking off like a frightened spider.

Alison and Blake chased after Luther, but before we joined them, another raucous crash sent Hunter teetering. I reached for him, but he drunkenly backed over a raised root and tumbled down into a brook. We had been walking along an escarpment, but the dense fog had hidden the ledge.

I called to Hunter from the drop-off, but my voice echoed back without a response. The last distant glimmers of Luther's flash-light disappeared into the mist, and with them, Alison and Blake. Another terrifying *whump* warned me not to stick around to meet the one making all the noise. I skidded down after Hunter until I hit the bottom and crashed on my shoulder a few feet away. Searing pain tore through my arm.

I coddled the injury and got back on my feet. "Hunter!" I called, my vision unable to penetrate the impassable mist. "Hunter!"

The ground quaked again. I covered my mouth and pressed against the wall. No telling what that thing up there was. More trees shuddered and broke around the top of the scarp. Waiting for the others carried potentially lethal consequences, but darkness curtained everything, making unplanned movements aimless. Hunter had disappeared far too quickly, though—I had to get going in case he was in danger. Moonlight squirmed through the mist, sparsely lighting the forest floor, but the scrambled moonbeams did little to help me find my way. I stretched my arms out and felt for anything.

Hoofs clopped through the forest, briefly stopping as a horse neighed in the distance. Then a golden light pierced the mist, so bright it hurt my eyes. The glowing orb hovered in place until I approached it, then it darted away, hoofs beating the ground as it zipped through the darkness. Adrenaline kicked in and I flew into pursuit. Even with the light guiding my way, the mist still made the underbrush unnavigable. I banged my foot against a thick shrub and fell on my stomach, but the light didn't stop moving, and I hurried back up and kept after it. A powerful *whomp* from behind me rocked the ground, the violent tremor sending me stumbling. Still, I kept my footing and pushed forward, shoving past over-grown bushes and clouds of fog, following the faerie light until the monstrous rumbling tapered off. And I didn't rest my hunt until the light had disappeared, and I crashed into something dry and wiry. I searched for the golden ball, listened for a running horse, but found neither.

The semispongy wall I'd crashed into sprang back to normal if I squeezed its surface, but if I closed my fingers around it too hard it seemed to crack. As my eyes adjusted, I found myself standing before a barrier of dried vines. No way to tell how far it stretched in either direction, but I quickly discovered a hole along the bottom, level with my foot. A light vibration coursed from the floor up my leg. That thing in the forest was still looking for me. Stopping meant death, I was sure of it. I crawled into the tunnel. The tight squeeze proved difficult, with stiff knotted vines prickling my hands the whole way through, but I emerged on the other side in a fogless grove with a crystalline pool that glimmered in the moonlight. Right then I remembered Tiffany's story about a magic wishing pond and a unicorn hidden deep in Darkwood Forest. My thoughts dawdled on the glowing light and the running horse that led me here—not that I normally placed stock in legends, but for a wizard trapped in a dream prison, it didn't seem too farfetched that a unicorn had guided me here. Now to learn if this magic wishing pond was legit.

I cupped water into my mouth and wished for all this to be over and for us to be safely back with our families. Nothing happened, though. But something strange stirred in me. It felt like a sapling in my chest, seeing the sunlight for the first time. It spread its roots throughout my body, and as those shining rays caressed the young tree, she took hold and grew stronger. *Magic.* Golden energy pulsed in my veins and rushed to my fingertips. Again, the world was like clay waiting for me to mold it. The pond had returned my magic.

My wizard senses, keen and sharp again, immediately picked up the others. Alison and Blake were safe with Luther, but Hunter's aura was in the opposite direction. He needed me. Wizards' powers knew no parallels in Everywhen, and I didn't know anyone with more experience fighting monsters in the dreamworld than me. With my abilities finally restored, that big stompy thing out there didn't stand a chance—at least, I hoped it didn't.

I crawled back through the hole into the misty forest. Happy to use my magic again, I flicked my wrist and made a glowing orb—it was the first spell I'd ever learned. Magic didn't come easy outside of Everywhen. Spells required great focus, and stories about kids accidentally turning light orbs into haywire fireballs abounded. The results: always catastrophic, and usually deadly.

Not far into my search for Hunter, I stumbled over a depression on the ground shaped like a giant human footprint, but with no toes. It stretched at least a dozen feet across. My mind exploded imagining what the foot's owner looked like. Then Hunter's familiar voice let out a deep, guttural "uuugggggghhhhhh." I'd never been so happy to hear someone groan. He leaned against a tree with his head, spitting out the last remnants of whatever he just finished throwing up. I gently touched his shoulder, and he screamed and fell backward.

"Johnny?" He shielded his eyes from the bright light with one hand and wiped away the dribble on his mouth with the other. "You got your magic back?"

"It's a long story." I helped him up. "What happened after you fell down the slope?"

"I don't know. I started walking around in the dark, then I got really sick and wound up here."

Crows loudly abandoned a treetop in a squawking flurry as the ground rattled. Another shake brought caution. The one after, concern.

"We're leaving, c'mon."

Hunter wasn't in the best shape to be running, but impending doom has a funny way of making one fully functional. We got roughly three feet away before a whistling sound cut through the air, and two branches fell crashing to the ground in front of us. Something unseen had sliced them off. We about-faced and fled in the opposite direction, then several misty tentacles shot out of the darkness and came at us like bullets.

"Drop!" I yelled. One tentacle cut through Hunter's arm as we hit the ground. He covered the wound and screamed. We didn't have time to lie there—I hurried to my feet then yanked Hunter up beside me and charged toward Alison's and Blake's auras. Hunter fought to keep pace even though his wound bled angrily. "Just a little more," I told him, stealing a look back—whatever was after us had flattened every tree in its path. A spinning log came hurtling at us through the opening. Hunter and I dove, and the log flew by overhead. Then a second uprooted tree barreled toward us. "Stay down!" I said.

Whatever pissed-off giant was throwing trees wasn't going to stop. I got to my feet, formed a light sword, and sprang into the air when the next trunk came. Time slowed down around me, and with magically enhanced precision I sliced the log in two. Once my feet hit the ground, I snatched Hunter and rushed us behind a fir. Another flying log shattered against our cover. Hunter pulled his jacket over his head and let the debris roll off. We hid there until it seemed the monster had ceased. I peeked around the corner for any more projectiles, and finally glimpsed the creature: it rose taller than the trees around it, a reptilian beast with human-like arms and legs and a head like a Komodo dragon. Its skin was a whirling mass of smoky tentacles, screaming faces occasionally surfacing along them.

Like all creatures in Everywhen, it lacked an aura, so gleaning information from it was impossible. I realized it had been invisible to me until I restored my wizard senses—just like the Void-spawns in the real world. We didn't have a prayer against that thing, so we fled.

The monster took a hulking step forward and its footfall rumbled the ground and almost knocked us off our feet. I glanced back and saw it drive its hands into the earth, puncturing through soil and bedrock for a grip. Then the beast lifted the floor like a carpet and slung a hellish tsunami of dirt and rocks at us.

"Don't look back!" I told Hunter. But he didn't listen, and when he peeked behind himself, he saw the soaring wall speeding toward us.

"What the fuuuuuu—" He screamed as we bounded through the forest like wild rabbits. We reached the vine wall.

"What're we going to do?" he asked.

The hole to the magic pond was gone, so I searched for a new way out, too preoccupied to explain anything. He impatiently eyed the rapidly approaching avalanche. "J, what are you doing? We're going to get crushed!"

I headed left along the wall, following my wizard senses until I found another small hole. "Here, Hunter!" I scuttled into the opening.

Hunter didn't have time to crawl, sliding in like a baseball player. The earthen tidal wave smashed into the wall behind him and filled the tunnel with dust. I covered my head, but the debris still flew up my nose. Even Hunter, who'd guarded his head with his jacket, ended up choking on dirt. The horrible shaking slowed to a feeble tremble then vanished completely. My throat ached from coughing so hard, and I'm sure Hunter's didn't feel much better. A slight aftershock hit the tunnel, threatening to cave the whole thing in, but it only caused some dirt to trickle down from the ceiling.

"You okay?" I asked.

"Yeah, you?"

"I'm good. Let's get out of here."

We crawled until we reached a thin spot in the wall. Even though the vines felt like brambles cutting into my skin, I ripped them away and widened the hole. Once the branches had thinned enough, I shoved my way through to the other side. Hunter came out after me and brushed himself off. Our journey took us into a fogless boscage with perfectly lined aspen trees arranged into rows. An eerie stillness pervaded the grove, as if the place lay frozen in time, whisked away from the changing hours and seasons. High above, the night sky—the stars themselves had vanished, leaving behind a shadowy nothingness. Strangely, though no moon stamped the sky, a light still permeated this place: a dim umber glow, hazy and dreamlike. Truly this place responded to its own strange physics. My wizard senses told me we stood between unknown possibilities. It felt like I was being torn in two directions, but this place pulled me into millions. Indeed, we'd found the verge—the verge between worlds.

The ground underfoot felt like ash, and a sooty stench clung to the air. Either the Institute didn't know about the verge, or they didn't have a proper way to seal it up. Knowing that, and that they'd botched our mind-wipe, gave me confidence that the Institute wasn't an undefeatable monolith. Wizards, with all their miraculous abilities, were still just woefully flawed humans.

Alison's voice broke the quiet, calling for Hunter and me. I followed her aura until I found the others.

"Johnny, what happened?" Alison asked when she saw me.

"Hunter fell off an escarpment and we got separated. What was that monster out there?"

"Perhaps a Void-spawn indentured to the Institute," Luther said.

"I've never been foolhardy enough to study it closely. It's time." He reached into the air and parted reality to one side like a curtain. A hole in the fabric of space appeared, and beyond it a stygian corridor with billowing black curtains for walls. An ominous feeling poured out of the opening like a warning. Walking into that passage was unpredictable, possibly even dangerous.

"This is a rather common manifestation of the cave," Luther said. "There's no telling what you'll find navigating the Cave of Miracles. To keep wizards from freely traveling between worlds, the cave plays tricks on them, so they'll become lost inside forever. Your powers should return to you beyond the threshold—they should flow from you as easily as they do in Everywhen. Remember to push through whatever strangeness you find within. Wizards are masters of their own destinies. If you get lost, just search for one another's auras. After this tunnel, we will arrive somewhere in the City at the End of the World."

"What's that?" Alison asked.

"It is every city that ever was, ever will be, and ever has been, collected like puzzle pieces in one place. A world trapped somewhere between dreams and reality. The location in which you'll emerge is likely to be random. Remember to track one another using your auras. Do not, under any circumstances, use magic within the city. It is forbidden." He gave us one more wary scan. "This is all I can offer before we enter." He looked unsure about going in with us, but we'd come too far and he knew we couldn't turn back. Our escape had thrown the Dreamhaven into high alert.

Luther stepped into the opening and vanished.

Alison started into the passage, briefly glancing back at the Dreamhaven—saying goodbye before walking into the corridor with Blake. Hunter entered ahead of me, and I followed.

Chapter 10

The Cave of Miracles lay between worlds like the thread on a spider-web adjoining two pearls of water. Its blustery walls resembled satin sheets, with a phantasmal yet forceful touch. I wanted to stay on a narrow path because I dreaded getting lost, but these corridors denied our passage. Their disorienting folds wrapped around me, swallowed me, and stole Hunter from my grasp.

"Hunter?" I called, fighting against the twisting curtains. But they spun me in circles and I became lost in their curves and bends. They surrounded me, melting into pure darkness. Fear compelled me to keep moving until I appeared suddenly in my old living room in Chicago. Right behind me, I spotted Dad in his recliner, his dormant eyes absorbing images dancing on a television set. I was overcome by horror, thinking that the Dreamhaven impostor had followed me. Then I recalled Luther's warning: *To keep wizards from freely traveling between worlds, the cave plays tricks on them.* The cave wielded Everywhen's madness amplified.

Dad remained motionless, not responding to me or the TV or anything. Worse than a copy—a husk. A memory that forgot to fade. I reached my index finger toward his cheek and made an indention in his skin. Then his head exploded into a million hairy moths. The monstrous little things skittered all over me. One landed on my nose. I focused on it—its tiny face looked like mine; it stared at me with my own eyes before its face transformed, resembling my mother's. And with another shift, it turned to television static. I closed my eyes and told myself it wasn't real. When I opened them again, I was still standing in my old living room. The floor lurched forward, going vertical, sending me sliding, crashing into the bay window. Nothing but darkness outside—the Void's gaping maw, waiting for the glass to break and drop me. But the room fussed like a hyper child refusing to stay in one place. It turned upside down, throwing me onto the ceiling. The world threatened to continue spinning, so I pressed my eyes again and remembered that my powers expanded limitlessly in the dreamworld. I didn't need much to summon myself back in the black-curtained hallway.

A hand landed on my shoulder, triggering panic. "Johnny!" Hunter said, sounding perfectly sober.

"You're not drunk anymore? How do you feel?"

"Fine. It's like nothing was ever wrong with me."

The Dreamhaven's laws seem to have faded when we crossed the threshold into the Cave of Miracles. Our dream bodies changed into real ones, and all the clothes from the dreamworld became real too. Wherever the Institute had been keeping us, the cave's magic transported us from that place and dropped us here—wherever *here* was.

"Hunt, let's hurry and find everyone before we get lost in this place forever."

We pushed through curtains until we found ourselves in a building with exposed brick walls and rafters with visible piping. Gnarled witch faces and gilded Venetian masks hung next to princess dresses and jester suits on gridwall panels and garment racks. A twenty-something woman slumped lazily behind a counter wreathed in colorful string lights and Mardi Gras beads near the front. She pulled her hair up into a taut bun, leaned forward, and squinted at us. Hunter and I were partially hanging out of a dressing room. The cave's winding black labyrinth had disappeared.

"A costume store?" Hunter said.

"Where are we?" I asked the clerk.

She gave a clueless shrug. "Brooklyn?"

I sensed the others' auras, and tapped a knuckle against Hunter's arm and checked his face to confirm that he was feeling the same thing. He nodded knowingly, and we headed for the door.

A steam cloud swept past us as we walked outside. When it cleared, the road before us appeared split between two worlds: one side, ours, had an asphalt street with yellow lines painted on it, a stop sign around the corner, and a light directing traffic; on the other side, the road was cobbled, and people in Victorian clothing were walking alongside horse-drawn carriages. A fourteen-year-old newsie stood on a wooden crate, hawking newspapers. He was too far away to glimpse the headlines.

The glare from the sunlight hurt my eyes. It was brighter than the sun in our world.

"Johnny, where are we?"

"Luther said that after we left the Cave of Miracles, we would come to the City at the End of the World."

A brass machine standing barely a foot tall, with flat feet that chattered like gag teeth and a big round nose, scuttled across the pavement in front of us. Its jerky body swayed side to side as it hustled to join three other machines like it. Each one resembled an upside-down bucket, and metal swoops under their noses imitated moustaches. They gathered around a hole in the sidewalk. One machine came apart into segments, like a toy. A hose emerged from inside it and started pouring wet cement into the spot. Another one came apart and smoothed the cement with a concrete placer that extended from a pole within its body. The machines made chirping noises and disbanded in opposite directions once they'd finished. Disbelief froze me in place. Hunter nudged me and we started moving again.

We kept to our side of the road and followed the others' auras west, to the crosswalk. A golden machine hovered in the intersection and directed traffic there. Its crude metal body lacked arms— its simple rounded head rested between two spherical shoulders, and its lower body widened at the top but drove to a point at the bottom, like an upside-down pyramid. Underneath the machine, a spinning halo two feet in diameter hummed quietly nearly a foot off the ground.

"What the hell is that thing?" Hunter said.

"What the hell is anything in here?"

Anachronisms abounded in the strange city. While we waited on a modern-looking street corner, a short way down, to our left, the city grew older. The cement buildings turned to brick and bore dated signage. One lit up marquee read *LG Stone Fine Dressing*. A guy with a flattop strutted down the sidewalk carrying an '80s-style boom box on his shoulder. Even more unusual, every car in traffic exhibited impenetrably smoky windows. Hunter hunched next to a brown sedan and used his sleeve to clear the glass on the passenger side, but no matter how much he rubbed, it stayed opaque.

The light changed colors, but traffic didn't move. The cars, and their drivers, colorlessly emulated life on our world. Same for the nineteenth century set piece across the street: That newspaper boy would stand on that same corner, peddling that same paper, forever. Time had no meaning here. No one here intended to go anywhere. Ever. The City at the End of the World was like a bunch of Lego pieces jumbled in a toy box, with nothing coherently stacked to resemble a "real" world. Or maybe my pale human reasoning simply failed to grasp the scheme behind its arrangement.

Hunter and I crossed the street, and although the era stayed the same, our surroundings changed to resemble Chicago, not New York. Alison, Blake, and Luther loitered at a hot dog stand on a corner northwest of us, not too far away. Luther no longer wore his Dreamhaven disguise. He looked like the same old sinewy man I'd met long ago.

"I would kill for a hot dog," I said, holding my stomach.

Hunter pointed to the others. "Let's go hit the old man up for some food."

Alison looked relieved to see us approaching. "J, you scared the crap out of me. You've got to stop disappearing like that. Where'd you go?"

"A . . . costume shop?"

"We popped up in the backroom of a sporting good's store," Blake said.

"Hey, old man," Hunter said, evoking a sinister glare from Luther, "buy us something to eat. We're starving."

It took Luther a second to recover from Hunter's impudence. "I'm not here looking for a snack." Luther returned to the scraggly haired man behind the cart. "BJ—"

"That guy's name is BJ?" Hunter said, cracking a smile.

Luther kept a harsh eye on Hunter. "BJ, have you seen any agents around?"

"Not today."

Luther thanked the vendor and headed up the sidewalk, toward another crossing.

"Who was that?" I asked as we followed. "What is this place? What were all those machines back there?"

"Perhaps one question at a time?" Luther said.

"What about that guy, who was he?"

"An informant of mine. One of the city's many denizens."

"Do these people really just . . . *live* here or something?" Alison asked.

"*Exist* is a more appropriate term. Yes, most of the entities you see exist here and only here. You may run across the occasional wizard, but it's extremely rare."

Blake caught up to Luther and walked beside him. "You called these people . . . *entities*?"

"They are conceptuals—archetypes of people that may, can, or do exist."

Lego people living in a Lego city, I thought to myself.

Alison looked back at the hot dog guy. "What was that guy an archetype of?"

"A nosy food vendor who knows more than he should."

"What about those robots?" I asked.

"We call the small ones 'hobs.' I've never seen them do anything but maintain the city. The larger ones we call 'guardians.'" Luther stopped at the crosswalk. The light was red for us, but the cars weren't moving. Hunter put a foot forward, ready to cross. Luther blocked him with his forearm. "If you break any of the city's myriad rules, including using magic, which is banned throughout, the guardians will remove you, often casting you back to where you came from."

Hunter, acknowledging Luther's warning, stepped back.

"Who made them? Who made any of this?"

"Do you know the story the Institute tells of how the world was made?"

The light turned green. Luther walked across the street, heading for a four-story building. We followed, me reciting the creation myth as I knew it: "The Creators escaped the Void and tried to make a paradise of eternal love, but the Void-spawns hunted them down and destroyed their paradise, so they used the cogs and wheels they'd made and built a new world—our world. That clockwork is the vivit apparatus. The Void-spawns chased the Creators into our world and hunted them down, but then the Void-spawns got stuck and couldn't go back to the Void, so they became mortal. Wizards are probably their descendants."

"I'm not inclined to trust most of the pseudo-religious fluff," Luther said, "but I think there are *some* scientific accuracies in that legend. This world is a toolbox of concepts. Governments exist street to street, and likewise laws and logic also exist street to street. The laws and government in one part of the city, won't be the same as those in another. If the Creators did indeed exist, this city was the model for every city that would ever or *could* ever exist.

"Oneironauts who have spent extensive time exploring the city tell the same myth: The Creators built the city, set in motion all the clockwork to run it, then left. I've, admittedly, learned very little about the city. Exploring it is dangerous. The city is like Everywhen in that it is always changing. Without a plan, it would be very easy for a wizard to get lost here forever."

Like in Everywhen, the vivit apparatus held no command over the city's physics. The city not only occupied a nexus between worlds, it was the first city—no, the first *anything* ever created, in any existence. I recalled those machines Luther had called hobs fixing the hole in the sidewalk earlier. The city ran itself using two mechanisms: one to protect and one to maintain.

We reached the run-down four-story building. Its darkly tinted windows made it difficult to see inside. The numbers *60139* were engraved on a brass placard near the entrance. Luther walked up the stoop and entered. A cardinal-headed creature read a 1987 *Sports Illustrated* magazine behind the reception desk in the lobby. Atop a three-tier filing cabinet behind the birdman, a miniature TV blared the 1987 World Series. Luther marched ahead, down a hallway and toward an old cage elevator.

Hunter stopped me, drawing my attention to the birdman. "The heck is that?"

"A Cardinals fan?"

"Come along," Luther said, annoyed with our gawking. The birdman turned a page in his magazine. The crack of a baseball bat echoed behind him.

We caught up with Luther and boarded the elevator. He pulled a lever that pivoted on a half wheel, and the elevator's metal doors screeched shut. The rickety thing rattled up a few stories, vibrating our teeth the whole way.

"How did you find the Dreamhaven?" Blake asked.

"Rumors that the Institute used a dream prison in Everywhen have been circulating for quite some time. I came to the City at the End of the World and did some investigation, and discovered a portal in the neighborhood we were just in."

"So, there're multiple entrances into the Dreamhaven?"

"As you witnessed, more than one portal *out* of the Dreamhaven exists, so more than one leading in is only logical. Regardless of which portal you use to enter, you always come out through a different one on return. Thanks to you I've learned another secret—large parties can get separated in the Cave of Miracles."

The elevator stopped and Luther slid open the doors. He walked us down a long hallway to a door with no handle at the end of the passage.

"Yes, here," Luther said. Using his fingers, he traced a circle over the door then marked three dots in the center. The formation turned into a glowing sigil that quickly disappeared. Out of the door grew a brass handle with a simple knob and a keyhole. Luther unlocked the door and opened it. "Sanctuary is through here."

Chapter 11

An armoire connected the doorway in the City at the End of the World to a cozy study in Sanctuary. With everyone already through, I closed the armoire then opened it again curiously, but no hallway in the City at the End of the World waited on the other side. Now, I found shelves filled with books. In fact, books occupied almost every shelf in the office, and a large Persian rug covered the floor. A pedestal desk sat in the northern corner, tall windows in a row behind it. The three o'clock sun lay in the west, its warm rays dancing across the lavishly varnished furniture.

"The portal to Sanctuary is so close to the Dreamhaven. How come the Institute hasn't found it yet?" I asked.

"Even if they had, they don't have the spell or key to open it."

"Are there other ways into the City at the End of the World?"

"You've no doubt heard the saying, 'To find a thing in Everywhen, one need only look for it.' The same is true for the city. That's how

I found it. I put the portal to Sanctuary close to the Dreamhaven's entrance because I didn't want to risk getting lost."

Nephelie, Aquila, and Linh walked into the office. Aquila's long brown hair fell straight down her tanned back, and she wore a black tank top with leather pants. She looked like someone who got piss drunk in dive bars and arm wrestled every guy who measured a few inches taller than her. That may have been true, but I'd only ever seen her crack jokes, not skulls.

Nephelie wore a long black dress that showed off her strong arms, and her locks were bundled atop her head, tied with a blue-and-green ribbon. Although her crimson eyes were intense—shouldering a rebellion carried a lofty emotional burden—her rich ochre skin was soft, like combat had never grazed her.

"Oh my God!" Linh said when she saw us. Linh had been one of my closest friends at the Institute. She wasn't tall, but she packed a lot more personality than people twice her size. Her black hair had grown out to her shoulders, and she was wearing a purple T-shirt and some jeans. Linh had led me to Luther Dorian, and she and Aquila had been the ones to help us escape. We parted ways shortly before I went to Gaspar's hideout. She probably didn't think she'd ever see us again. "How'd you all get here?"

Nephelie didn't know what to make of our intrusion. Aquila, however, had a funny look on her face. "You again? Luther, what's going on?"

"I found them in the Dreamhaven . . . *aware*," Luther said.

"That's never happened before," Nephelie said.

"I know. They asked me to get them out."

"Aquila," Nephelie said, "can you take the children into the dining room and see if they're hungry? When they're done, Linh, please show them to their rooms."

"Okay, everyone," Aquila said, standing by the open door, "file out."

Linh looped her arm around mine. "You've got to tell me every-thing." We started out the door, but Luther and Nephelie stayed behind to talk. Already keeping secrets. I wanted to hang around and listen, but "get them something to eat" hadn't been the worst thing I'd heard lately.

An old foyer awaited us outside Nephelie's office. I'd seen enough houses like these back in Chicago to recognize the ornate, Victorian interior. A grand staircase split the main hall in half and joined the manse's two wings, with Nephelie's office in the upper right-hand corner. Adjacent Nephelie's office, in the southeast corner, a wide entry led to a dining room. An antechamber ran between the front entrance and the foyer, and a closed door lay on the foyer's west-ern side, across from the dining room. Linh let me go and started talking to Blake. While no one watched, I crept off to investigate the closed door.

Discovering the door unlocked, I stole a peek inside. A few short bookcases rested their backs against the walls, and a wing chair sat on a rug near a latticed window. Two young boys and a girl read quietly around a table. The children's bored faces told me everything about their reading material. One child lazily browsed a book with the words *Science and Health* on the cover. I gathered the others were also textbooks. Aquila cleared her throat at the dining room's entrance, arms folded over her chest, an eyebrow cocked at me. "They need to study. Life doesn't stop just because we're in a war." I closed the door quietly so as not to alert the children, then walked into the dining room. We congregated at a long table, near a window overlooking a cliff and a large body of water. Aquila left the room once we all took seats.

"So *this* is Sanctuary? What's the deal with this place?" Alison asked.

"It's like . . . a home for underage wizards," Linh said. "Since they're not old enough to take care of themselves, once the Defectors get them out, they bring them here. The Defectors are broken up into cells, and Nephelie doesn't really run her own cell, but she runs this place and oversees a lot of larger operations, so the Defectors also treat this place like a central hub."

"Cells?" I asked.

"Yeah. It's how the Defectors are arranged. There's a core group of cells, but new, unaffiliated cells pop up all the time. Supposedly the Defectors are organized that way so if one cell gets captured, the Institute can't read their minds and uproot the whole rebellion."

"But don't plenty of Defectors know where this place is?" Alison said.

Linh pointed to a small magic circle carved into a wooden pilaster. "They have those sigils all over Sanctuary. The Defectors can activate it to move the whole place."

"Move it?" I asked.

"Through teleportation."

The Defectors moved Sanctuary around to keep it hidden. Clever.

"Why keep a bunch of kids in the central hub of a rebellion?" Blake asked cynically. To him, good guys in the war between the Institute and the Defectors didn't exist. Like the Institute, the Defectors wanted something. He just didn't know what yet.

"This is the safest place for them *because* it can move around."

"What happens when they become adults?"

"They can choose to fight with the Defectors, and the Defectors will help them secure housing and jobs and stuff."

Aquila returned with a pot of dumplings floating in steaming vegetable broth. She placed a stack of wooden plates on the table, and a ladle and some metal spoons. My stomach growled when I saw the shimmery, golden soup. "Serve yourselves," she said. We descended on the food like locusts, ladling spoonfuls into our bowls and shoveling plump dumplings into our mouths. No one said much while we were eating.

When we finished, Aquila cleaned up and Linh led us upstairs, to the left wing. There was a round stained-glass window over the landing where the staircase in the foyer split. The image depicted two dragons, one light one dark, bound in fire-breathing combat. The same image on Luther's pocket watch.

We headed down a long hall, toward our room. The first door we passed on the right side of the passage was open. Inside, two kids—a brown-haired boy and a girl with black pigtails, each no older than six—jumped on a bed, screaming as they beat each other with pillows.

Linh stopped at the door. "Hey, Aquila's going to yell at you guys." The kids let out another wild screech and hopped off the bed, speeding past Linh into the hallway. Linh sighed and we continued to our room.

"How many kids are here?" I asked.

"Ten, counting you guys. There were eight a while ago, but Pollux and Castor both turned eighteen and left."

"They didn't become Defectors?"

"Castor's a pacifist. Pollux wanted to join, but Castor talked him out of it and they just left."

"And the Defectors just let them go like that?" Blake asked.

"This isn't the Institute. What're they going to do, force them to become Defectors?"

"What if the Institute captures them? Won't they find this place?"

Blake's vigilance amused Linh. "It can move, remember?" She led us into an empty room at the end of the passage. "Here we are."

Two bunk beds juxtaposed each other on opposite sides of a window. The not-too-distant crashing of waves and cawing seagulls revealed that we were close to a large body of water. Sanctuary presided over some steep cliffs to the north and pine forests to the south. It didn't have any neighbors either—the Defectors liked their privacy.

"How do they choose where to move the house?" Blake asked, staring out the window with me.

"The Defectors do a lot of research before they move Sanctuary. They use scouts to find new locations. I don't know all the details, but they make charts and stuff Nephelie uses to map out where the house will go next," Linh said. The Defectors lacked a strong central structure, but they worked well in tandem. It made them unpredictable. That was their greatest weapon against the Institute.

The sun had started its downward journey toward the horizon, smearing the sky with pinks and oranges, the room a pleasant glow. "I think there're some spare pajamas. I'll get them for you." Linh ducked out.

Blake splayed himself on the bottom left bunk. Hunter wrapped his arms around me and pulled me into the lower bunk on the right. I fell on top of him, so he grinned and planted kisses all over my face. I sunk into his chest and let his gentle heartbeat soothe me. Alison peeked her head out the door, checking for Linh. "We're the oldest kids here."

"Looks like it," Blake said, arms folded under his head. "Is it weird that I still feel tired?"

Alison came back into the room and checked the small cabinet under the window, but there was nothing inside. "No, I get it," she said, her attention drawn outside. "My body feels weak."

"Did you get your memories back?" I asked.

"Yes!" she said. "This big light pillar shot down from the sky and busted through Veles Hall's roof, then the Institute went nuts. Smiths were crawling everywhere. We saw them pull you two out of your room and drag you to the Heka Building. I was about to march in the Heka Building and be all like 'can I speak to your manager,' buuuuut"—Alison spun toward Blake like she had an axe to grind—"doofus here thought it'd be a better idea to cut a deal with Aiden."

I knew where this was going. Aiden, leader of the Legacy of the Crowns, hated Blake after he'd embarrassed him during a wizard duel.

"What was the deal?" I asked.

"I told him we'd stage another wizard duel, and I'd let him beat me if he helped us get inside the Heka Building."

"What happened?" Hunter asked.

"He walked us into a trap."

"Did you forget to mention the part where I told you that asking Aiden for help was a bad idea?" Alison said.

Blake clamped up, embarrassed. "Alison warned me about Aiden. She said we could find some other way."

"How did you guys end up in the Dreamhaven with us?" I asked.

"I don't know. Last thing I remember is those agents spraying us with that smelly, green stuff."

Linh walked into the room with a few towels and some pajamas. "There's a bathroom at the end of the hallway if you want to take a shower."

"So where are we?" Alison asked. "Like . . . in the US . . . or Canada or whatever."

"Michigan, I think. Somewhere along Lake Superior. About six hours north of Chicago."

"Linh," Luther called from behind, startling her. She spun and found him standing in the doorway. "Please, go make sure the other children have had dinner." Linh caught her breath and left. Luther clasped his hands behind his back. "Children, before you do anything else, I'll need you to follow me upstairs."

We followed Luther into the hallway. Alison gave me a skeptical look. "What do you think they're going to do?"

"Hopefully not sacrifice us to something."

Luther led us to the other wing. We passed a small infirmary halfway down the hall, then Luther grabbed a cord dangling from the ceiling. He pulled down a trap door and ladder leading to the attic, then scurried up like a mouse. Blake climbed the steps with no problem, then Hunter. Alison found the shaky steps wobbly but managed. I, with my grace and luck, drove my foot through one of the rungs and almost fell. Luckily, Alison caught me by my sleeve. Once in the attic, Luther showed us to a wide-open space around a large circular array, which had been drawn on the floor in white chalk.

The ring looked familiar, then it hit me: the sigil under the Keep—the Legacy of the Crowns' dorm—the one Crowns used to induct initiates into the Legacy. While not resembling the sigil perfectly, it was a close enough match. This one had a heptagram like the one I'd seen on Luther's pocket watch.

"What is this thing?" Blake asked, eyeing the symbol.

"It is our own Legacy array, constructed long ago to overwrite the death curse."

I'd forgotten that the Institute had marked us for death. The Institute had been arranged like a giant magical array, and when you stepped inside, the circle placed a death curse on you. When the Institute activated the death curse—the results were self-explanatory. They used this curse to mark non-Lineage wizards, those who hadn't been born into magical families. Gaspar had called it a *quelling*, a rare but occasional purge conducted to "maintain order in wizard society."

"You knew we were marked the first time we met, and you let us go anyway?" I asked Luther.

"We tried to bring you here, but you went after Gaspar instead. We couldn't risk showing you the array and then having the Institute find out about it when they recaptured you." Luther regarded the circle fondly.

"If this is a binding circle, then this will bind us to a task."

"There is no stipulation. We do this ritual with anyone that we help escape the Institute. Be aware, the ritual is not perfect, and if you reenter the Institute, the curse will overwrite this spell and mark you again, unless you're a Legacy wizard." Luther turned his focus on Blake. "You do not need this ritual because you are marked with the sigil of the Thorns, and the death curse will not work on you.

"Please stand in one of the triangles in the larger circle," Luther said, stepping into a smaller circle at the top of the array. We walked into the larger circle, each taking our place in a different triangle. The old man raised his frail hands and weaved his fingers through the glowing machinery of the vivit apparatus. He tampered with the clockwork until the rings shined crimson. A wind swept through the room, and into my ears crept the faint sound of people marching and yelling. I saw protesters fiercely clashing with police; tanks, one after the other, rumbling down empty streets; and a tattered flag waving in the air amid a sea of corpses. A feeling of triumph pulsed through the horrifying visuals, like an underlying theme: *To die for this cause is great.* My heart, once sad and weakened by the events in the Dreamhaven, grew hardened, angry. Vengeful. No longer was it good enough to merely flee the Institute; I wanted it destroyed.

The rings stopped glowing. Luther pulled his hands from the golden machinery and it vanished, except for the circles still crudely drawn on the floor.

"Was that it?" Alison said. "No more death curse?"

"No. I've overwritten the curse with our own seal," Luther said.

We returned us to our rooms, changed by the ritual. I couldn't stop thinking of how much I hated the Institute and everyone who worked there. The receptionists, the teachers, the deliveryman—every single cog and wheel that kept that machine running. I wanted to visit misery upon all those people. To slake my thirst for revenge with their blood.

"J," Alison said, drawing me out of my frenzied thoughts, "look at my aura. Tell me what it looks like."

Alison and I closed our eyes across from each other. Immediately, the same visions I'd had during the ritual flooded my mind: people yelling in defiance, street clashes, feet marching, and bottles shattering. Was endless warfare the freedom the Defectors spoke of? Even if we chose not to fight, like the two boys who had left before we arrived, we were Defectors. Their enduring struggle had marked our lives forever.

Chapter 12

Our first night in Sanctuary, I caught Hunter sneaking out of bed and followed him. I found him sitting on the half landing. Moonlight passed through the stained-glass window, refracted into a dozen pale beams that showered him in airy colors.

"Hey," I said, dropping down next to him.

He shot me a smile, but it hurt him. "Hey, J."

"Is your head hurting again?"

He threw an arm around my shoulder and pulled me close. "No." Another stabbing pain shot through his head.

"Did you take any medicine?"

"It'll go away. They never last that long."

"Don't you think you should talk to Luther about it?"

"About a headache?"

"About a headache you brought here from the Dreamhaven."

"It's just my sinuses, J—I always get like this during the spring. Plus, that's not why I woke up."

"Why did you?"

"I had a nightmare. . . about the Void." Hunter never spoke timidly, but right then he hushed his voice, like he feared the Void itself would hear him and come looking for him.

"Can you . . . can you tell me about it?"

He didn't seem like he wanted to relive those feelings, but Hunter never backed down. His courage always got the better of him. "It was . . . dark and lonely . . . but I could feel it in my head. The Void. It said things to me."

"Like what?"

"It told me to join it. It said that I could never escape and that I should serve it for all eternity. I think it wanted to eat my soul."

"Why didn't you . . . join it?"

Hunter looked at me, a warmth burning in his eyes. "Because I wanted to be with you again."

We kissed then, under the moonlight, and I urged him back to bed.

Over the next five days, I kept thinking about Mikey. Although he'd enabled our escape, his reasons for helping us lay mired in doubt. Did our escape serve some greater design, or did he help us just because? My cynicism told me to dismiss the latter, but that would've been premature. I didn't know enough to speak on his motives.

Alison's sharp commentary died down after the Dreamhaven. She didn't have her HRT, and I thought that was making her nervous, but she stayed quiet even after Aquila got her some medicine from the neighboring town. No one else noticed her subtle mood shift, but too many times I watched her bite her words and become lost in thought, a vacant look in her eyes like her soul had gone back to the Dreamhaven. Part of me worried she'd go into Everywhen and find her way back.

Hunter's headaches persisted, as did his nightmares, but he repeated the same lie about sinuses and lingering anxieties. Not wanting to break his trust, I didn't tell the Defectors about any of it.

The Defectors taught us that American wizard society had been organized into a series of confederations, called Assemblies, and that each of these Assemblies was divided into six regions: Mid-South, South East, North East, Midwest, Pacific Northwest, and South West. Each regional Assembly was different, but they were all led by magisters. These magisters worked in tandem with the Institute to adjudicate local issues. Magisters numbered anywhere between three and nine to an Assembly, and they were always members of a Lineage in good standing with their Legacy. The Defectors kept these magisters' identities a closely guarded secret. No one needed a vengeful Defector in a bloody haze, jeopardizing months, sometimes years, of careful planning.

Every five years, Lineage wizards in good standing with their Legacies gathered in a great convocation called *The Grande Assembly*. The Grande Assembly chose leaders for its ruling body, the High Council, from the most powerful and influential in wizard society. And though these candidates didn't need experience as magisters, choosing someone who lacked such merits constituted a dangerous political faux pax. They called these leaders Prefects of the High Council, and they chose new regional magisters and also acted as the Marduk Institute's administrators. These prefects served until the next Grande Assembly, but the Defectors assured the ones residing had been there for at least two decades. Rumors about the shadowy admins swirled around the Institute, but no one had ever seen them. Even the Smiths spoke about them like they were urban legends.

Most wizards, Lineage and non-Lineage alike, didn't know the Institute's true purpose. To "proper" wizard society, the Institute offered disadvantaged wizards a shelter. For older non-Lineage wizards, the Institute provided invaluable services that helped them survive: housing, training, free food, medicine. As far as the Lineages saw it, non-Lineage wizards had it easy. Ordinary humans should only be so lucky. But we knew better. We, like the shadowy admins, knew the Institute's true purpose was to kill non-Lineage wizards, and to train Lineages to shepherd them until execution day. Although Gaspar had argued the quelling existed to maintain the hierarchy in wizard society, with Lineages at the top and non-Lineages at the bottom, I doubted it was that simple. Things rarely are.

I woke up to Aquila painfully prodding me in the ribs. Our daily routine began anew: Wake up early. Do a bunch of pointless chores. Rinse. Repeat. She'd been alternating responsibilities among us each day. The one thing no one wanted to hear was, "You've got babysitting duty." That meant you had to watch the kids in the reading room all day. It was more like psychological torture than a job.

"Come on, sleepyheads. We've got a long day ahead of us." She poked me again when I didn't move. "Come on. Get up." I groaned like a zombie and slowly rose. Hunter did the same.

Aquila charged us with fixing breakfast after we cleaned up. Hunter's camping experience made him a perfect candidate for manning the skillet. What I lacked in camping experience

I made up for in my amazing scrounging abilities, so I got to gather ingredients. The pantry's nearly barren shelves told me the Defectors needed to restock their supplies—and I didn't know how they planned on doing that. It cracked me up to imagine Aquila using her powers to trick Postmates into delivering us groceries. Luckily, I found pancake mix in the cupboard. Hunter and I whipped up a batch while Alison and Blake set the table, then we plated the pancakes and seven children—four girls and three boys—came running in. The kids asked us about our adventures, and Blake embellished the details and turned our few (horrifying) experiences into exciting stories.

The kids were a menagerie of life experiences from all over the United States, their stories just as interesting as ours. Their ages ranged between eight and eleven. They spoke fondly when they talked about Aquila because it was she who rescued them. But they also didn't mind sniping her for her overbearing personality. They didn't say much about Nephelie, except that she always worked. Before we ruined it, the Defectors used to run a robust liberation network within the Institute. Now that Melchior knew their scheme, they wouldn't be able to sneak out any more kids for a while.

After breakfast, Linh headed upstairs to attend to the rooms. She got the easiest job because of her seniority at Sanctuary. Foisting babysitting duty on someone gave Aquila a perverse rush. Today, she assigned that duty to Blake. Everyone who "won" that (not-so) coveted position also got Aquila's complimentary gum stick, which she said helped stave off the edge. Blake huffed, grabbed the gum, and put it in his mouth. Then he left for the reading room, looking back at us sadly as he opened the door.

Aquila pulled Alison and Hunter into the kitchen and handed

them buckets and scrub brushes. "You two have the floors today." Alison's dewy-eyed expression melted into a nasty glare that Hunter echoed. I imagined two pit bulls barking viciously at each other. There weren't two people in the world more different than Alison and Hunter. They'd be fighting before day's end.

Aquila walked me through the kitchen to the laundry room, and through there to the garage. The whole place stunk like engine oil and Lake Superior—a fishy, moldy smell—and the temperature dropped ten degrees. Boxes piled to the ceiling filled the space. A few sported the word *Junk* in thick, black Sharpie while others were labeled *Housewares*, *Kitchen Appliances*, and *Bathroom Supplies*. An old green truck was awkwardly parked there, stuffed black trash bags littering its cargo bed. Aquila switched on a hanging lamp in the garage and handed me a box of trash bags.

"We've been trying to clean up in here forever. You can just throw all the junk in the trash bags and toss them on the cargo bed. If you'll break down the boxes afterward, that'd be great too."

Busy work. They didn't really need the garage cleared out; they just wanted us out of their way. Most days Nephelie and Aquila locked themselves in the office, where they planned their next scheme. Luther, however, stayed gone, slipping into the armoire in Nephelie's office every morning like clockwork.

I dug through a soggy box labeled *Junk*. Not that I thought the Defectors would've thrown away anything important, but I hoped they had. There was nothing in the box except for old, mildewed newspapers and wires for machines that didn't exist anymore. The next box had broken picture frames, tarnished silverware, a busted VCR—more of the same. Fifteen minutes (and a whole box packed with rusty lunch tins) later and I still hadn't found anything. Disappointed, I filled up the first bag and tossed it on the cargo bed, and repeated the process. Before long, boredom settled in and curiosity overtook me. They hadn't left us alone since we got here, so I hadn't been able to investigate. Now was my chance. I snuck up to the laundry room door and peeped inside.

"It's going to take us forever to clean the floors if you do it like that," Alison said.

"This is how you're supposed to clean floors," Hunter said. They were arguing. Just like I'd predicted.

"Poor, feeble boy. Don't you understand it would be easier if we just did it like this." Alison dumped the soap bucket all over the floor.

Hunter was aghast. "How're we supposed to clean that?"

Alison did a quick search and spotted a broom. She snatched it and scrubbed the floors. "See," she said, stepping on the sudsy tiles, "easy peasy." Alison miscalculated a step and slipped. Hunter tried to keep her from falling and they both went down. They overheard me giggling behind the door.

"Get off me, Alison," Hunter said struggling to get up.

Alison crawled off Hunter and picked herself up using the sink as an anchor. Hunter got to his feet but stumbled on the slippery floor. He balanced himself against a chair to keep from falling again.

"Johnny"—Alison hopped over the spill—"what're you doing?"

"I thought I'd go look around."

"I'll cover for you," Hunter said.

I headed into the foyer and spotted Nephelie's office—empty. Sanctuary served as the central hub to countless Defector operations, and Nephelie played an integral role in their leadership. That guaranteed I'd find something useful among all those books and documents. I hurried inside.

Wall to wall, the office stretched wider than I remembered, so big I didn't know where to start. My eyes snagged on a picture sitting on a shelf near Luther's cabinet: a young Nephelie standing arm-in-arm with Aquila, the Keep towering behind them. Their past as Crowns lay cloaked in mystery. Did both their bloodlines belong to Lineages? Had they betrayed their families to fight for the Defectors?

Nephelie never smiled, but she cheesed hard in the pic. An innocent warmth pervaded the image. But time changes everything, including the people in that picture. Nothing else on the shelf caught my attention. Next up: her desk. The drawer on the upper right-hand corner squeaked out, and inside I found some well-organized paperwork. Ordinary stuff like maintenance bills. In the next drawer down, a supply list:

> *Laundry detergent*
> *Fabric softener*
> *Food for that cat hanging around outside*
> *Wood cleaner*
> *Paper*
> *New pillowcases*

And it kept going. Nothing interesting. No secret magical weapons. No pet Void-spawns to do all the dirty work. Running a rebellion was a lot more boring than I had imagined.

The door to the office opened. I quickly crawled into the leg nook and hid. A few clunky footsteps sounded, then the door closed.

"What's up, Neph?" Aquila said.

"Maleeka contacted me. She said her and Penn ran into some

witch-hunters in Menominee, told me the hunters had been chasing them for miles. It looks like the witch-hunters ran them off the road near a cemetery just within city limits." Witch-hunters didn't sound like good news, especially when you considered *we* might be the witches they were hunting.

"Sounds like they're in Maple Grove. That's not far from here."

"She said her and Penn were able to save a few pieces from the shipment, but most of it was lost in the wreck. Can you find them? I'm going to contact Estaban and see about another shipment. If things get too hairy, get out of there."

"Even if it means leaving them behind?"

Nephelie didn't respond. The Defectors were nothing if not expedient. A minute later, the office door opened and closed again. They had left. The name Maleeka sounded familiar. Blake and Linh had mentioned her before—they all came to the Institute around the same time, but Maleeka escaped before them. From what I remembered, though, she had mysteriously vanished.

I left the office and lured Blake out of the reading room and told him everything. Epiphany and dread swirled on his face in equal parts.

"Do you know when Aquila's leaving?" he asked.

"No clue."

We ran into the antechamber and cracked the front doors. Aquila got into a gray sedan parked out front. It looked as old as the truck in the garage, and its undercarriage dipped when she took a seat. Blake pulled out the gum in his mouth, balled his hand around it, and closed his eyes. The car grumbled to life and its exhaust pipe poured out gritty smoke. Blake tried to fling the gum but it clung to his hand. His face contorted furiously. He shook the gum loose, and before the car tottered off, he threw it and it stuck to the back bumper. Aquila headed to the road between Sanctuary and the forest, took a left, and the car wheezed loudly as she sped off.

"Why'd you do that?" I asked.

"I put a locator spell on the gum, should help me track Aquila's car."

"What're you going to do?"

"I'm going to go find Maleeka."

"But Aquila—what about the witch-hunters?"

"Johnny, you heard Nephelie. Maleeka's in trouble. And the Defectors won't do anything to save her if it isn't convenient."

Blake's sudden willingness to go up against witch-hunters we knew nothing about surprised me. He didn't get into fights without knowing the odds. Even with his life on the line, his guilt-born desire to protect others informed his actions. Reservations aside, we were friends and I wouldn't let him go alone. "I'm going too."

"What're you two doing?" Alison said from behind us, Hunter next to her.

"Blake's friend is being chased by witch-hunters."

"What's a . . . *witch-hunter*?"

Blake told us that the Institute hired other wizards when its resources were stretched too thin. Trained agents were a valuable commodity. They took months to train, and the good ones—rare because the job was so dangerous—spent years developing their talents. Outsourcing to mercenaries allowed the Institute to save its agents for more important roles.

Bratty Lineage wizards would never soil their persnickety hands "witch-hunting." Non-Lineage wizards, however, lived a perilous existence outside the Institute's walls, facing myriad dangers, not least among them poverty. Lacking their former support structures forced many non-Lineage wizards to seek employment with the Institute, for safety and financial benefit. If they rejected the Institute's employment, for whatever reason, few options remained. Witch-hunting, however, allowed them to survive on their own terms, and it paid handsomely. Likely, the Institute removed the death curse as an added benefit, but I didn't know that for sure.

"Aquila said the cemetery wasn't far from here. Let's get going," said Blake.

"What about Linh?" Hunter asked.

"She'd probably just rat us out. Let's leave her here," Blake said.

"Wait a second," Alison said. "We can barely use magic. How the hell are we going to deal with witch-hunters?"

"Tenacity?" Blake said with an uncomfortable grin. In a straight-forward fight, our chances against those witch-hunters looked dismal, but Blake refused to leave Maleeka out there alone.

"Look," I said, "we beat that sandman, didn't we?"

"Kind of. Your boyfriend sort of . . . *died*," Alison said.

"I'm good, though," Hunter said optimistically.

"See. He's good. Plus, we got out of the Dreamhaven, didn't we?"

Alison patted my shoulder. "I'd believe that hopeful optimism of yours if your leg wasn't shaking so hard, J." My leg had indeed rattled the whole time. I made it stop. "Anyway, I'm not short on bone-headed courage. But if we all end up dead, I'm going to haunt you guys in hell."

Blake's spell allowed him to use his wizard senses to follow the gum on Aquila's bumper. For him, it was like a towering light in the vivit apparatus, an immense glow visible for miles. Without looking into the clockwork, Blake's wizard senses registered it as a sublime feeling, like experiencing a revelation, and that feeling grew the closer he came to it.

The forest provided the fastest route to the cemetery. Taking the truck in the garage would've alerted Nephelie, so we decided to walk. Being this close to Lake Superior, storms buffeted the forests, uprooting trees and leaving them partially tipped up. Mushy detritus covered the forest floor, making our quick journey a slog. We found a short, wrought-iron fence around the cemetery and easily scaled it.

Blake huddled us together before going any farther. "Those witch-hunters could be anywhere," he said. "I wouldn't head straight for Aquila's car. We don't know where one of them might pop up."

"What's your plan?" Hunter asked.

"It'll be easier for us to sneak around if we pair off in teams of two."

"I'll go with Alison," I said.

Blake and Hunter gave me a funny look, which Alison took quite personally. "Why're you two looking at us like that?"

"What're you two going to do," Hunter said, "have Alison snark them to death?" Blake chortled loudly then took one look at Alison and sucked in the rest. Even Hunter clamped up when he saw the scowl on my face. We didn't find Hunter's joke very funny.

"I mean—you know," Hunter said, "we're a team and all, but like, me and Blake do a lot of the heavy lifting. Just being honest." His decision to dig in his heels left me glaring. "We just don't want you two getting hurt, that's all." Wrong thing to say to someone like Alison. Few things gave her a rush like proving people wrong.

She scoffed loudly. "We don't need you two to protect us. Come on, J, let's go ahead and give our lovely *boyfriends* a head start. They'll need it." Alison haughtily tossed her hair over her shoulder and we walked away. "Can you believe those two?"

"Sadly, yes." The late morning coolness gave way to noon's warmth. "You've been kind of quiet . . . since we got to Sanctuary, I mean."

Her brown eyes walked silently among the tombstones. "Hmm," she said, my words finally reaching her. "Sorry."

"You don't have to be sorry. But . . . do you miss the Dreamhaven?"

She watched her feet. "I don't know. Maybe. Kind of."

"Are you mad at me . . . for making you leave?"

"No."

"So, what's wrong?"

"None of this even feels real, you know? It's like we just go from place to place, and I still don't understand why any of this is happening. And I . . . I still just want to see Mom's grave. I want to move forward, but I can't. It's like there's this unfinished chapter of my life, and I can't start the new one until the old one closes."

"I guess I feel the same way."

"Do you think they feel lost too—the Defectors, I mean?"

Before responding, I spotted a blond man in a black turtleneck walking suspiciously through the cemetery. He immediately triggered my wizard senses. His aura popped and fizzled like faulty electrical wiring. "Ali, look out," I said, pulling her behind a tombstone and ducking. We peeked around the corner and watched the guy. He continued scouting around, his eyes creeping toward us. No doubt his wizard senses had picked up on us too. "Ali, gloss your aura."

"What?"

"Just—imagine you're invisible. It'll make it so he can't see our auras."

A wizard's powerful aura left traces on the vivit apparatus—it looked like gold paint on the clockwork. Wizards' auras also emanated a strong emotional current, and other wizards easily sensed that energy. Linh once taught me a technique to hide my aura called *glossing*. A wizard need only imagine themselves going invisible to silence their aura's emotional frequency. This made it harder to detect us using the wizard sense. Extra steps were needed to clean your aura's residue off the vivit apparatus, but we only needed to make our auras undetectable.

Alison and I squeezed our eyes shut, clenched our teeth, and huddled together tightly. In my mind, my skin grew translucent like water then slowly faded until I disappeared entirely. Certain the spell had worked, I peeked around the tombstone at the blond wizard again. Alison kept her eyes closed, too afraid to look. The blond wizard stopped walking and donned a curious look on his face. His senses no longer detected us and that confused him. He turned in a circle, giving the cemetery a wary scan. Then he pulled out a phone and started texting. I decided against sending Blake a psychic message because the glossing spell required my full attention. Reading the blond wizard's thoughts was also tempting—uncovering his allies and their plans could save us later—but it risked exposing my identity and location when he inevitably sensed it. He lowered the phone and carefully read his environs once more, then tucked it away and resumed walking, face still drawn into an anxious pucker.

Blake, I said with my mind, *I think we found one of the witch-hunters. It's a tall guy with blond curly hair, and he's wearing a black turtleneck.*

Blake and Hunter didn't know the glossing trick. If we didn't act quickly, the witch-hunter would find them. *Thanks for the head's up*, Blake said.

"He's going to find Hunter and Blake," I said.

"We've got to stop that guy." We used the headstones for cover, creeping behind the witch-hunter as he made his way through the cemetery. "Can't you just make one of those light sword things like when we fought the sandman?"

"It's not that easy in the real world. I'll mess it up and blow us up or something."

We hurried behind a tombstone planted in shaky soil. Alison pressed her hands against the headstone as she ducked, but she exerted too much force and it toppled over loudly, scaring us to our feet. The fright broke my concentration. Having heard the commotion, and probably sensing our auras too, the witch-hunter turned and gave us a wild look.

"Someone's ghost grandma is going to drag me to hell," Alison said, regarding the broken tombstone, not yet noticing the witch-hunter.

"Ali," I said, tugging her sleeve.

Alison looked up and saw the witch-hunter. "Hey," Ali said anxiously. "We're just . . . lost . . . looking for our friends. Oh, friends," Alison called sheepishly. "Friends?"

"Run!" We darted in the opposite direction. But the witch-hunter disappeared into a shadowy cloud and reappeared in front of us. We staggered back as he widened his arms, ready to grapple us. Alison pushed me out of the way and swung her foot into his groin. His eyes crossed as he grabbed himself and groaned painfully.

"Bet you don't have any magic for that," Alison said proudly.

"Ali," I said, prompting her to flee.

We resumed our frantic dash, but dried vines sprouted out of the ground and ensnared our feet. I jerked my leg up and snapped one vine, but dozens more crawled out to replace it. Alison dropped to one knee and tore at the vines, even gnashing them apart with her teeth. Still more came, winding around our legs and dragging us to the ground. Our only choice was to lay there immobilized.

The blond witch-hunter calmly strode toward us. Scruff peppered his young jawline—he looked no older than twenty-two or twenty-three. A risky job like witch-hunting required an athletic build—combat with other wizards being implied in the job title—but his gangly body didn't lend itself to heavy physical exertion. His long, dirty nails and wrinkly clothes said he spent more time behind a computer barking orders at his *Fortnite* raid group than at a gym. Then again, the studiousness needed to understand magic's intricacies made nerds perfect wizards.

I balled my fists and tried to yank my arms free. "Stop moving," he said. The vines tightened around my wrists. He controlled them without having to move even a cog in the vivit apparatus. As expected, his magical knowledge easily surpassed ours. Two shadowy clouds burst into the air behind him and two more witch-hunters emerged: a surly looking, middle-aged woman with wavy black hair that fell in tresses around her shoulders, and a bald man around the same age with a black cross painted on his face that stretched from his forehead to his chin.

"Who the hell're these kids?" the woman said in a husky, gruff voice. The old nicks and cuts on her skin told an allegory, each surely tied to a different wizard. The lesson they conveyed: Those who spend their lives destroying others wreck their own lives in the process.

"I don't know," the blond witch-hunter said. "They were following me around. They're wizards. Do you think they're with those Defectors?"

"I didn't see them in Menominee," said the man with the cross on his face. A man with his imposing physical stature was what I imagined when I heard the term *witch-hunter*. The crusty paint on his face chipped off in flakes. His air-starved pores rejected the marking—he'd paint it back on if needed. Maybe he used it to scare his quarries, or maybe he wore it because his fanatical nature demanded it. Either way, he scared the hell out of me.

The three witch-hunters trained their eyes on us. A creeping feeling on my nape warned me to guard my mind.

"These runts won't let me read their thoughts," the gruff woman said.

"Throw them in the trunk," the man with the cross on his face said. "We'll contact Žižek and see what he wants to do with them." *Žižek?* That name sounded familiar.

The man with the cross on his face swung his hand down and materialized a light sword in his grasp. He pointed it at my face. "We're going to tie you up. Don't make us kill you."

They ripped off the vines then placed Alison and I back to back and tied us together with hemp rope. "You fixing to throw us on a train track?" Alison said.

The gruff woman got in Alison's face. "Don't tempt us." Then she picked us up by our feet, and the man with the cross on his face lifted us by our shoulders. They lugged us through the cemetery until they reached a black Impala parked in the gravel just outside the front gate. The blond witch-hunter popped open the trunk and the other two lowered us onto a wet spot that smelled faintly like gasoline then shut the lid. Their feet crunched on the gravel, audibly at first then disappearing as they moved away from the vehicle. Alison and I squirmed, hoping to loosen the rope.

"Who the hell is Žižek?" I asked.

"Probably the Smith that hired them."

The rope tethered us like a chain. If we started slinging around spells, we risked drawing the Institute to our location. Plus, I only knew the light sword spell, and casting that—or even just harnessing aspects of that spell to burn away the rope—while lying on a gas stain in a confined space sounded like a galaxy-brained idea. *Blake,* I said with my mind, *the witch-hunters have us. They've locked us in the trunk of an old, black Impala parked outside the cemetery.*

Sounds like you two needed Hunter and me after all, Blake said, his thoughts smug and self-satisfied. *We'll come and try to get you out.*

Shouldn't we contact Aquila or something?

I don't think that's a great idea. It might only complicate things. Just hang in there until we show up.

"Blake and Hunter are on their way," I said.

"No way! You told them we got captured?"

"What else was I supposed to do?"

"Certainly not give those two wannabe-alphas an ego boost. Ugh. We're never going to hear the end of it."

The trunk opened and the same menacing Smith who had masked himself as my dad in the Dreamhaven loomed over us, the man with the cross on his face and the gruff woman standing to either side of him. Then it dawned on me: *Žižek,* the name the witch-hunters mentioned earlier. It was the name on that Smith's tag. I had glimpsed it before he vanished, after Alison hit him with the fire poker.

"Well, well, well," Žižek said with a pleased look on his face, "we meet again."

"You know these two?" The gruff woman asked.

Žižek smiled. "We're acquainted."

"Didn't I kill you?" Alison said.

He didn't look too happy with that response. "We'll need to take them to a secure location." He reached into his jacket and pulled out a canister and sprayed us.

Chapter 13

Light glared in my eyes as the eirineftis haze slowly lifted. The bright afternoon sun beamed down through missing patches in the vaulted ceiling overhead. A finch chirped unseen among the decaying rafters. Damaged stained-glass windows bordered the long room's perimeter and a few broken-down pews lay piled in the northeastern corner. They'd left us tied up in a shambling, old church, lying on the unsteady, rain-brined floors, and I was stuck facing a wall.

The gruff woman's voice cut through the silence. "Are we getting paid for those kids too?"

Alison squirmed behind me, fighting to disentangle us, but her noisy efforts threatened to draw our captors. "Don't make so much noise," I whispered. She stopped moving.

Johnny, Alison said in my head, *close your eyes and let me try something*. That suggestion didn't inspire much confidence, especially since I couldn't see Žižek or the witch-hunters. Regardless, I did as she said, and Alison showed me the world through her eyes. The man with the black turtleneck leaned against a column, playing on his phone, while the gruff woman and the man with the cross on his face spoke to Žižek.

"I don't have the money. You'll have to wait until my boss shows up," Žižek said, raising his shoulders innocently.

"You mean you didn't even bring the money to pay us," said the gruff woman.

"No."

The man with the cross on his face snatched Žižek's lapels and reeled him in. "You mean you want us to wait here until your boss shows up to pay us?"

"I can't pay you if I don't have any money."

"Can't you guys just teleport those vans wherever you want?" the gruff woman asked.

"No. The big ups don't like when we fling magic around like that. It confuses the sensors."

"The sensors?"

"The magical sensors the Institute uses. That's why I asked you to refrain from using a lot of magic." If the Institute required that Smiths investigate everything that triggered their sensors, it made sense minimizing magical outbursts helped conserve their manpower; after all, like Blake told us, the Institute lacked unlimited resources. Even their magic failed to make them invincible. Alison and I learned that when we found a rat infestation in Dedi Hall— the adult housing unit on campus.

"How long until your boss gets here?" the woman asked.

"Not long," Žižek assured them, but he was lying. We were all the way in Michigan, and the Institute was somewhere in northern

Missouri, in the Ozarks. It would take hours for one of those extraction vans to get here.

"Why don't you keep looking for those Defectors I hired you to find?" Žižek said.

Alison stopped showing me her thoughts. Everything got quiet, then an engine revved, and wheels softly grumbled as they treaded out over dirt.

Those witch-hunters are gone, Alison said.

Blake, I called, *we're in some old, abandoned church. It's missing part of the roof. Those witch-hunters left and now there's only one Smith here.*

Got it.

I'm not waiting around for Blake to come save us, J, Alison said. *Come on. There's a piece of glass near us, help me get to it.* Alison bumped me with her shoulder and started wriggling across the floor. I followed her lead. With constant exposure to the savage Lake Superior storms, the church's miraculous survival testified to its sturdy construction. Still, the moldering floors creaked every inch she crawled. Alison stopped moving.

That Smith is coming toward us.

"You two really dinged me up back in the Dreamhaven," Žižek said. With my back turned, I couldn't see Žižek, but I heard the rickety floor groaning under his footsteps. His shadow swallowed us, its shape suggesting that he'd crouched. Alison shrank against me. "Imagine how excited my boss is going to be when he finds out I have you two. I might even get a paid vacation."

"You're telling me you guys don't even get paid vacations?" Alison said sarcastically. "Some benefits package."

"You're funny." Žižek's shadow grew tall and rigid again. He rattled something, sounded like a can. "I'd keep you guys asleep until the boss gets here, but I'm running low, and I need to save the rest just in case."

Žižek walked away. I listened until he stopped moving. Alison went back to slithering us across the floor. My shirt's hem snagged on a piece of rotted flooring and a splinter tore into the fabric. She inched a little farther and the material ripped loudly. There was no way Žižek hadn't heard that. He cleared his throat and my mind went into overdrive: *This is it. He's going to come over here and finish the job he started in the Dreamhaven. We're screwed!*

Calm down, J, Alison said in my head.

Get out of there!

Sorry.

As if getting my ass dragged across this splintery floor hadn't been bad enough. Žižek stayed motionless, though, but if we kept moving, he was going to catch us. Alison stretched her fingers toward a sizeable shard, but it was too far away. She kept trying for it until the piece wobbled in place and scooted across the floor. She was moving it with her mind. It slowly found its way into her hand, then she set about cutting us free.

Nice trick, I said.

I've been practicing.

I lifted my upper body and peeked over her. It didn't give me a perfect view, but at least Žižek came in sight. He faced the church's ramshackle entrance, his back against the corner of a broken-down pew. His cold disinterest reminded me that catching us held no personal value to him. It paid the bills, nothing more. But something in his voice said it thrilled him, gave him a twisted rush. The ropes slackened and fell.

Let's take him out, Alison said, crouching. We shrouded our auras and completely blocked our thoughts. Žižek kept his back to us, still looking into space.

How? I asked.

I don't know. Can't you just make one of those light sword things?

I told you, Ali. Not in the real world. Let's just knock him down and steal his can of eirineftis.

Good plan.

We scurried up behind him like a couple of mice. I rammed my shoulder into the hollow behind his knee, forcing him to clutch the pew for balance, but the corner snapped off and he fell to the floor. Alison leaped on him, flung open his blazer, and snatched out the can. She depressed the valve in his face, but it only hissed— the can was empty. Žižek smacked her aside. I ran to help but the floorboards under us collapsed and dropped us into the crawl space beneath the church. The fall left me on my back, dazed.

Johnny! Alison's psychic prod snapped me back to reality. She waved for me to duckwalk beside her. Together, we hastily crept across the gently sloping ground. The roomy crawl space's ceiling stretched almost a foot above our heads, making movement easy. *Look there*, she said, pointing to a crevice in the back. Wherever that hole led, it beat staying here.

Žižek stomped his foot, and a rock spike shot up from the ground in front of us. We scampered around the spike and took cover behind it. Žižek dropped his head through the hole in the church floor. "Come on, you two. You can't hide forever." We stayed hidden until Žižek pulled his head back through the hole. Then we resumed speeding toward the fissure in the back. Using the slits in the floorboards, I tracked Žižek's movements, but he skipped about wildly and erratically, making him difficult to follow. I switched my focus to ahead of us to check my footing, but when I set my sights back again, looking for him, I didn't see him. He'd vanished.

A handful of feet away from the cleft, his shadow fell over us.

Fear froze me in place. He looked down at me through the crack, donning a sinister grin. His face moved around like shifting clay and turned into my dad's. "What's the matter, Juanito"—his smile widened—"you scared?" Another spike lanced out of the ground and sliced my leg. I screamed and pulled my knee to my chest. The gash was shallow, but long and bloody. Several more earthy lances speared up in a procession, crisscrossing one another on their way to skewer me. I rolled toward the crevice and kept rolling until I fell into the cranny and tumbled downward.

"Johnny!" Alison called after me.

The world spun around like a clothes dryer. Then the sun came in view and I felt grass under me—the hole led outside the church. Like a speeding barrel, I tumbled until I lost momentum and crashed at the bottom of the hill, landing in some bushes near a tree line. I lay there, head spinning, body ravaged with pain.

Alison popped into sight and reached down. "Johnny, come on, get up!" She helped me up, and I hobbled alongside her into the forest. I looked back: a hole in the church's foundation hung over a dirt slope leading down to the tree line. We sprinted deep into the forest then hid behind an outcropping near a stream to catch our breath.

"How'd you get away?" I asked Alison between gasps.

"I followed you—just, you know, a little more gracefully." She looked at my wound. "Ouch."

The cut burned, but there was so much pain all over my body it registered as little more than a whisper in the noise. I slid down the rock face until I sat on the ground. Alison checked around our hiding spot for Žižek, then she crouched next to me.

"Don't die on me, J," Alison said.

Although the cut didn't look that bad, my head still swam, hinting at heavy blood loss. My discomfort grew when an uncharacteristic cold settled over me. The warm spring temperature didn't warrant any sudden chills. Fifteen minutes later, Blake and Hunter showed up. Hunter saw my injury and the blanched, sweaty look on my face and commenced drawing a healing circle in the dirt.

"Don't worry, J," he said with reassuring cheer. "We'll get you fixed up real quick."

Alison recounted our adventure to Blake. "Did you guys find Maleeka?" she asked once she'd finished.

"Not yet."

Hunter completed the circle then helped me into it. Within seconds the wound had healed, the soreness disappeared, and my body temperature regulated. The blood loss still left me feeling weak, but I could power through it.

Blake pointed westward, over the treetops. "Aquila's car is that way. I can still see the light beacon. Let's get going before that Smith or those witch-hunters find us."

Aquila's car was abandoned on the roadside. We checked it for signs pointing to where she'd gone, but we didn't find anything. Frustrated, we trekked back into the woods and kept looking for Maleeka. My weak body demanded food and my throat yearned for a drink. It was nearing late afternoon, maybe four, and we all desperately needed a break and some nourishment. Hunter's headache kept him quiet.

In a clearing near an underused stretch of road, we found a derelict barn with parts of its roof caving in. Blake suggested we hunker down inside and rest. No one felt strong enough to argue back. He pulled on the ratty barn door, dragging it across the dirt and revealing two people already hiding inside—a girl our age, with black and copper box braids, a sharp angular face, and a tawny complexion, and a guy, androgynous, with messy black hair and broad, sturdy shoulders.

The girl saw Blake and her mouth fell open. "Blake?"

"Maleeka!" Blake ran to her. The other person, clearly Maleeka's ally, Penn, kept a safe distance, studying Blake warily. Penn wore a dusty leather jacket scraped all over.

"*Jode*, man, close that door before you get us killed." Maleeka hurried us into the barn and slid the door shut.

"Not really very safe you know," Alison said, "leaving the door unlocked like that."

Maleeka gave Alison a sassy look then turned her attention back to Blake. "What are you doing out here? I thought you were still at the Institute?"

"We were trying to find you. Heard some witch-hunters were looking for you."

"You got us a way out of here?"

"No, we were hiding out for a minute. We haven't had anything to eat or drink in hours."

Maleeka nodded to Penn. "Hey, do we have any extra supplies?"

Penn approached two tactical backpacks lying in a corner. If the only supplies that survived their run-in with the witch-hunters nested in those two bags, Sanctuary's thinning supplies were about to get a lot thinner. Penn retrieved four water bottles and some vegetarian jerky, and passed it all around.

"Who're your friends?" Maleeka asked Blake while we ate.

"That's my girlfriend, Alison"—Blake pointed to Alison—"and these are my friends, Hunter and Johnny."

Maleeka didn't care about Hunter or me. She set her razor-sharp gaze on Alison, starting at her shoes then working her way up. "Hmph. She looks like your type."

"What? Drop-dead gorgeous?" Alison said.

Maleeka smiled. "A smart ass."

"Who says you can't have it all."

Maleeka turned her umber eyes to Hunter and me. "You two are cute. How did you find us?"

"We were at Sanctuary," Blake said. "Johnny was snooping around when he overheard that some witch-hunters had chased you and Penn down. When I found out you were out here, I had to come look."

"Where's Linh?"

"I didn't tell her we were coming. I was afraid she might tell Nephelie."

"So you came out here without their permission?"

"I couldn't leave you alone out here with those witch-hunters."

"What were you two doing?" I asked Maleeka.

"We were working with a Defector cell in Chicago called Threnody. Nothing dangerous, though. Estaban made us run supplies to other Defector cells in the area. Our main job, though, was making sure Sanctuary was stocked while it was here. We'd never had problems on any of the supply routes before, but this time, those witch-hunter *pendejos* found us in Menominee and didn't stop chasing us."

"Who's Estaban?"

"He's the leader of Threnody, one of the most important Defector cells in the country. Anyway, there's a storehouse in Chicago where we keep all our supplies, and we do shipments once a month to all the local cells."

"How does Threnody get more supplies for the storehouse?"

"Lie, cheat, steal, whatever. I don't deal with that side of things, so I don't know anything about it."

Maleeka knew a lot about the Defectors, and she didn't mind sharing it. She told us she met Penn at Sanctuary, and that Penn didn't say much because his violent extraction left him so traumatized he stopped speaking. Penn didn't hang around the Institute long before he'd hitched a ride on a delivery truck and escaped. He made it to North Carolina before two Smiths almost caught him, but Nephelie and Maleeka saved him and brought him to Sanctuary. Penn's loyalty to the Defectors burned as hot as his hatred for the Institute.

"What do you know about Aquila and Nephelie?" I asked, thinking back to the picture in Nephelie's office.

"Not much. Nephelie used to be in the Legacy of the Crowns, then she fell in love with Aquila, who was non-Lineage. Somehow, they found out about the kill curse. Nephelie helped Aquila escape the Institute, and they joined the Defectors. Together with Threnody's leader, Estaban, they established Sanctuary. Nephelie's almost as quiet as ol' Penn here. Almost."

Maleeka told us that before Pollux and Castor left Sanctuary, Nephelie offered them a job running supplies. They refused, so she appointed Maleeka and Penn instead. Even though such responsibilities rarely found themselves allocated to such young Defectors, they hungered to prove themselves. The Defectors depleted their manpower in operations against the Institute, and that forced Maleeka and Penn to work as the only supply runners for a long time. Other Defector cells in the area relied on them exclusively for supplies, so when the witch-hunters helped the Institute destroy the supply lines, they found themselves susceptible. Sanctuary's role as a children's shelter made it especially vulnerable. If the Institute had uncovered Maleeka and Penn's roles as supply runners, then surely Threnody's storehouse—no, all of Threnody, lay open for attack. The Institute severing the Defectors' supply lines made dealing with the individual cells much easier. Sanctuary, however, proved trickier because of its ability to move around. But if Threnody now lay in ruins, Sanctuary's diminishing resources promised a short-lived resistance.

"Why didn't you tell Aquila you were here?" Blake asked.

"We did. She was coming to get us, but she ran into those witch-hunters. She told us to stay put until she came."

Tires rolled onto the rocky dirt outside and squealed when they stopped. Aquila returning right then seemed fortuitous. Hunter approached a wall and peered between the planks.

He turned back, a frenzied look on his face. "It's those witch-hunters!"

Car doors slammed shut. The barn's front doors were the only way in and out.

We were trapped.

"Move to the wall back there," Penn told us.

"We can't fight them, Penn," Maleeka said. "They're—"

"All of you!" Penn said. "Get back!" Penn's demands confused us, but fear trumped my desire for debate. Alison, Hunter, and I all backed into the corner with the two backpacks. Blake and Maleeka didn't move, though.

"Penn what're you going to do?" Maleeka asked.

"I said get back!" Penn swung his arm and a gust pushed Maleeka and Blake off their feet and into the corner with us. Penn turned his attention on the barn doors, widened his stance, and shaped his hands into claws, holding them perpendicular at his side. Cogs and gears gathered between his hands. The wheels melded together like molten gold, and the blob expanded and contracted until it became a more intricate machine: a ball of wind. But Penn didn't stop there. The new machine's spinning pieces moved faster, heating up, going from a bronzy-gold color to reddish orange before transforming into a more convoluted machine: a fireball. Sweat beaded on Penn's brow, his face filled with uncertainty. He quickly moved his fingers around the new machine, but he didn't understand the sequences to make it work, nor did he know how to control its mass, its heat. The new machine's complexity doubled with its size, and its parts whirled furiously, teetering and shaking erratically—the fireball turned haywire.

"Penn, what the hell are you doing?" Maleeka screamed. "Stop it!"

The barn doors creaked open, and horror washed across the faces of the witch-hunters when they walked in and saw Penn standing there with a haywire fireball in his hands.

"Get down!" Maleeka yelled.

We hit the ground and covered our heads. Penn's fireball grew into a blazing supernova, so bright and so hot it provoked us to shield our eyes. The spell exploded with a monstrous volcanic roar, its heat lashing out and spreading throughout the barn. For a minute, the bolide threatened to consume everything, but the fires didn't reach us. My ears rang after the blast, but after several seconds the ringing died. Sputtering flames spat and hissed all around me, and the fire's menacing heat stroked my skin in waves. Too close for comfort.

Maleeka knelt and cried near Penn's mangled body. The explosion had ripped off the barn's front and flung the cross-faced man through the Impala's windshield, his body covered in repulsive, oozing burns. Likewise, his allies lay burned to death in the grass outside. A light rain started—a cleansing shower to quell the fires.

Aquila's car pulled up roadside. She emerged and ran to the barn. The devastation stunned her, but still she reacted with haste. "Grab their bags and go put them in the trunk. Then get inside and wait for me," she said to Hunter and I. Aquila's had to deal with similar situations before, that much was certain. She handed us her car keys, and we left to gather the backpacks. After collecting them, we stuffed the bags in the trunk and waited for Aquila to return. Alison and Blake joined us first, and then we all awkwardly crammed together in the backseat. Aquila came out of the barn then, holding Maleeka's hand. Maleeka looked back, surely not wanting to leave Penn's body behind. Besides costing Penn his life, the poorly planned magical outburst threatened to summon Žižek, if not the Institute.

To any non-wizards investigating the scene, it resembled a gas explosion. The Impala lacked tags and probably other paperwork. The severe burns on Penn's body also made him unidentifiable. He would become a nameless casualty at the bottom of a filing cabinet in a police station. *Fight 'til you die.* That same harrowing fate awaited all Defectors, including us.

The windshield wipers squeaked loudly, drowning Maleeka's quiet sobs. The time on the radio read *5:30.* Blake pressed his forehead against her chair and rubbed her shoulder with one hand. She didn't move an inch, not even her violent crying evoked a spasm. Hunter sank down and leaned against me. It looked like his headache was getting worse. Aquila sped us back to Sanctuary.

Upon walking in, Nephelie gave us a nasty look, but her anger subsided when she saw Maleeka in tears. "What happened?' Nephelie asked.

"Penn cast a fireball, and killed the witch-hunters and himself in the process," Aquila said.

"What?"

"The Institute's going to be here before long. We have to move Sanctuary."

Nephelie didn't waste time asking questions. We followed as she walked into her office and dragged the Persian rug off a hidden magic circle scored into the floor. In the vivit apparatus, a boiler-sized engine floated down as if through the ceiling, hovering a few feet above the seal. Nephelie operated the machine, and a low hum filled the air as the symbol flashed blue and glowed, sparkling glimmers dancing around it. The tiny halos etched all over the house—into the bottom baluster on the staircase, on the high beams in the dining room—all shined the same color, and the light grew until it painted everything in azure. Not knowing Sanctuary's next location filled me with dread—they'd not gotten the supplies they needed to care for everyone. The Institute's plan to uproot us and leave us flailing in the dark had worked. When the ring in Nephelie's office stopped glowing, so too did all the smaller circles. Nephelie slowly lowered her hands and the machine vanished, her face awash in concern.

"Where'd you move Sanctuary?" Aquila asked.

Nephelie left the office and headed through the antechamber. She flung open the front doors, ushering in an arid wind. Outside was a vast desert, covered in scrub grass and cactuses, with a few fold mountains on the horizon. Disbelief hit me like a battering ram. Everyone else looked uneasy about Sanctuary's new location too. "The Sonoran Desert," Nephelie said. "A few miles north of Blythe, California."

Alison stepped outside and spun around, scanning the barren landscape. "You put us in the middle of a desert?" It certainly didn't seem like the best idea, especially considering our diminished supplies.

"We couldn't stay around Chicago."

"So you moved us to a *desert?*"

"Sanctuary is climate controlled. Treat it like a camping trip."

"We're running out of supplies, Neph," Aquila said quietly, like she didn't want us to hear.

"There're a few Defector cells out here we can collaborate with."

A few children trickled out of the reading room, curious. Linh slowly made her way down the staircase toward the foyer. Maleeka's dour mood brightened when she saw Linh. She ran past us to join her.

"The circles in the book room were glowing, Mrs. Nephelie," a boy said. "Did we move again?"

"Go back in the reading room, James," Nephelie replied gently. "The rest of you go in there, too, except Maleeka."

"No way," Alison said, storming back inside. "We have a right to know what's going on."

"Just like you had a right to go out there and almost get yourselves killed?"

"We found Maleeka didn't we?"

A tense silence developed. "James, go back into the reading room with the other children."

James grumbled and did as he was told.

With the children gone, Nephelie said, "I've tried contacting Estaban, but I'm not getting a response. I've also contacted six other Defector leaders in the Chicago area. Every time, nothing."

"I think those witch-hunters chasing us down are part of some big Institute scheme," Maleeka said. "The Institute cut off the supply lines—they've probably made moves against the smaller cells too."

"My thoughts exactly."

"What do you think happened to Estaban?" Aquila asked, voice hushed, like she was afraid to hear Nephelie's answer.

"I don't want to make too many assumptions. In the meantime, I'll contact our Defector allies in this region and see if we can't get a supply convoy out here. We have enough food and other supplies to last us a week—two if we stretch them—but we'll need more resources soon."

With the Defector cells in Chicago and the surrounding areas most likely destroyed, Maleeka craved answers. Hell, everyone did. But Nephelie and Aquila locked themselves in the office to wait for Luther, whose investigations in the City at the End of the World kept him away. Hunter got another strange headache and headed upstairs to lie down. I joined him, wanting to keep close. Everyone else gathered in the bedroom too.

Maleeka leaned against Blake's bunk while he perched on top of it, next to Alison. Linh leaned up against my bunk on the floor next to me. Hunter lay on the bed behind us, softly groaning in pain.

"I just want to know how any of this happened," Maleeka said.

"Didn't you join a Legacy, Blake?" Linh asked.

Maleeka's eyes turned sharply to Blake. "You joined a Legacy and you didn't tell me?"

"What does that have to do with anything?" Blake said.

"You could be working with the Institute," Linh said.

"That doesn't even make any sense," Alison said in a viciously defensive tone. "Blake didn't know anything about Maleeka, or the Defectors in Chicago, or any of this shit. If you're trying to say Blake is a traitor, I think you'd better mull that over a little more."

Everyone got quiet. Linh and Maleeka saved their rebuttal. Nothing prevented the Institute from attacking us, and that made everyone nervous—a few times, I caught myself staring at the door, waiting for Smiths to burst in. Everyone's anxiety unavoidably led to a spike in tension. Our desperate search for answers in such a dire situation inclined us to a few dust-ups. People blame each other when answers run low, and we didn't know anything.

"I didn't mean to imply anything by it," Linh said after the pause.

"Let's go see if Luther's gotten back yet," Blake said.

Of course, even after Luther returned, Nephelie and Aquila still refused to tell us anything. They stayed in that office plotting the whole day while we ran Sanctuary. Hunter's head hurt too much for him to help. After dinner, Aquila asked Maleeka and I to clean up the kitchen. I gathered a few plates and silverware off the table into a small stack and placed it next to Maleeka while she rinsed them off in the sink.

"I'm sorry about, Penn," I said. She didn't say anything back. I got the impression Maleeka didn't like showing vulnerability. Her dark eyes always flitted about, though, like she didn't know how to stop thinking. "What do you think Aquila and Nephelie have been talking about with Luther?"

That question perked her interest. "I got a little bit out of Aquila before she left the kitchen. She and Nephelie are headed out in the morning to meet up with some Defectors, hopefully to pick up supplies."

"Has the Institute ever waged this kind of attack against the Defectors?" She sponged a plate clean then kept wiping it like she forgot what she was doing. Water ran off the scars and scratches on her fingers. Those aged marks made her hands look like they belonged to someone older.

She shook her head.

"Are you scared?"

"We're Defectors. This is just the way things are. You pray every day the Institute won't take you, but if we're being honest, I'd rather die than go back to that place. So, I guess no, I'm not scared, because I can't afford to be scared. Because if I waste time being afraid, that's one more minute the bad guys get to kill me."

Fighting the Institute hardened children, made them into the young warriors the Defectors didn't debate about weaponizing. That's probably why Maleeka didn't say much about Penn's death. Somewhere in her soul, she had been expecting this day. This was no clean, ordinary fight. Our struggle positioned us against a system that sought no less than our total annihilation. Maleeka might've been only sixteen, but her battle scars—from her fingertips to somewhere deep in her soul—looked like they belonged to someone much older.

The following morning, Aquila got us all up as usual. Alison and Blake got ready and headed out, but Hunter didn't move. I shook him to see how he felt, but he rolled over, shaking and convulsing, his arms limp as foam bubbled from his mouth.

"Hunter!" I said. Having heard me, Alison and Blake came back into the room. I scooped him into my arms, but his violent, jerky motions made him hard to hold. His body trembled and shook, then stopped. Blake helped me slide Hunter off the bed and onto the floor, where we rolled him onto his stomach so he wouldn't choke. Blake picked him up and carted him out. We rushed to the small infirmary in the east wing, and Blake unloaded Hunter onto a bed.

"What's wrong with him?" I said, crouching beside the bed.

Maleeka checked him with her wizard sight. "I don't know, but his life force is fading."

"What do you mean?"

She didn't respond.

Linh said, "I'm going to go get Nephelie and the others," and left the room. I held Hunter's hand. Not knowing what ailed him filled my mind with the most frightening scenarios. I quickly drove away those thoughts to fend off panic. My survival thus far depended on me switching emotional gears when things got tough. The Defectors demanded their members keep a steely resolve—the same resolve Penn showed when he cast the fireball.

Nephelie, Aquila, and Luther all rushed in and approached Hunter's bed. Reaching into the vivit apparatus, Luther fiddled with a small but very intricate machine hovering over Hunter's head. Nestled deep in the clockwork underpinning Hunter's mind, an inky blob stretched and recoiled, alive.

"What is that black thing?"

Luther backed away. "I'll need to go into the study and do some research. The rest of you stay here."

I stayed rooted at Hunter's bedside while an unpredictable emotional panoply hit me in waves. Alison and Blake remained close, sitting on two metal chairs in a corner. Luther walked back in around seven and motioned for me to follow. Alison and Blake rose to join, but he only needed me. He led me downstairs, into Nephelie's office. Nephelie and Aquila had gone out to wait for the local Defector faction. Luther asked me to explain everything leading up to our imprisonment in the Dreamhaven. I told him about the cintamani, about bringing Hunter back with Gaspar's notes. I even mentioned Hunter's strange, recurring headaches. Luther never betrayed his thoughts. He remained quiet as I spoke, a hand on his chin and his eyes to the floor, deep in contemplation.

"I'm going to be direct with you," he said when I finished. "Once something goes into the Void, it can't just come back. Surely, Gaspar must've mentioned that in his notes."

My cheeks flushed. Even if Gaspar's notes had warned against bringing people back from the Void, I wouldn't have paid attention. Hunter had saved me from the Sandman, and I'd owed it to him.

"Hunter isn't the first wizard to have conjured a cintamani. History is defined by wishes that changed things completely. I've found numerous entries about the cintamani and the ways that wizards have tried to cheat its cost. What you did ranks among them."

"Someone's done this before?"

"Over the years, the Defectors have come across quite a bit of literature we believe the Institute has tried to hide." Luther opened a book on Nephelie's desk with the name *Hanno Scherrer* scrawled across the top. Entries handwritten in German filled every page in the book. Luther turned to a page marked *August 9, 1887* near the bottom.

"Hanno Scherrer," Luther said, "belonged to a secret, dynastic wizard line known as the Knights of Lemuria, during a time known as the Third Magus War. I know they didn't teach you about the Magus Wars at the Institute, and what information we have is fractured, but we know the Third Magus War involved two warring factions: the Knights of Lemuria, and another faction we have less information on called the Malebranche. Scherrer was studying alchemy in the Black Forest, obsessed on using a philosopher's stone to end the war. He used his daughter's soul to make one. He then used his wishes to change the tide of the war. From what we've pieced together, the Knights of Lemuria were able to defeat the

Malebranche. Afterward, they established a great wizard assembly whose sole purpose it was to defend the world from such wickedness, should it ever crop up again.

"Scherrer was a hero to wizardkind, but no one knew that he had sacrificed his own daughter to save the world. Guilt-ridden, Scherrer began investigating how he might retrieve something from the Void." Luther flipped through some pages, coming to a diagram that resembled the magic circle I drew to rescue Hunter from the Void. It was Gaspar's Unwinding spell.

"Scherrer arranged a spell to fish his daughter out of the Void. He succeeded. Many joyous months passed. But the Void always reclaims what belongs to it"—Luther swiped through the book—"and the girl became ill. Scherrer described it as a darkness in her mind that slowly spread to her soul. The term Scherrer settled on was *Void-touched*. He said his daughter had become Void-touched, a sickness that rots the soul into nothingness. He learned that, in time, she would die and be returned to the Void. Slowly, her body crumbled while her mind wasted away. Scherrer was forced to watch every dreadful moment."

"What does that mean?"

"That means there is no way to save the boy. His soul is being eaten by the Void, and it's destroying his body too. In fact, the reason his memories were missing when you first encountered him in the Dreamhaven might be directly attributed to the Void-touch. That is why he's been experiencing headaches: it's destroying his mind. In time, he will die."

"There's got to be a way to help him!"

"What're you going to do?" Luther asked, voice bubbling with ire.

"I don't know. I'll figure it out. I'll go somewhere. Do something!"

Luther closed the book. "Don't you think you've done enough?" It was clear he blamed me for Hunter's condition. The guilt he laid upon me weighed heavy as a boulder. He waited for me to ask questions, but I didn't. "I'm leaving to continue my investigations in the City at the End of the World. I'll be back later this evening."

Luther pulled out his key and unlocked the cabinet. An empty hallway in a run-down apartment appeared on the other side. The same apartment we'd used to reach Sanctuary. He crawled inside and closed the door behind him. I opened the doors after him, but the cabinet had reverted to normal. Luther had vanished, leaving me alone in Nephelie's office; he didn't care to deal with my emotional outbursts.

My eagerness to rescue Hunter had brought him back cursed. It fell on me to fix this; it fell on me to undo the curse and save his soul once more. This time for good.

I opened Hanno Scherrer's notes again and read. It didn't take long to find a passage where Scherrer described visiting his daughter in Everywhen, shortly before she died. According to the notes, while she lay dying in the material world, her soul waited somewhere known as the Night City.

Scherrer performed a dream rave with his daughter and joined their minds, making it easier for him to visit her in the Night City. While there, he studied his surroundings. He said a powerful Mara called *the Nightmare King* ruled the Night City. The Nightmare King warned Scherrer that the city's true ruler, though, was Death itself, and that if Scherrer didn't stop coming to see his daughter, eventually Death would claim his soul too.

When Alison had trapped herself in Everywhen, Blake had taken us to the Night Market, a bazaar in Everywhen where Maras traded in peculiarities. There, Linh told me about the Night City—

she said it existed like a border between Everywhen and the Void. If our souls returned to the Void after death, it made sense that a dying person's soul waited in the Night City, on that border, until their final moment. If I ever wanted to see Hunter again, I needed to unite our minds through a dream rave and seek him in the Night City. Once I found him, I intended to bring him back. I'd reached into the Void once and pulled Hunter out, and I would do it again.

I hurried back to the infirmary and found Alison and Blake waiting for me. I told them everything Luther had said, but I didn't bother mentioning Scherrer's notes—I'd already forgotten most of them. They shared a concerned look.

"You're not thinking of going in there after him, are you?" Blake said.

"It's about noon. Aquila and Nephelie won't be back for a while, and Luther's gone too. If I'm going to do this, I need to do it now."

"You don't *unite* with people who are dying. It'll kill you."

I didn't respond.

"Johnny, are you crazy?" Alison said. "Are you seriously thinking about uniting with Hunter so you can visit him in . . . *the Night City*? That sounds like a cheap '80s porn."

"I'm not just going to visit him. I'm going to get him out."

Blake grew visibly frustrated. "If you go in there, you aren't coming back."

"Johnny," Alison said, "you're not going in there. Hunter's going to die, and if you try to save him, you're going to die too." Alison's voice grew shaky. "You're not going in there. Do you hear me?"

Blake's stare hardened. He knew my desire to save Hunter wouldn't falter, no matter how much they pleaded. "Ali," I said, "Hunter sacrificed himself to save me. I'm not leaving him in there. I fought the Sandman in Everywhen, and that monster in the Dreamhaven. I can save him. I know I can."

Blake responded well to conviction—seeing the passion in my eyes stirred him. "Then I'm going with you," he asserted. "You helped me save Maleeka. And Hunter's my friend too."

Alison glared at us. Anxiety made the air turgid. The legendary Night City was the only place in all Everywhen—possibly in all creation—that wizards outright avoided, for any journey into that cursed place promised sorrow, pain. It was the lone cliff overlooking the endless Void, the last stop on a ghost train to the abyss, and if the stories were true, none returned.

Alison, having lost the will to keep arguing, merely shrugged. "Whatever. Count me in."

I nodded to Hunter. Blake picked up his legs and helped me lift him to the floor. Alison was already lying down. We joined her and formed a cross with our heads touching. No turning back. We closed our eyes and fell asleep.

Chapter 14

A doddery suspension bridge stretched over a yawning chasm, the cables connecting its adjoining towers covered in black rust—even its pillars were decrepit vestiges. At the bridge's end, a shadowy city rose into the inky pall, an ianthine haze glowing behind it. The city's crumbling towers leaned against one another, their foundations creaking loudly. A preternatural silence permeated all around me—ominous, like the hush before a coffin closes. Neither Alison nor Blake stood at my side. Getting separated happened all the time when traveling with others into Everywhen. Still, the fear this place inspired made the loneliness more unsettling. Behind me, even more darkness. I stepped toward the bleakness and caught myself nearly walking off a cliff and retreated from the edge. A few rocks skittered off the ledge and fell into the abyss below. I was on a round platform connected to the bridge, like a chunk of street torn off the Earth and launched into space.

Hunter cautiously ambled across the bridge, heading toward the city like he was lost. He looked off to the right, over the edge.

"Hey, Johnny," he called out, voice shaky with fear.

"Hunter?" My voice echoed like I was shouting into a cavern, but he didn't hear me.

Hunter cupped his hands around his mouth, his back still turned to me, and called, "Johnny, where are you?" His voice bounded off the darkness same as mine. The fear in his words climbed, his fevered search for me revealing nothing. "Johnny? Why's it so dark? Where am I?" Hunter walked into the creeping gloom along the bridge, and it swallowed him. I ran onto the bridge and called for him, praying my voice reached him, but the mournful vale around the bridge engulfed me and plunged me into darkness. The ground under me became like mud, sticky and thick. I thought up a light ball, but nothing happened. I tried again, but the spell failed a second time. Magic should've been easier to use in Everywhen, not harder. Even though my spells didn't work, my wizard senses detected Alison and Blake's auras, so I headed toward them. A mucky, splashing noise resounded, like an alligator slapping its tail against the water, but it proved difficult to locate. Somewhere, out there in the darkness, something was moving. A few quick breaths helped me regain my focus, but my wizard senses grew weaker. Like a jamming signal scrambling a radio message, some great force was dampening my magic.

The sploshing noise came closer. It sounded big. Much bigger than me. Then something smooth and rubbery brushed against my leg. It didn't feel like a snake because snakes don't have joints. This felt more like a thin, spidery limb, but it measured much longer than an ordinary limb. I stilled my movements and silently begged for it to leave. No telling what horrible thing squelched around in the darkness out here. If I didn't need to save Hunter, I would've woken myself up. The creature resumed moving, far enough away that I felt comfortable letting out a breath. I needed to hurry out of here before that thing came back. Too much noise threatened to draw it to me, so I stepped delicately. If I didn't get through this supernatural darkness, I'd never see Hunter again. That thought was enough to keep me plodding forward until darkness lifted like a sheet and I found myself standing in an alley with a dead end at my back. Heavy raindrops pattered on every surface in the alley, and from the trash cans seeped a rank odor. If this was the Night City, and thereby just an extension of Everywhen, even though none of this was real, it still stoked the senses in all the same ways.

Dying streetlamps lit the path ahead, their gleam illuminating the black walls. A wasting tabby cat hollered and leaped off a trash can, sending the lid crashing to the wet pavement. The alley curved into another, and that one morphed into yet another—a nightmarish twisting maze that led to a rainy street teeming with people swathed in black, rain-soaked capes. They walked close to one another, some heading north, others south, all oblivious to the raging storm. No telling where their journey ended, or if it ended at all. To match the weary denizens, I imagined myself wreathed in similar garb. Unlike my failed light ball, however, I managed the transformation. Whatever force weakened my magic here didn't seem consistent. Sometimes it stopped my spells abruptly, other times it flailed, and my magic pushed through. I stepped into the crowd and weaved between the mysterious figures, heading toward Blake and Alison's auras. The cloaked figures paid no heed to my presence; their march was unphased as I moved among them. If I stopped walking, they bumped into me and kept going. The buildings along the street climbed high into the darkness above like never-ending skyscrapers and bore no signage. Even the crowd congesting the thoroughfare ignored their existence, no one entering or leaving any one. The street functioned like a set for a strange scene, nothing else.

Blake and Alison's auras grew near, so I sped up my pace, then everyone in the street stopped moving and looked at me. Their cowls didn't hide the ghoulish creatures underneath. Inside their hoods, they looked like ordinary people. I didn't know whether to continue or not, but soon their unflinching gazes turned black with chastisements. Without speaking, they whispered: "How dare you come here looking for him?" A hideous woman with long black hair and coarse, pocked skin laughed. She opened her mouth wide, and I spied a canary tied to her tooth, a few inches from her face. It flitted wildly, fighting to escape, but the string around its leg held tight. Slowly, the woman's horrid tongue, riddled with pustules and meaty, throbbing veins, crawled out of the corner of her mouth and slithered toward the canary. I turned and ignored the spectacle. The Night City wanted to lure me into its hypnotic mind games, so I forced myself free. A sickening crunch echoed behind me, and the woman cackled again, hideously, her voice like a howl into the Void. I shoved past the robed figures and followed Blake and Alison's auras to a dead-end alley with a flickering streetlamp spotlighting a hole in the wall. It looked like someone had made the opening with a blowtorch, its edges perfectly smoothed.

"Hello?" I called into the hole.

"Johnny?" Alison's voice echoed back.

I crawled through into a room with black walls and checkered floor tile. In one corner, a person with a face shaped like a deep bowl, wearing a robe that dangled off their emaciated body, with a blue patchwork quilt strewn across their lap. The stranger pointed to another niche where an empty rocking chair swayed furiously. Flashes like lightning sporadically lit the nook behind the seat. In the room's center, a narrow golden beam struck the floor, coming from a tiny hole too high in the ceiling to reach.

"Johnny!" I heard Alison's voice again. This time it came from the ceiling. I approached the beam and pressed my hand to it. The ray bent like a flimsy wire. I tugged it to make sure it was sturdy, then I tightened my fingers around the line and pulled myself up. Dream physics made my body weightless. I reached the hole and poked a finger through, and it tore like a balloon—the whole ceiling was like a thin rubber sheet. I ripped the hole even wider and a torrent of gray sand exploded through the opening and flooded the room. I swam up through the sand until I popped out of a shallow dune.

The world had transformed into a black sand beach, with basalt columns of different heights scattered throughout. Blake and Alison talked near an incline leading up to a shaky old pier. The dock stretched out over atrous water that gleamed with a silver sparkle, even though no moon cast such a glow upon it. A well-appointed wherry bobbed lazily at the end. I stumbled across uneven rocks and sandy dips on my way to join them.

"Jesus, J, you scared the shit out of me!" Alison said upon seeing me.

"How long have you guys been here?"

"We just got here," Blake said.

"We were in some gross, underground, crypt-maze thing," Alison said.

Blake pointed at the wherry. "I think we're supposed to get on that."

Hunter's aura felt like a distant memory, something sweet on the turgid air. It pulsed in the darkness on the horizon, beyond the ocean. We traveled to the pier's end to get a better look at the boat. A gilded scrollwork pattern snaked around its shiny black hull. In its spacious cockpit a fancy rug was strewn across the bottom boards. At the back, a cuddy with a brass lantern hung over a lavish bench, covered in jeweled pillows.

The helmsman, a darkly robed figure whose face was hidden under a heavy cowl, didn't look up at us. The coxswain drummed its long, pale fingers on the oar in its hands. We boarded the boat, and I camped on the bench in the cuddy with Alison. Blake, however, kept vigilant, arms folded over his chest, body directed at the ferryman.

Churning waves lapped the hull, splashing like something moved under them. Just below the surface, a pale, ghoulish creature with skin that resembled heavily incised clay floated lifelessly. Its hair swayed like cobwebs in the shadowy water. But it wasn't the only one of its kind down there. I hurried away from the edge, eager for the boat to move.

"Okay," Alison said, halfway between irritated and creeped out. "How do we make . . . *them* move the boat?"

The boatman ferrying souls across an acheronian river was a cross-cultural archetype, such as Charon, who traveled the dead across the River Styx into the Underworld. Everywhen resided among humanity's collected dreams, so it seemed reasonable that early wizards exploring the Night City discovered this Stygian boatman and brought back stories to the real world, only for those tales to give rise to said myths and legends. It was likely the other way around too: This figure existed not because it had always been here, but because humankind had dreamt it up. Everywhen was a perpetual chicken-egg conundrum.

"It's taking us . . . to the Underworld, right?" I asked. "How's that story go again?"

"Charon's obol," Alison muttered, thinking to herself. "A coin! Give them a coin."

Blake imagined up a penny then placed it in the spirit's cold hand. The boatman closed their spidery fingers around the coin and vanished it. Then they used their oar to push off from the dock. My thoughts stayed on Hunter as we quietly floated into the abyss. I hoped for a short voyage. Alison stayed wordless. Her silence, a rare thing indeed, signaled immense anxiety. Blake's, too, seemed concerned, but his mind likely churned out strategies, not fears.

"Are your powers acting weird?" I said to them both.

"Like, not acting at all?" Alison said.

"It's weird. It's like sometimes I can use them, and sometimes I can't."

"It's been happening to me too," Blake said.

"What do you think is going on?" I asked.

"I don't know for sure, but we aren't going to have much luck finding Hunter without them."

The oar's somber slush became the only sound we heard. It felt like that for a while. Then a strangeness caught my eye, breaking the monotony. Another black ocean hung high above us, and in its bleak waters, ghoulish bodies, like the ones floating under us, hovered languidly. I shrank down next to Alison, alerting her to our ominous ceiling. Stricken with horror, she pulled me close. Blake noticed the panic on our faces and looked up. He looked uncertain.

"What the hell?" Alison said.

A terror possessed us as we expected the roof to come crashing down. But the water never moved, nor did the bodies suspended in it. The oarsmen moved us out from under the celestial ocean, and a clear look back revealed the massive hovering water cube under which we'd traveled. The dreamworld's bizarre geography left us speechless.

We didn't travel much longer before a gray beach on a not-too-distant shore came into view. The ferryman guided us there and moored the vessel. Then they struck their oar against the bottom boards, hurrying us to disembark. Alison jumped off the boat, making a small splash as she dropped and starting for dry land before Blake and I had even turned.

"Are we going?" she said. We joined her on the shore, and the ferryman pushed off the bank. "That was creepy."

Blake left to explore while we watched the ferryman slowly disappear back into the darkness. He took a few shaky steps up a sandy slope. At the top, he put his hands on his hips and said, "No way."

We joined him on a hill overlooking a vast clockwork junkyard. The landfill was covered in broken machinery, with knolls and hills and skinny, towering junk pillars that protruded out of the landscape like hundred-foot-tall fingers. Although no sun hung in the sky, everything was perfectly visible as if bathed in midday light. It seemed, judging by the horizon, that the sea of brass metal pieces never ended; however, Hunter's aura glimmered faintly, somewhere beyond this place. We trekked down the hill and started into the metalwork wasteland.

The machinery underfoot jingled and shifted unpredictably. I thought about using a spell to help traverse this no man's land, but the Night City's spotty magic barrier made it impossible to predict what would even work, and now was no time to investigate the barrier's limits. Blake took big, heavy steps and plunged his feet firmly into the ground to steady himself. I stretched my arms out at my sides and tightrope walked so as not to trip on the uneven footing.

One wrong move and we could find ourselves plummeting into a sinkhole. Alison stumbled over a dip herself and nearly fell face-first on a pile of sharp, broken wheels, but Blake caught her in time and helped her upright.

"Do these pieces make you two feel weird?" Alison asked.

"Yeah," Blake said. "Like the vivit apparatus."

Strangely, I knew what she meant. The vivit apparatus felt like possibility, like the world existed as one big "what if" and you controlled the power to answer the question. This ancient place failed to hide its connection to a distant past. In my mind, I saw the shadowy Creators—whoever they were, whatever they were—painstakingly assembling the universe like a clock, starting with the City at the End of the World, and all the parts they didn't want or need they tossed into Everywhen—here. A close-enough inspection even revealed a slight gleam to them, like tarnished brass that needed a good polish. But that's how this place differed from the vivit apparatus—its machinery lay dead.

A tremor shook the ground. We all stopped moving to keep balance. The ground trembled briefly then stopped, but the sudden quake left us puzzled.

"Do you think we stepped on a sinkhole?" I asked them.

"Johnny," Alison whined, "please don't say stuff like that." Then the ground shook again, throwing us all off balance. "Oh god, we're going to fall in a sinkhole and die."

"Calm down," Blake said, holding himself steady and studying our surroundings. "Let's get close." At his insistence, we inched together until we were standing back to back. The commotion grew until the land swayed like waves on an ocean.

"Look!" Alison said, pointing at a serpentine shape moving beneath the machinery.

A clockwork worm burst out of the ground near us, flinging machinery in every direction. The creature measured as tall as the Sears Tower, with a conical drill for a head and a hulking body made of jumbled cogs, wheels, and springs. All the leftover magic in this place had crashed together to form this monstrosity, and it looked committed to keeping us from progressing.

"That thing's going to dive for us," Blake said, already preparing to dart.

"We'll never get away. It's huge!" Alison said.

The worm drove its spinning head toward us. I dug my feet into the ground, tensed my legs, and bounded like a spring, landing far away from the beast. It noisily tunneled underground and vanished. I had managed a spell to empower my jump—the inconsistent force affecting our magic had wavered again. Alison and Blake must've fled in another direction because I couldn't find them. The creature partially surfaced again about twenty feet away and plowed toward me. I readied another jump, but my foot got stuck in the machinery. I pulled to free my limb with no success. As the worm neared, the ground undulated relentlessly, making it difficult to stand. I gave another stalwart tug and dislodged myself, then leaped again as the worm tore up the ground behind me. The creature noticed this and submerged again.

The Night City's magic barrier failed to keep me from strengthening my physical abilities, so I focused instead on finding Alison's aura with my wizard sense. It manifested behind a rounded junk pillar. I jumped over there and found her peeking around a corner, immersed in her search.

"Ali," I whispered.

She startled and put a hand to her chest. "Jesus, J. Now is *not* the time."

We hid together, both of us searching for the worm. "Where'd Blake go?"

"I don't know."

I stood. "I'm going to go look for him."

Alison yanked me back down. "Are you high, J? Let's just . . . wait until that thing pops out again."

We waited ten minutes before I started to grow impatient. "We can't just sit here." I rose to my feet again. "Plus, don't worry. We can . . . kind of use our magic."

"J!" Alison called as I walked away from the pillar.

The worm didn't emerge. I signaled for Alison to follow, but she hesitated, stepping only halfway out before nervously rushing back to her hiding spot.

A vortex formed in the ground a few feet away. Its powerful suction pulled everything toward it. I readied another jump, but this time my jeans snagged on a broken cog. I jerked up, but the fabric ripped, throwing me off balance. My fall didn't scare me nearly as bad as when the junk carried me into the whirlpool, though. I flipped on my side and twisted and turned my leg, but the sharp metal trapping me in place cut my foot. The whirlpool's sides grew nearly perpendicular, but my caught foot kept me from falling into the pit. But the faster the whirlpool moved, the more the parts holding my foot loosened their grip.

A massive drill emerged from the vortex's center, gnashing everything that tumbled into it, crunching like a monstrous garbage disposal. The cog stuck around my foot slacked then rolled into the pit. I held on tenuously to the whirlpool's sides, but the shifting metal sliced up my hands and I lost my grip and fell. Machinery spun around me in a disorienting eddy, but before getting pureed I crashed against a large gear that had fallen into the pit. The oversized machine part grinded against the drill, but it was too large to get minced. I latched onto it for safety. I sped around the whirlpool twice before the giant worm explosively surfaced and sent me spinning through the air, still clamped onto the gear. The creature's clamorous rise destabilized the junk pillar Alison had been hiding behind, and it collapsed on top of the monster with such force the creature returned underground.

I waited for the gear to stop spinning, but when it did, the velocity yanked me off and sent me plummeting to the ground. Blake caught me midjump and we landed safely next to Alison.

"We can't beat that thing," Blake said. "Let's get out of here."

We jumped like grasshoppers through the machine wastes, fleeing the pursuing monster. But no matter how quickly we moved, the worm stayed close behind, angrily smashing through junk pillars and anything that got in its way. Our escape terminated at the edge of a gorge. Though I saw land on the other side, harnessing enough magic to bridge the rift with a leap looked impossible. We were cornered, and the worm continued to drive toward us, only a few hundred feet away.

"What the hell do we do?" Alison asked.

With nowhere left to run, I jumped off the cliff.

Chapter 15

I was dropped in the middle of Fuller Street, right before the cul-de-sac where Dad and I used to live in Chicago. But something about this place didn't sit well with me—it was like a grim reflection, with a pitch-colored sky that hung over everything like a funerary veil. A small fire raged on a split-level house's lawn to my right. The home's windows and doors were boarded up. I used to pass that house every day after school, on my walk home. It didn't have any tenants because the sharky landlord had chased them all out. A black mailbox used to sit at the driveway's entrance, but there was nothing there now. Weak fires also burned on other yards throughout the neighborhood, and hollowed-out, battered vans littered the streets. In the distance, screams rose into the night.

Gunfire rattled close by. Convinced a roving band of killers was about to make me target practice, I took cover behind a sedan parked along the sidewalk near the split-level. I snuck around the vehicle and spied three young guys standing in the street, dressed in black SWAT armor and carrying AR-15s in one hand and beer in the other. They were celebrating—what they were celebrating I didn't want to know. I could only imagine the horrifying things they'd been up to. One fired another volley into the air and laughed loudly, and his drunken friends hooted and cheered him on. The three horsemen of the suburban apocalypse. All they needed was a disconcerting fixation with Levitical law to make this nightmare complete. Each gunman had an average build, but one was taller and gawkier than the others. They hid their faces behind balaclavas. I leaned forward for a better look.

"Look, boys, we got a kicker," one yelled upon sighting me.

I ducked as he fired, metal shards sparking off the trunk.

"Time for a game of smear the queer!" said the one who had fired.

His friends chuckled at his anemic wit. I was unimpressed, but more importantly, I was scared shitless. The two other gunmen slowed to load their weapons, giving me time to bolt across the lawn, toward the split-level's back gate, which was locked. I scaled the fence. Gunfire sounded behind me—I didn't have long to seek refuge. I made my way around the house to the back, where I spotted a patio door. Thankfully, it slid aside easily and let me into the kitchen. Although the inside was dark, fires outside, visible through the windows, gave me enough light to spot a staircase.

Since the Night City's magic barrier failed to stifle my spells in the junkyard, I wondered if I could cast a fireball here. I set about imagining the flames appearing in my hands, but nothing happened. The barrier's power again suppressed my magic. That simplified my choices: I ran upstairs and hid in the first room I saw—it had a king-sized bed in it, another door leading into a bathroom, and a bifold closet against the wall. The dreamworld existed in flux, and portals connected these ever-changing realities. I checked the bathroom for a way out, but it was just a bathroom.

Someone caved in the front door downstairs.

"Where are you, little piggy?" a voice bellowed from downstairs—the one who'd spoken earlier. His two accomplices snickered, then a clamor erupted in the kitchen. It sounded like they were crashing appliances and metal utensils against the floor while hollering glee-fully. Loud thuds in the stairwell—a gunman was coming upstairs. I didn't have time to investigate the closet, so I scuttled under the bed and pressed myself flat against the floor. The footsteps stopped at the bedroom door, which creaked open, revealing a pair of combat boots.

They plodded across the carpet, walking around the bed. Downstairs, the gunman's allies continued to trash the kitchen, shattering plates and clanging pans, doing everything in their power to be obnoxious.

I saw then as Alison carefully peeked her head out of the bifold closet.

The gunman marched into the bathroom and audibly tore down the shower curtain.

I wriggled forward, poking out from under the bed. "Psst, Alison!" She didn't hear me, though. Alison shut the closet door again, and I wormed back under the bed before the goon came back out of the bathroom.

He circled the room like a shark. Even under this much dark-ness, my hopes of reaching the closet before getting shot seemed foolish. He idled around the foot of the bed before moving to the door. His boots paused midstep and turned to face me. He rattled something on his gun and a spotlight struck the floor and swept toward me. *Shit*. I sucked in a deep breath and tucked my arms under my chest, trying to shrink. But I couldn't get small enough the evade the light. The beam hit my eyes, and I resigned myself to death.

"Stan!" a voice called from downstairs. The gunman quickly moved the light away, and I let out the breath. Alison popped her head out of the closet again, and although the gunman was only momentarily distracted, I took my chances and crawled out from under the bed and bolted for the closet.

"There you are!" the shooter said, raising his gun. But I was already gone.

Inside the closet was another world stretching far back, every foot punctuated with a new row of clothes. Alison pushed past blazers and button-ups and dresses, pulling me in deeper. I kept looking back to make sure nobody followed us. The gunman's voice echoed: "You can't hide in there. You can't hide anywhere. Nightmare King's going to find you."

The Nightmare King. That name jogged my memory. Hanno Scherrer, the wizard who sacrificed his daughter to create a cintamani, had mentioned the Nightmare King in his notes. The powerful Mara that ruled over the Night City. Scherrer never mentioned encountering a magic barrier in the Night City, though, but he did say the Nightmare King urged him to stop coming there. And if you wanted to dissuade a wizard from visiting, hampering their magic in such a dangerous place provided a good start.

"What the hell's that guy talking about?" Alison asked.

I changed the subject to avoid getting sidetracked. "Where's Blake?"

She shoved aside a fur coat and a Hawaiian shirt. "I don't know," she said curtly.

"What's wrong?"

Alison stopped walking. Hesitated. "Nothing's wrong," she said and kept moving.

Navigating the crowded closet, with its low ceiling and close-together walls, proved uncomfortable, but it took more than some Everywhen strangeness to get Alison acting so temperamental.

"I've known you my whole life," I said. "I know when you're being weird."

"This is a weird time to get all mushy, J."

"Ali—"

"Fine! How do you think it makes me feel coming to this place after Mom died?"

Her words cut like a knife. "I told you . . . you didn't have to come."

"That's reasonable, right?" she said. "You thought I'd let my best friend, and the only person I have left in the world, come here alone?"

"Are you mad at me?"

Again, she paused and considered her words. The anger that had swiftly flared in her died down just as fast. "I didn't want to leave that place, J."

"The Dreamhaven?"

"Yeah."

"It was a trick, Ali."

"I didn't care."

The scene around us changed in a blink. We were standing in a funeral parlor, with eight wreaths gathered around an open coffin sitting at the room's head. Chairs lined the walls, leaving a wide-open space for mourners to gather and approach the casket. Alison's uncle Eddy leaned forward until his chair's legs hovered off the ground. He had been the youngest of her mom's brothers and sisters, at least six years younger than Cecilia. Alison always said he never did anything for anyone without a price. Her floral print–obsessed, middle-aged aunt Rebecca walked up beside him and rested a hand on his shoulder. Rebecca married a church-going man who constantly extolled the values of a good Christian life. Alison's mom, her educated sister, hated the ogre and had slowly grown apart from her sister. When Alison came out, Rebecca rejected her and Cecilia cut her off altogether. A few other guests dawdled in the room, but I only recognized Alison's grandma.

"It's all right, sweetie," Rebecca said to Eddy. "Cecilia can finally rest. The cancer was brutal."

Rebecca's words came as a shock. The Institute had kidnapped us before Alison's mom died, so Alison never got to attend Cecilia's funeral. She started toward the coffin. I wanted to stop her, tell her this place played tricks on people, but I didn't. Her grandmother lingered near the coffin, covering her mouth with a handkerchief while sobbing. When she finally walked away, Alison moved closer. Her mother Cecilia lay inside, her head rested on a cream-colored pillow. She looked peaceful, as though she drifted in a dreamworld as lovely as the lilies and oleanders gathered around her. A few tears dripped on her cheek as Alison cried over her.

Alison rested a hand on her mother's chest. The mortician had restored much of Cecilia's beauty. Her brown, wavy hair—which resembled Alison's—fell in gentle curls around her face. She was gowned in a luminous blue dress, like the sky after a rain. Alison kissed her own fingers and placed them tenderly on Cecilia's lips. I rubbed Alison's back, then dropped my hand next to hers and looped our pinkies.

"I thought I'd be less angry when I finally saw this," she said.

"Well?"

"I'm not any less angry." She chuckled bitterly. "In the Dreamhaven, I ran away from all this. I was with you and your dad, and everyone liked me, and I got to pretend I was living the life I wanted. For a minute, I forgot how the Institute took everything from us."

"We're Defectors, Ali. We can finally get revenge—"

"You don't want revenge any more than I do. You just want to go back home." She was right—her words stung like a reopened cut. "We've been fighting our whole lives. We didn't have to fight in the Dreamhaven. You could've dated Hunter and lived with your dad and been happy."

"I have you . . . and I have Blake, and we're going to get Hunter. We'll find a new way to be happy."

She went perfectly still, then cried deeply. But her tears didn't burn with anger; she was letting go—our old lives were gone. Our old families were gone. This was our new life, and we had a new family. Blake. And Hunter. And Ali. And me.

Chapter 16

Like the Dreamhaven, the Night City manifested as a dream within a dreamworld, neither subject to Everywhen's laws nor those of our own world. But where the Dreamhaven sought to mimic our reality, the Night City warped like images in a funhouse mirror. Its physics didn't follow any preestablished rules, nor did its logic. The City exhibited its own intelligence—and not just that, it freely ransacked our minds and used our thoughts to adjust itself, becoming unpredictable. It dropped us into Cecilia's funeral to test Alison's resolve, but she emerged feeling like a chapter in her life had finally closed. Now she moved through the endless closet with eagerness, backfiring the Night City's ruthless trickery.

The closet world stretched the length of several houses. I stopped once and studied the sleeve on a silky blue blazer. The fabric turned black and disintegrated in my hand. Everything behind us was slowly withering into dust.

Alison and I squeezed together around a narrow opening at the closet's end. A peek through the gap revealed a moldering library with dim, greenish lighting and bookstacks that towered infinitely into the darkness above. We were nestled between two shelves in a winding aisle that curved left and right. The air stunk like parchment and mold. Alison nudged aside the bookcase to our left and widened the opening, then pressed a toe on the wooden floor. It let out an exasperated groan. She pulled her whole body through the crack, and I followed close behind.

"Where the hell are we?" Alison asked, swiping her fingers across the books on a shelf.

"A library?"

"No duh, J. Why a library? Why here?"

"Let's just keep following Blake's aura and get out of here."

"Is your magic working?"

"Just my wizard sense."

"I wish I knew why our magic didn't work right in this place." I kept my theory about the Nightmare King quiet. Going off on a wild goose chase after this Nightmare King wouldn't help anyone.

This place was a font of dead secrets, the old books on every shelf brimming with mysteries. Books arranged into columns on the floor cluttered its serpentine aisles. On our way through the skinny, twisting passages, I skirted my fingers along the books' dusty spines, looking for anything indicating what knowledge they contained, but not a single title graced any of them. Curiously, I snatched a book off the shelf to determine its contents myself, but an indiscernible language appeared in its pages. Linh once showed me how to unscramble foreign languages using my wizard sight. I closed my eyes and prodded the magic barrier with my mind, testing for an opening. It didn't feel as strong here as it had, and when I looked back down the nonsense briefly blurred then words moved around until they became readable.

The book detailed a great civilization, Mu, that once floated high above the Earth. Its society lay divided among a small minority privileged to wield magic—the elites—and the masses who lacked access to wizardry. These rulers also tasked the underclass with serving them. Two other phrases stuck out: *Lemuria* and *Magus War*, terms I'd encountered when talking to Luther and in Hanno Scherrer's notes. Supposedly, the civilization was destroyed during the First Magus War. Luther's account of Scherrer mentioned that he'd belonged to a dynastic order called the Knights of Lemuria, who had used a cintamani stone to end the Third Magus War by defeating a mysterious group called the Malebranche. Scherrer's notes made little mention about the knights themselves, though, nor did they ever mention a First or Second Magus War.

I hurried next to Alison with the book still open. "This book has some pretty weird stuff in it."

"This whole place has *some pretty weird stuff in it.*"

"It talks about an ancient civilization that floated above the Earth, and the *First Magus War.*"

"Didn't you say Luther mentioned something about a Magus War?"

"Yeah. Supposedly, there were other floating cities too"—I flipped to the next page—"and they were all at war. Lemuria, Buyan, Atlantis . . ."

A shadow whipped past, drawing our attention to a tall, hooded figure who came to stand before us. The figure's face stayed hidden under a heavy cowl, like the boatman. It extended one large, pale hand toward me. The gloomy specter terrified us into remaining still. It gradually folded back all its fingers except for the index, which it pointed at me.

Alison looked down. "J, I think the creepy librarian wants their book back."

The robed figure didn't intend on letting me out with the book in tow. And sitting down for a reading session while Blake and Hunter were lost in the Night City wasn't an option. I handed the book over, then the specter whooshed away, disappearing completely. That book stayed on my mind, though. Who knew how many wizard secrets hid in a place like this—secrets the Institute sought to suppress or destroy.

We hurriedly followed Blake's aura, both eager to quickly escape the archive, until we found a door riddled with splintery cracks.

"He's . . . through here?" Alison asked.

"Feels that way."

She reached for the knob and opened the door. The world around us became a disorienting whirl of colors, like lights blurring as you spin on a merry-go-round, and just as quickly everything stopped and we found ourselves on a stage facing a tiny bar. Strange patrons gathered at a dozen round tables close to the stage. A bearded man with a cowboy hat rimmed with crocodile teeth sat at one table, a wall of snowy television sets stacked on top of each other behind him; and a couple wearing gas masks and sharing a nozzle relaxed at another, our reflections hanging in their lenses. Nearby, a jittery old man wearing suspenders and a bowler perched at a stool onstage, screeching out discordant notes on an accordion. He stopped suddenly when we walked in. It looked like we'd stolen his thunder. He lowered the instrument and gave us a dead glare, with lifeless fish-like eyes.

"I think he wants us to get off the stage," I whispered.

Blake talked to a bartender, whose head resembled a smudge in a dirty mirror, at a counter behind the sitting area. Alison and I got off stage and joined Blake. He looked relieved to see us. The old man quickly returned to churning out painfully dissonant tunes.

"Took you two long enough," Blake said.

Alison looked back at the shaky old dinosaur onstage. "Where exactly are we?"

"Just some bar in the Night City."

"Why're you here?"

"Looking for information."

Alison looked annoyed with Blake's response. "You didn't think to come look for us?"

"I knew you two could handle yourselves."

"I *guess* that's an upgrade from earlier."

"What were you looking for information about?" I asked.

"I was trying to figure out why our magic wasn't working. Supposedly, there's a powerful Mara that rules over the Night City called—"

"The Nightmare King. I read about him," I said.

"Where?" Blake asked.

"Luther had a book. It belonged to a wizard named Hanno Scherrer. In it, he talked about the ruler of the Night City being a Mara called the Nightmare King."

"You keeping anything else from us?" Alison asked. The bartender wiped out the inside of a tumbler and watched us talk.

"No. I forgot about the Nightmare King until that gun nut said his name."

"Why didn't you tell me back there?"

"Because I didn't think—"

"*Anyway*," Blake interrupted, "the bartender said the Nightmare King keeps an anti-magic spell around the whole of Night City."

"Why doesn't it always work?"

"No clue. Either way, we need our magic at full capacity if we want to find Hunter. Let's go find this Nightmare King first and see if we can't get it to drop the spell."

"Oh sure," Alison said, "we're just going to walk up in his big, nightmare-y castle and ask him to drop the spell, no prob."

"That's exactly what we're going to do," I said.

"How? How are we even supposed to find this Nightmare King?"

"You need only look for a thing in Everywhen to find it," the barman said. He set down the tumbler but left the washcloth inside. Then he pointed down a hallway leading to the club's entrance. "The Nightmare King will know you are looking for him."

"Let's not keep him waiting," Blake said.

I felt it as we approached the entrance: dreadful eyes on my nape. The Nightmare King's ominous aura lurked behind those doors. It felt like horrible sadness. The Night City mourned eternally, and at the heart of all that misery, the Nightmare King ruled on a throne of tears. Merely mentioning the Nightmare King had conjured it, and now it coiled deep around our minds. And without our magic, we were helpless to stop it.

Blake furrowed his brow. "Do you both feel that?"

"The Nightmare King knows we're looking for it," I said. We pushed open the doors and found a glittering hotel lobby on the other side.

Alison stepped forward and scanned the space. "A hotel? Is it going to room service us to death?"

"It could crush us in an elevator?" Blake said, walking up beside her.

"Guess it didn't get that nickname for nothing. I bet this thing's a ball at parties."

Fluted ionic columns stood atop sandy marble floors. Art Deco sconces fixed near their tops filled the room with a pale yellow-orange light. A chandelier sparkled gently overhead. At the far end, an unattended reception desk. Our feet clacked against the polished floor, echoing throughout the eerily quiet space. Elevators with wrought iron half dials over their doors lined the walls. The Nightmare King didn't lack a dramatic flair. Unfortunately, its "humble abode" didn't really give off a warm and comforting vibe. Alison pulled herself halfway onto the reception desk and peered into the office in the back. A stopped clock hung on a wall behind the desk—even its pendulum hung perfectly still in the center. Alison got off the desk and slammed her hand on the service bell, but nothing happened.

She turned and leaned back, elbows on the countertop. "So, this Nightmare King invites us in here then leaves us downstairs. Rude."

A ding from behind—an elevator door opened.

"Maybe it has some manners after all," Blake said.

We walked to the open lift, then gathered around the elevator and peeked inside. Alison gave a grim look. "Didn't you say something about getting crushed in an elevator?" she said.

"We don't have any other options," I said, and walked into the elevator. They shared a nervous glance then followed me in before the gate closed. After a sudden jolt, the brass dial above the doors started moving to the right. The Nightmare King's aura grew more oppressive with every floor we climbed. It filled the cab with a sense of impending doom. Alison sighed heavily and played with her hair—she always did that when she got nervous. A loud screech frightened us all, followed by a soft violin coming through a speaker high on a wall. It played a gentle, melancholic song.

"I feel like we're on the Titanic while it's sinking," Alison said.

"I love that movie."

"Rose could've saved Jack."

"No, she couldn't—the door wasn't buoyant eno—"

"She could've moved."

The car churned to a halt and a chittering filled the air, almost loud enough to drown out the music. Blake and Alison gave apprehensive looks that made my skin crawl. The noise grew. It sounded like millions of tiny, skittering feet.

"Why'd we stop? What the crap is that noise?" Alison muttered.

A cockroach flew out of a vent near the speaker—and not just any roach, a big fat city roach four inches long. It flittered toward me and I nearly hyperventilated. Few things filled me with utter revulsion and horror like city roaches did. I swatted wildly until it flew past me and landed on a wall. Another cockroach crawled out of the vent and took flight. Alison screamed when she saw that one join the other. Then the grate fell, and roaches spilled to the floor in the hundreds. Alison and I huddled together in the farthest corner from the roach pile. Blake moved back, too, but he was more cautious than afraid. One roach landed on my left arm and bit me—I freaked out and swung my arm, flinging the little monster. Hundreds more cascaded out of the vent; the hungry black heap continued to grow.

I looked up and saw a hatch on the ceiling. "Blake," I said, pointing to our escape route. "Boost me up."

Blake took a knee and let me sit on his shoulders, then he lifted me toward the hatch. I weighed more than he expected—he wobbled to the side and nearly dropped us, but I pressed my hands against the ceiling and balanced us until he regained his center. Alison rose up on her tiptoes in the corner, withdrawing from the spreading mass. I pushed against the heavy hatch, gritting my teeth until finally it opened, clanking loudly against the cab's roof. I reached through the opening and planted my forearms on the ledge before reeling myself up, then lay on my stomach and reached down.

"Come on!"

Blake lowered a knee again and waited for Alison to climb on his shoulders, then hoisted her up. He winced as roaches started biting his legs, but Alison grabbed my hands in enough time. I held her steady until Blake regained his composure enough to maneuver her directly under the hatch. She scrambled up onto the roof with me.

"Ali," I said, "hold me down while I reach for Blake." Alison wrapped her arms around my waist and secured me, and I lowered my upper body through the opening. Blake didn't see me, though, as he was too busy kicking and swinging as the roaches covered his legs and started for his midsection.

"Blake!" I shouted. He spotted me hanging through the hatch and jumped, and I snatched his hand. He weighed so much that he almost pulled us all down into the cab with him. Alison quickly tightened her hold, and I reeled him up until he was able to sling his arm over the ledge and pull himself the rest of the way up. A few cockroaches flew up through the opening, but we slammed the hatch shut once Blake was through to prevent any more from following.

"J!" Alison tugged on my sleeve and made me look up. Another stalled elevator was suspended in the shaft, twenty feet above. The doors to floor twenty-eight were wide open just below it. Our elevator groaned to life and resumed climbing, threatening to crush us. When floor twenty-eight's landing was within reach, Alison and I jumped and hauled ourselves through the opening. Blake leaped, but his fingers slipped and he fell back onto the elevator with a loud clunk.

Alison sprang to her feet. "Blake!"

Blake barrel rolled through the gap between the lift and doors and hit the floor next to us with inches to spare. The doors slid shut, and a noisy metal clamor followed.

"Gah. That was so messed up," I said, standing and sweeping my hands through my clothes, still feeling like cockroaches were crawling all over me.

Floor twenty-eight's landing was tucked in an alcove between two converging hallways. A framed canvas painted all black hung over a leather bench opposite the elevator doors. Alison eyed the art. "Someone should tell the Nightmare King's interior designer about pastels."

Blake looked around the corner, down the hallway to our right. The passage stretched about forty feet before hanging left and continuing. The corridor to our left mirrored the one to our right. "Right or left?" Blake asked.

"The Nightmare King's leading us to him," I said. "Why else would those doors have been open?"

"So regardless of where we go, it all leads to the same place," Alison said. "At least Mrs. King makes it easy for us." She headed down the corridor to our right, and Blake and I followed.

The corridor's dingy wall lighting turned the passage a dim orange, causing the gross beige wallpaper to take on a yellowish hue. If nothing else, the Nightmare King understood mood. Every step forward, its powerful aura filled my chest with a stomach-rending sadness that made me feel sick. I pushed out the feeling, but its lingering impression left me thinking about Hunter. Doors with unmarked brass plaques lined the hallway. I jiggled a door handle as we passed, but it didn't open. We walked left at the corridor's end and spotted another curb farther down, heading left again. We took that and kept walking until we found another corridor, this one turning right. We navigated the cavernous paths, one after another, going in circles, trying to reconcile the Escher-esque warren. The entire time, I got the feeling the walls were inching nearer to one another. Without windows, the space's claustrophobic tightness only increased. A deathly *sswwwffff* caught my attention, but I didn't know where it came from. The noise sounded again and continued. It was the walls—the walls were closing in.

"Run!" I shouted.

Alison and Blake looked at me strangely before they realized what was happening. We dashed into the next hallway, but the walls there started advancing on us too. We charged down the passage, but my foot caught on a nail sticking out of the carpet. I lost balance and crashed to the floor. The nailhead had pierced through my shoe and snared the rubber, making it difficult for me to stand. Alison ran back when the walls were only inches away from one another and dragged me along with her, leaving behind my shoe.

The walls finished sliding together, blocking off the hallway behind us. It took us all a moment to gather ourselves. Strangely, my shoe reappeared on my foot.

"What is this thing, a Batman villain?" Blake said.

"It's messing with us," I said. "It controls this world. We don't have any magic. It could've killed us if it wanted to." I shouted to the ceiling, "Stop messing with us and just show yourself already!"

Two darkly colored doors appeared at the end of the passage. The Nightmare King's palpable aura swelled behind them.

"Those weren't there before," Alison said.

"We've got to be careful," Blake said, but I ignored him and walked toward the doors. "J, we don't know what's behind there!"

"Yes, we do. It's the Nightmare King."

"It could be a trap—another hallway full of tricks."

Although his words didn't sway me, a dreadful feeling hit near the doors and gave me pause. It was like I was swimming in the ocean while sharks circled under me. But Hunter's aura was drawing near. I shook off the discomfort and opened the doors. Before me, a hall of mirrors branched in two directions. Each pane of glass distorted me in different ways, some stretching tall and thin, others round and squat. Alison came up beside me. "This . . . doesn't look like a hotel room."

Blake walked up on my other side and studied his own twisted reflection. "Let's stay together."

Alison and Blake walked in one direction, but I caught my reflection giggling in a mirror in the other and decided to investigate. The closer I came to the reflection, the less it looked like me. Its sunken eyes had shadowy circles, skin gray as a corpse's. I turned to call for the others, but a mirror wall had appeared behind me. Now all that awaited me was the path leading to a dead end. All my reflections burst into snickering, some covering their mouths and whispering to the others. Their indistinct words transformed into a roaring hiss that filled the chamber. Then one reflection walked into another mirror and melded with the doppelgänger there. The other reflections did the same until only one remained in the dead-end mirror. I approached and got a better look: it had jaundiced eyes and a snarling mouth full of big, crooked teeth. Its dark, ashen skin looked desiccated, as though partially mummified.

The look-alike stepped through the mirror, and the glass rippled like water as it emerged changed on the other side. It grew taller, donned a sharp suit, and its head transformed into a billowing cloud of black smoke with a pair of glowing yellow orbs for eyes. Its monstrous mouth—too wide for any human—twisted into a smile. The creature's feet hovered off the ground, but only slightly. In a familiar teenage boy's voice, the monster said, "You've lost your friends."

"Are you the Nightmare King?"

The monster closed the space between us. I moved back until I bumped into a mirror. I was cornered. It loomed over me, its hideous shadow swallowing me.

"I am."

Chapter 17

The Nightmare King beckoned for me with his long fingers as he floated back through the mirror. I feared I would be endangering Alison and Blake if I resisted him. I followed through the mirror and stepped into what looked like an unfinished bathroom, with a wall covered in white tiles and wooden floors that looked partially sanded. The Nightmare King took his place near a window and stared at the nothingness outside, his fingers threaded behind his back. He exuded graveness even though he sounded like a child. It came as no surprise the Night City's ruler—a witness to the endless march of souls into the Void—embodied such solitary sadness.

"Why are you looking for me?" he asked.

"I'm trying to help someone, but I need my magic to do it."

"And you believed the laws of the Night City would bend *just* for you?"

"Please. He needs my help."

"Why should I care?"

"Because I'm not leaving here without him. He's like family to me."

"Family? What's that? Is it a fruit? A pile of string?"

How was I supposed to explain what a family was? Families weren't always the same. Someone could get married and have kids, even get a dog, but that doesn't make a family. I'd been in one of those families before. I'd had a mom and a dad. Then everything fell apart and we drifted away from one another. But that wasn't like Hunter, Ali, Blake, and me. I would never have made it through the Institute without them. How do you explain that to someone? You might as well ask a bird what freedom is—the bird can't tell you. It only knows that when it takes off into the sky, the wind carries it higher. It can go anywhere. And that's what a family does: it carries you higher.

"It's . . . not easy to explain."

The Nightmare King stared at me with glowing yellow eyes. "If you can't explain it, then how do you know it's real?"

"You can look inside my head and see what it is, can't you?"

He went quiet. "You have relationships with multiple people in a group."

"No. That's not all it is. It's something more."

"Then what? I have never had a family before. How can I believe you if I've never experienced the same thing?"

"I don't know. I guess I just . . . I have faith . . . that it's something more."

Again, he didn't respond. It was like he was trying to gauge whether I was being sincere. How far removed from human thinking was the Nightmare King that a concept such as family struck him as disingenuous?

"Perhaps, a wager?"

"You want to make a bet?"

He pointed to a door behind me. It flung open, slamming against the wall. A powerful gust blasted into the room. Beyond, a short hallway stretched into a larger space, what looked like a squalid apartment's living room. A door on the wall facing me opened. Blake walked in first, then Alison to his left. Bewildered looks dressed their faces. They opened their mouths to speak, but some unseen barrier kept their words from me.

"Are they your family?"

They split up to investigate. It's funny how when you see someone and you know all their little traits, watching them from a distance makes them more endearing. "Yes."

"Would you give up anything for them?"

"Yes."

"Fine then. If you can keep that promise, I shall lift the spell; however, you mustn't tell them of our deal. Now, step through the door."

I walked through, and the door slammed shut behind me, announcing me to Blake and Alison, who startled and spun toward me. Alison came around the corner to my left. "Where the hell did you go?"

I almost told him that I'd found the Nightmare King, then I remembered our bet. Better to keep them from asking too many questions. "I got lost." Blake eyed me suspiciously. We'd encountered our fair share of malevolent lookalikes. I didn't blame him for scrutinizing me.

"Why did you leave us like that?" Alison demanded. I kept quiet, and she pressed me further: "Why, J?" She folded her arms over her chest and gave me that shrewd older-sister look.

Before I could answer, Hunter walked in through the door Blake had used. He curiously scanned the room before spotting me. A ticklish feeling spread through my chest, my fingers, my feet. My body kicked into motion before I fully processed what I was seeing.

I rushed over to him and ran my fingers down his cheeks, painfully choking back tears. "Hunter?"

Hunter looked around again, confused. "Johnny, where are we? What's going on?"

I put my arms around his waist and buried my face in his chest, rubbing my cheek against his soft cotton shirt. Hunter clasped his hands around me, rested his chin on my shoulder, and hugged me back.

"Johnny, what's wrong?" Hunter asked.

I gently pulled away. "Don't you remember anything?"

"No," he said, shaking his head.

"You're in a coma. Luther said you're . . . 'Void-touched.'"

"What's that?"

Blake's doubtful expression became a cynical glare. "He said that when you went into the Void, it marked you, and now it's trying to suck you back in. Where were you?"

Hunter shrugged

"Okay," Alison said, "it's nice we're all reunited, but the Nightmare King hasn't lifted that spell and we're still stuck in this"—she scowled at the room—"*place.*"

"Nightmare King? What is this place? Are we . . . in Everywhen?" Hunter asked.

"We're in the Night City," Blake said, walking to the front door and opening it. "We can't just wait in this room."

We all peeked our heads out the door. No horrifying, twisted dungeon awaited outside the room, only an ordinary, run-down hallway. Blake strode out confidently and Alison chased after him, giving me an addled look as she passed.

I would've happily stayed in that room, hugging Hunter.

"We should follow them," he said, "before we get left behind."

The hallway was all wrinkly stucco walls with chipped paint, and the light fixtures in the ceiling showered the passage with a sickly, flickering yellow glow. A smell like stale cigarettes permeated the air, and no matter how far we walked, we never came across another room. Our destination remained uncertain, like another encounter with the Nightmare King, but Hunter's hand in mine brought me peace. I recounted everything to him. He listened, face stricken with wonder. Blake and Alison's underwhelmed reactions implied they didn't trust him—they kept quiet as we walked. I only attributed so much to their suspicions, though, the rest I relegated to my own reservations: they were the dishonest ones; in fact, it was plausible they worked for Nightmare King.

Blake and Alison stopped walking. The hallway in front of us warped and distorted, spiraling like a corkscrew.

"What the—" Alison said.

"Let's go," Blake said. He walked forward until he was horizontal, then vertical; gravity imposed nothing on his movements. I got dizzy when I thought about walking in circles, but we needed to find the Nightmare King to leave this place.

Hunter held me back, and Alison and Blake walked farther ahead. "I don't like this," he said. "Where are we going?"

"We're looking for the Nightmare King, Hunt, so he can break the spell and we can get out of here."

"Why're you all convinced this is the way?"

The thought never crossed my mind. Blake had marched ahead with confidence, and we followed unquestioningly. This spiraling corridor made no guarantees—it could lead anywhere. Slowly, the walls around us blurred like a smudged oil painting, every color blending and swirling. I searched for the Nightmare King's aura but didn't find it. Strange considering it permeated the entire Night City.

"I can't feel the Nightmare King's aura," I whispered to Hunter.

"What if he's purposely misleading us?"

"Who? Blake?"

"Yeah?"

"Why would he do that?"

"Are you even really sure that's Blake?"

I'd already thought as much. Hunter saying so only reified my distrust. Something in Blake's gait was off—too certain. Back in the real world, he was sure of himself, but this sure? And Alison's doubtful silence. True, she grew quiet with discomfort, but this quiet? In the Dreamhaven, my wizard sense parsed real from copy, but here I couldn't know if they were real or merely the Nightmare King in disguise. Then I recalled our bet. Was this all part of the Nightmare King's gambit?

Hunter nudged me, leaned closer. "I say we tell him we're heading back. We can figure out a new plan before we can't turn back at all." I looked behind us. That was certainly easier than interrogating Blake.

"Hey, Blake, we should head back," I said.

"What's wrong?" Blake said. "This is the way."

"How do you know?" Hunter said. "Can you even pick up the Nightmare King's aura?"

Aggravated, Blake pointed at Hunter. "What's your plan?"

"We head back and figure out some other way to find this Nightmare King dude."

"This is the way."

"How do you know?"

"Because I can still feel his aura."

It was strange that Blake sensed the Nightmare King but I didn't. Was this a trick? Was the Nightmare King confusing us with his magic, spinning us in circles like children on a roundabout?

"How come you can feel it but we can't?" Hunter asked.

"What do you mean you can't feel it?" Blake said. "Can you feel it, Ali?" Alison slowly nodded. "I don't know why you guys can't sense him, but we can."

"How do we know if we can trust you?" Hunter asked.

Blake gave Hunter a fierce look. "What's wrong with you, Hunter?"

Hunter set his jaw. "There's nothing wrong with me. What's wrong with you?"

Tensions flared. My muscles stiffened.

"Nothing's wrong with me, Hunter. Why're you acting weird?"

"Maybe it isn't Hunter at all," Alison said. "Did anyone ever think about that? I mean he's supposed to be deeper in the Night City, isn't he?"

"Maybe *you* aren't who you say you are," Hunter said to Alison.

"Well, there's two of us and one of you."

Hunter's rosy cheeks went ashen.

"Leave him alone!" I said. "Did you two forget we came here looking for him?"

Alison put her hands on her hips. "Johnny, are you being serious?"

"Why wouldn't I be? Everyone needs to calm down. We're not fighting. We're friends."

Blake cut his eyes at me, then Hunter, but never said a word.

"We need to get away from these two, Johnny," Hunter said.

"No!" Blake said. "We're not splitting up."

Hunter cupped my hands in his. "Come on, J. Don't you trust me?"

Blake seethed. "I said, you aren't leaving."

"See, Johnny," Hunter whispered, "he's trying to keep us on the wrong path. We shouldn't trust them."

"What're you saying to him?" Alison asked.

"Nothing. Come on, Johnny, let's go back." Hunter wrapped his hand around my arm and urged me, but he didn't pull. Blake maneuvered around Hunter before I could move. "Get out of our way, Blake, or I'll make you," Hunter said, balling up his free hand.

Blake's body went rigid as a marble statue. "Try me."

Hunter let go of me and shoved Blake's chest, and Blake pushed him back. Hunter swung at Blake's head, but Blake stepped back and avoided the right hook. Hunter raised his fists and took another shot, but Blake dodged again—he never lost his temper. But Hunter had pushed him beyond his limit and he threw a jab of his own and clocked Hunter in the mouth. Hunter grabbed his jaw, blood trickling from his busted lip.

I blocked Hunter with my body. "Blake, stop!"

But Hunter shoved me aside and flew at Blake, fist raised. Blake side-stepped Hunter and tripped him. Hunter stumbled, and before he could get his bearings Blake spun around and punched him, knocking him off his feet and bloodying his nose.

My mind whirled. Blake and Hunter always got along. "Get off him!" I pulled Blake's shirt until it tore. He moved away, and Hunter wiped his nose on his sleeve and got to his feet, ready to keep fighting. "Hunter, stop!"

"Don't worry," Hunter said, "I got this, Johnny." Hunter charged again, and even though Blake tried to dodge, Hunter calculated his movements and redirected his fist into Blake's cheek. Blake then grabbed Hunter's shoulders and they tumbled to the ground, rolling around, each struggling for the upper hand. Blake won out and pinned Hunter, straddling him. Then Blake started to wail on Hunter.

"Help, Johnny!" Hunter cried while struggling to block his face. Alison watched helplessly. She wanted this to stop as badly as I did.

I had to act, so I focused on the light sword spell. The Nightmare King's tight reigns felt like a plastic sheet over my face—magic was like oxygen and I was suffocating, but I needed to pull through, to rip the sheet off my face and harness my powers. For Hunter. For Blake. For Alison. For me. Surging energy into my fingertips, I fought against the Nightmare King's powerful stranglehold, forced my magic to pool in my hands, and when it waned, when I could feel the Nightmare King tightening his grip on the threads that held his spell together, I fought even harder. So hard the cells in my body felt ready to burst and set me ablaze, and when I felt the Nightmare King's clutch weaken, I shattered through his spell and sparks fired from my fingertips, coalescing into a glowing light sword. The swords' warmth filled my hands, unaffected by the Nightmare King's indomitable hold. I had broken his spell.

Alison's face flushed with shock. "Johnny, how did you—what're you doing?"

Blake saw me coming toward him with the glowing weapon and scooted across the floor, away from Hunter.

Hunter looked to me, bruised and bloodied. He set his stormy eyes on Blake, his sweetness souring into cruelty. "That's not Blake, Johnny. Kill him."

Blake kept quiet, staring at me defiantly. I clenched my hand around the energy sword.

Alison shielded Blake with her body. "No way, J! This is crazy."

Hunter joined me at my side. "They're both trying to trick us! Kill her too!"

Both hands around the hilt, I pointed the blade at Alison and Blake, and lowered my gaze. Alison looked terrified. But was she faking it? Behind her, Blake glared at me, daring me to lash out at them. I steeled myself.

Then I did the most horrible thing.

I turned and drove the sword through Hunter's stomach. Tears gathered in his frightened eyes when he realized what I had done. Uncertainty drilled into my aching heart. But I pushed the sword deeper, searing flesh, vaporizing bone. Killing him.

"Johnny," Hunter said with a painful gasp, "why would you . . ." His words tapered off, and his skin blackened like charcoal. Smoke billowed out his mouth and he crumbled to the floor like ash. I lowered the blade and my head. The smoke that had seeped out of him floated in the air then transformed back into the Nightmare King.

"How did you know?" the Nightmare King asked.

Stray tears slipped down my cheeks. "Hunter never would've asked me to hurt Blake or Alison. He would've been too afraid that they were real."

"You know your family quite well after all."

"We had a deal."

The Nightmare King's fearful gaze fell on Blake. "First, I have something I want to show you."

Chapter 18

Black stage curtains fell around us. The Nightmare King pulled one aside, revealing a dimly lit lab. Glass pods numbering in the hundreds had been arranged into rows throughout the facility. Inside each tube, people lay suspended in bright-green fluid. If not for that greenish glow, the lab would've been too dark to navigate. I didn't know if this was another trick, but the Nightmare King held the curtain open for us. No one wanted to be first, but Blake took charge, then I skittishly walked in with Alison. The Nightmare King dropped the veil, and the curtains vanished behind us.

A faint stench permeated the air. Eirineftis. The lab smelled like eirineftis. As Alison and Blake walked off to conduct their own investigations, I approached one of the pods. The chamber was connected to a life support machine, and a boy with a blond buzz cut and a scar above his right eye floated inside the tube. He had been stripped to his underwear and an oxygen mask was affixed to his face. I studied him more intensely until realization chilled me: the boy sleeping in the chamber had been Blake's foster brother in the Dreamhaven, Ben. I hurried to another tube and found Tiffany, and in another Scott. All the Dreamhaven's residents were gathered in this facility, kept in stasis inside these strange green pods.

"What is this place?" I asked.

"We are under the Marduk Institute's Heka Building," said the Nightmare King.

"What?" Alison said, voice high with anxiety.

"Yes."

Blake asked, "Won't the Institute know we're here?"

"These are only your dream bodies. Your real bodies still lay wherever you left them. The scientists at the Institute aren't omnipotent, and my magic is quite powerful." I reached out to touch the tube, but my hand passed through it as if I were a ghost. The Nightmare King had taken our dream forms into the real world. "Do not try to wake up," he warned. "Your bodies are under a spell until we are done here."

"Why'd you bring us to this place?" I asked.

"To show you."

"To show us what?"

"Everything."

"What is this room for?"

"It is where the Institute keeps the Dreamhaven prisoners."

Blake brought his face close to a pod. The green glow from inside illuminated his skin. "And this green goo . . . it's eirineftis isn't?"

"You already know," said the Nightmare King.

So, the Institute had stored us in tanks filled with eirineftis. No wonder our magic didn't work in the Dreamhaven.

"I found a . . . wishing pond near the verge. I drank from it and my magic came back. If the eirineftis is supposed to keep us from using our powers, how come my powers came back after I drank from the water?"

"Proximity to the verge may have given the pond anomalous properties," said the Nightmare King. A sound theory—as sound as any. A few pods didn't have eirineftis in them. I imagined those had Smiths sleeping inside.

The Nightmare King hovered over to two doors near a bio-metric scanner on an adjacent wall. The scanner buzzed, and the words *Access Denied* were displayed in red. He waved a hand and the scanner beeped, and *Access Granted* appeared. The doors *whished* open and air gusted into the room. I wanted to analyze everyone trapped in the lab, but the Nightmare King was already leaving and I didn't want to get left behind in this creepy place.

I walked up beside Blake and Alison as we followed the Nightmare King. "Why do you two think he's showing us all of this?"

"No clue. I hope he doesn't hand us over to the Institute or something," Alison said.

Blake's full attention stayed fixed on the Nightmare King—my words didn't even reach him. Something about the Nightmare King had burrowed deep in his mind. I drew Alison's attention to Blake, but his stark expression bewildered her, so I minded my business. A familiarity surrounded the Nightmare King—it disquieted me too. His youthful voice . . . I'd heard it before but couldn't remember where or when.

The light panels on the ceiling flickered when the Nightmare King passed under them. His immense aura—sadness, loneliness, fear—unsettled the whole building.

We entered a hallway with three pale scientists scribbling notes on digital pads as they stared through an observation window into an operating room. The Nightmare King silently moved past them, heading to an elevator at the end of a passage. With about as much sense as a mayfly, I stopped and peeked through the window. I was left breathless by the indescribable horror inside: A boy about my age lay split open, sternum to abdomen, on a medical table. Two surgical lights hovered over the boy. A surgeon wearing a black apron removed the boy's kidneys and placed them on an electronic scale. Another doctor overseeing the vivisection announced their findings as he keyed in data on his own pad: "Subject is sixteen years old. His powers have been active for two years. Kidneys weigh 125 grams." Next, the surgeon took out the boy's liver and set it on the scale. "Liver weighs 1,561 grams." The surgeon grabbed a drill off a table covered in medical instruments. He put the drill to the boy's head, but I couldn't keep looking. A high-pitched whirring followed. Had I been in my real body, I would've thrown up. Alison noticed the slight green hue to my skin and came over to investigate. She, too, peered through the window and gasped. Blake joined us and quickly turned away.

"What're they doing to him?" Blake asked, glancing between the ongoing vivisection and the Nightmare King. "Is he—" his voice dropped to a whisper "—is he going to die?"

The Nightmare King stopped moving but kept his back to us. "If he did, would it matter? Isn't that the point of the Institute?" Hands still clasped behind his back, he headed for the elevator. Although the Nightmare King sounded like a boy, he evinced an Institute scientist's cold detachment. The Nightmare King used his powers to circumvent the security card reader and entered the elevator. Alison remained glued to the observation window. It took a few tugs before she stopped watching.

"We need to follow him," I said, pointing to the Nightmare King. Blake waited for us in the elevator. Alison nodded weakly and swallowed, taking one last, fateful glance into the surgical room.

With us all in the elevator, the Nightmare King swept a hand through the air and the doors closed. The electronic display over the door ticked down.

"Where're we going?" Blake asked.

The Nightmare King didn't answer, though, and Blake didn't insist. We all went quiet. I was still processing the violence I had just witnessed—that boy could've been me, Hunter, or any one of us. He'd earned that cruel fate for being born a non-Lineage wizard. That had been his only crime. Gaspar's willingness to sacrifice people to destroy the Institute now made sense. My resolve to see this place burn to the ground had been solidified.

The elevator opened and the Nightmare King guided us into a dark, dome-shaped chamber with tessellated walls. Three somnambulist teenagers lay in glass pods angled at 120 degrees in the room's center. The tubes holding them, unlike the ones in which they kept the Dreamhaven prisoners, didn't contain eirineftis. Instead, numerous cannulas injected green fluid directly into their bodies. Keeping them submerged in eirineftis clearly didn't work to suppress their powers. Each unit was fixed with an EKG and connected to a complex, rounded machine that shot a blue light up to the ceiling. A screen on the oculus displayed fuzzy, distorted images.

Blake walked up to a pod, disbelief scrawled across his face. He muttered, "Mikey," as he stared into the tube. Mikey, the same name as the boy who helped us escape the Dreamhaven. The somnambulist who'd once lived with Blake, who killed Blake's best friend, Gerald, while possessed by a Mara. The boy's complexion was unnatural and pale green. One of his hands was wreathed in a thick, boney covering, and pointy scutes protruded from patches on his face, like an ankylosaurus. He was ossifying. The other somnambulists also had greenish skin covered in osteoderms.

"This is Mikey. This kid here is Mikey." Blake looked away from the chamber and gave the Nightmare King a dirty look. "Show me who you are. Who you *really* are."

The smoke from around the Nightmare King's head spiraled around his body, and when it faded, Mikey appeared in his place. He had icy-blue eyes that matched his jumpsuit, the outfit the Institute forced on all somnambulists.

"Mikey?" Blake said.

Mikey floated down until his feet touched the ground. "Yes."

"Why did I hear you over the radio in the Dreamhaven?" I asked.

"The Dreamhaven chamber is close. I used what little power I had to send out that signal. I hoped that if a wizard received the message and escaped, they would come back and help the others."

"What's happening to you? Why do you have . . . *bones* all over your skin?" Blake asked.

"Prolonged exposure to eirineftis can be quite deadly. The Institute calls it 'the green sickness.' First, the skin turns a greenish color, then the body begins to ossify until every part of it, including organs, is nothing but white, calcified tissue. I am the current Nightmare King, but when I die, another will take my place. Most likely one of these two."

The Nightmare King was nothing but an endless procession of dying somnambulists. Their final days were spent sitting as Death's right hand, a warden for dying souls. The Institute had continued pumping eirineftis into Mikey even after he'd started ossifying. That explained why his anti-magic barrier in the Night City had been so inconsistent: his magic had been waning.

"Why can't they heal you—with magic or something?"

"There is no magic that can cure a magical illness. Even those keen on the study of life magic do not understand the ways the cogs and wheels change and shift once one has acquired the green sickness."

"Why are they doing this to you? What're you doing down here?"

The chamber doors opened and the lights came on. Melchior walked in then with a man in his late thirties wearing a white suit. The man had short, black hair, and his powerful aura swallowed the room in otherworldly strangeness. In my mind, I saw a black expanse, cold and never ending, and in that darkness, trillions and trillions of eyes sprouted and watched me. Somewhere, far off, the discordant hum of twisted carnival music played. I didn't know what he was, but I wanted to run to the other side of the world just to hide. Once the doors closed, feathers sprouted on the man's face, and his head transformed into a horned owl with hungry yellow eyes. His fingers grew long and hooked, becoming razor-sharp talons.

The sight frightened the words out of us.

"What the hell is that guy?" Alison said, breaking the silence.

"A vampire," Mikey said.

Melchior and the owl-headed man approached the machine in the middle of the room. The three somnambulists writhed and thrashed, gnashing their teeth as if in pain. Slowly, the blurry shapes on the oculus took on defined forms, becoming soundless images. A brown-haired boy with bronzy skin walked across a city street with a backpack slung over his shoulder. I didn't know the city, but the old brick buildings towered, with stoops and fire escapes crawling up their sides and security bars on their windows. The boy stopped in the street, reached into his pocket, and pulled out a phone. He looked at the screen and scowled, then he started texting someone back—angry texting. At that same moment, a speeding gray sedan turned a corner down the street and hurtled toward him.

Inside the speeding vehicle, the driver struggled with a burger wrapper, too distracted to notice the boy in the road. The boy lowered his phone and, seeing the oncoming car, tensed his body and shrank. Time slowed down and the car came to a sudden halt. Confusion flooded the boy's face when he realized the driver hadn't hit the brakes. He neared the vehicle in disbelief, even touched it to make sure he wasn't dreaming, but it still didn't move. He ran across the street to safety, and the car resumed moving. The entire sequence replayed in the oculus as if it were a looping video. The somnambulists all spoke at once, each repeating the same words: "Demetrius Johnson. Age sixteen. Address: 3752 Hastings Street; Atlanta, Georgia."

Melchior depressed a triangular button pinned to his lab coat. The owl-man's face transformed again, feathers slipping under flesh, talons reverting into fingernails, yellow eyes shrinking and turning blue as he shapeshifted back into a human.

A Smith walked in. "Yes, sir."

"Demetrius Johnson. Age sixteen. Address: Hastings Street, 3752; Atlanta, Georgia," Melchior said.

"Yes, sir." The Smith left as quickly as he'd arrived. The vampire's face turned back into an owl head.

"What was that?" I asked Mikey.

"That was how the Institute finds wizards right as their powers develop. The magic ring around the Institute magnifies our magical sensitivity, and the Institute uses us and this mechanism to track them down."

The vampire spoke: "The time of the quelling is upon us. Mammon has grown extremely hungry. Only the souls of thousands of wizards will keep him sated, else he escapes his prison in the Dreamhaven and sets back our plans."

"Yes, Alichino," Melchior responded.

"How go the preparations?"

"As expected."

Contrary to what Gaspar had led us to believe, the quelling wasn't used to maintain the power hierarchy in wizard society; from the sounds of it, it was used to feed a monster trapped in the Dreamhaven. A monster called *Mammon*.

"I've heard tell that you've had problems with the rebels. A few escapees that encountered Mammon themselves in the Dreamhaven."

"Nothing we can't handle. Our operation in Chicago has routed the source. Furthermore, we've been able to uncover where the Defectors have transported their central hub, Sanctuary."

"Where?"

"The Sonoran Desert, thirty miles northwest of Blythe, California."

"What will you do?"

"Their Sanctuary is running low on supplies. They will need to contact the Defector cell in Blythe, which we have infiltrated. I've sent our agents to finish the job."

Alichino and Melchior started for the door. Before he walked out, Alichino stopped and looked around the room. His focus fell on Mikey, who stared back with icy hate. Alichino smiled and continued out the door with Melchior.

"What the hell was that all about?" Alison said, "and what did you mean when you said he was a vampire? Like glittering in the sun and drinking blood and stuff?"

Mikey watched the door like he waited for them to return. "Drinking blood, yes, but the rest is nonsense. Vampires are wizards who've made deals with Void-spawns in exchange for power. The wizard must join their soul with the Void-spawn and become what is known as a *dual-soul*. What they become can only be likened to a living god. The hunger for blood is a side effect of the wizard's union with the Void-spawn."

"Why was that vampire bossing Melchior around?" I asked.

"Because Alichino is one of the Institute's administrators. He is, in fact, the only administrator I've ever seen."

Blake walked back to the tube containing Mikey's actual body. "Will the Dreamhaven prisoners get the green sickness too?"

"No. We are exposed to a much higher dosage than they are."

"So, they're just using you guys like batteries for their magic-finding machine?" Alison said. It was crude, and insensitive, but completely true. "What about the quelling? And . . . *feeding Mammon?*"

"From what I've gathered, Mammon is a Void-spawn, a very powerful one. They keep it trapped in the dreamworld and feed it wizards to keep it happy, but every thirty years, the creature grows extremely ravenous and tries to escape. The Institute performs the quelling ritual and gorges the beast on souls to pacify it."

"How long have they been doing that?" I asked.

"I only know of two other times they've mentioned."

"When?"

"They didn't give specific dates."

"Why? Why're they keeping it in there? What plans might it interfere with?"

"That I do not know."

"Alichino said we encountered Mammon. Was Mammon that

giant monster that came after us when we were looking for the Cave of Miracles?"

"Although I've never actually seen it, I've sensed a powerful Void-spawn in the mist, so I assume so, yes. The mist in the Dreamhaven and that monster you fought were manifestations of Mammon."

"What if we stop the quelling?" Alison asked.

"The beast might escape."

"Then what?"

"I do not know."

The grim uncertainty in his response left my blood cold. Stopping the Institute's monstrous quelling meant unleashing a Void-spawn so powerful that it frightened even the demigod-like vampires. These Void-spawns were natural allies, but something had stoked a shadowy power struggle that led them to imprison one of their own. All so they could pursue plans unknown to any of us.

"So, is this why you brought us here?" Blake asked.

"No," Mikey said. "This isn't everything. Come"—he started phasing through the floor and into the room below—"I have more to show you."

We sunk through the floor intangibly and hovered down into a room filled with upright glass tanks, many much larger than the Dreamhaven pods. Each vat contained a bizarre creature floating in eirineftis. My wizard sense immediately told me the things inside the tanks were Void-spawns. Much like the Dreamhaven facility, this lab also arranged its tubes in rows, but being so large far fewer tubes occupied the space. The tank nearest where I landed held a serpentine monster with a face like a rooster—beak and wattles and everything—and sharp, raised fins that covered its scaly body. Cannulas stabbed into its flesh drew out a purple fluid that flowed into a quietly humming pump next to the tank. The purple liquid gathered into an obround-shaped glass chamber at the top of the pump. The next tank over contained a creature with a man's torso, but a face and wings like a bat. Its body was also riddled with cannulas extracting purple fluid.

"What are they doing to the Void-spawns?" I asked Mikey.

"They are withdrawing the raw materials they use to manufacture eirineftis."

"But this stuff's purple," Blake said as he leaned over and analyzed the first creature.

"Yes, before it's been refined."

The Institute captured Void-spawns and drained their blood to make eirineftis. They then used that eirineftis to seize wizards and other Void-spawns. One row over was a busted tank, broken glass jagged like sharp teeth. The pump connected to the tube was lifeless, but a clipboard dangled off its side. The first page header read: *Subject: 004199 Bandersnatch*. Scribbles loaded with scientific jargon followed. We had encountered a Void-spawn called the Bandersnatch when I first came to the Institute. At the time, I wondered if the creature had escaped. This left little doubt.

Blake walked up behind me and eased a hand on my shoulder. I gave him a pale look and handed him the clipboard.

"Bandersnatch," he said at a low rasp.

Below where the clipboard hung, a red tube extended from the pump and plunged into the floor. All the pumps had similar red tubes. "Where do these go?" I asked Mikey.

"Into Lake Misty," Mikey said.

"What do you mean?"

"The machine synthesizes eirineftis from the blood, and they pump it into the lake."

Alison made a grossed-out face. "Yuck! Why the hell would they do that?"

"Isn't it obvious?" Blake said. "People drink the water and it kills their powers."

"You mean they're using this stuff to keep people from becoming wizards?"

We gathered around Mikey. "Yes," he said. "Blake is correct. The eirineftis is pumped into Lake Misty, purified, and bottled in the Pura factory, then it is shipped all over the country."

"But not everyone drinks Pura bottled water," I said.

"No, but Pura has a contract with this country's government, so, one way or another, Pura's water finds itself in everything: food, drinks, even the manufacturing of plastic. The continued exposure to eirineftis keeps the masses from manifesting their powers, but it also withers their health." But the method wasn't foolproof—Alison and I had proven that. Of course, that's why the Institute existed, to pick up the stragglers and feed them to . . . *Mammon.*

The world around us melted away like an illusion, leaving us standing on a platform floating in a sea of darkness. Like many times before in the Night City, some unseen light illuminated everything, allowing us to see each other. The floating island wasn't remarkable—just a desolate piece of gray rock. The Nightmare King had transported us back to the Night City.

Mikey walked to the platform's edge and turned his back to the Void. "Go and tell the other Defectors what I've shown you. Hopefully this information will help them save the others."

"You almost killed us with your bugs and shrinking hallways," Alison said. "You could've just asked nicely."

"Forgive me. I wouldn't really have hurt you. I just wanted a bit of fun before I died," said Mikey.

"Charming. I bet you make friends easily."

Mikey turned his back to us and gazed into the darkness, like a child staring into the mouth of a well. "My time here is over. But where you go, no Nightmare King may follow, for there is something more powerful in the Night City than I."

His words triggered memories. Hanno Scherrer had written the same thing in his journal. The Night City's final guardian wasn't the Nightmare King; it was Death.

"What're you going to do?" Blake asked.

Inky tentacles crept up from the cliff's edge and slithered around Mikey's legs. "I've been sick for too long. Now, the Void must claim me, as it does all things." He paused as the tentacles climbed to his thighs; they wrapped around his waist, his arms. "You'd do well to turn away, Johnny. With your magic restored, leave this place. You can't rescue Hunter. The Void has already claimed him, and it will drag him back to nothingness." He waited for his words to settle on my mind. "Blake, I'm sorry. What happened to Gerald wasn't your fault. Stop blaming yourself. You don't have to be everyone's protector. Please, start protecting yourself."

"Mikey!" Blake reached for him, but the shadowy tentacles succeeded in pulling Mikey into the darkness.

Chapter 19

Hunter's aura was just beyond the darkness ahead. Stronger, closer—so close his minty breath rang fresh in my nose. Our quest to save him had detoured because we needed the Nightmare King, Mikey, to drop his magic barrier, and now that he was gone and his spell lifted, our powers were back. Only one obstacle remained: confronting Death itself. I had never planned to let Alison and Blake follow me this far. No matter what they did or said, I wouldn't let them come any farther. Rocks clumped together before me, shaping into a bridge that extended over the darkness.

"You two go back," I said, "you have to warn the Defectors that they're walking into a trap." I took a few steps onto the bridge.

"We do this together, Johnny," Blake started for the bridge, but the bridge snapped and moved away from the platform.

"Johnny, no!" Alison tried to grab me, but it was too late— her and Blake were already shrinking behind me. Going it alone scared me, but they had helped me enough. Only I could shoulder this burden, and I wouldn't let them risk their lives for my foolish endeavor.

The rocky bridge stretched so far ahead that its terminus didn't even register. Fear plagued my lonely walk, and in the darkness strange sounds, like those I heard in the mist back in the Dreamhaven, surrounded me. They took all forms, from trilling, low-pitched gurgles to reptilian growls and high-pitched whines, like babies crying. The Void's somber call reached for me. I uncomfortably wrapped my arms around myself and sped up. But no matter how far along the bridge I walked, I never came any closer to the end.

A crumbling sound came from behind. I turned and gasped when I saw a Goliath monster, human in shape, towering like a hundred-story skyscraper and hovering in the darkness. Its freakishly pale skin looked gnarled and twisted, as if horribly burned, and spidery blue veins crept around its chest and shoulders. An oily whirlpool sloshed in the middle of its chest, with tarry creatures that resembled people moaning and reaching out from it. Amid all their indistinguishable cries, they called my name: "Johnny." The hole in its chest created a powerful suction that pulled apart the rock bridge and swallowed it piece by piece. Its monstrous aura reeked of one thing: Death.

Its tornadic chest cavity threatened to suck me in and pulverize me. I broke into a desperate sprint. But no matter how far my legs carried me, the bridge stretched on infinitely.

An unfamiliar woman's voice cut through the air: "Johnny!" It distracted me and made me lose focus on the bridge spell. The rocks wobbled, ready to drop me into the Void. I kept running but tightened my hold on the magic holding the bridge together. A shadowy tentacle whished past my ear and embedded itself in the ground ahead. Great, the big scary monster had stabby tentacles.

The woman called my name again, this time more distressed: "Johnny!" Five more inky tentacles sprang out of the whirlpool on the monster's chest and flew toward me. Fear muddled me, and I lost the spell. The path collapsed. I imagined myself whipping through space and appearing in Alison's mom's attic in Chicago, then I crashed to the floor.

I quickly checked myself for wounds. Luckily, the creature's tentacles hadn't flayed me. Where was I? Frantically, I canvassed my surroundings—a darkened attic filled with wooden crates, old toys, and a few empty chests. It certainly wasn't Alison's mom's attic, but at least it wasn't the Void. It dawned on me then that physical space didn't exist in Everywhen. With my magic restored, reaching Hunter only required I will myself closer to him. The bridge had been a manifestation of that desire.

Behind me, a lattice window in a gable stared out across a ruined city. Rain buffeted empty buildings along the avenues of a war-torn sprawl, and debris congested the streets in big chunks. This was the city I'd seen on the horizon when I first came looking for Hunter. The lightless Void spread across the sky like a ceiling, but in the distance, it looked like a supernatural fire painted green-blue streaks that extended high into the darkness. Hunter was out there. I could feel him.

A hatch with a ladder led me down from the attic and into a murky hallway. Every door along the passage was locked, but at the end of the hallway I found an imperial staircase leading down to an entryway. This place was like a shadow version of Sanctuary. Two locked French doors barred me from the antechamber at the bottom of the stairs. I forced them open with a thought.

A woman wearing a silver hauberk and cuirass with a single pauldron covering her left shoulder waited in the antechamber, blocking the front doors. A tiara spiked with a single horn nested in her long white hair, and she carried a sword strapped to her hip. Her aura soothed me. It washed over me in comforting waves, told me I was safe around her. It reminded me of Hunter, but I didn't know why.

"I need to get past you," I said brusquely.

"I'm coming with you."

"What? Who are you?"

"You've met me before," she said. "My name is Amalthea."

The first time I came to Misthaven, Hunter introduced me to a kindly and mysterious old wizard named Alwina. Hunter had been working for her as a stable boy. She kept a unicorn named Amalthea at her farm. "But you're . . . not a unicorn."

"I take on many forms."

I remembered the strange light orb that had guided me through Darkwood Forest. The neighing of a horse and the clopping of hooves. "Were you in . . . Darkwood Forest? Did you lead me to the magic pond in the Dreamhaven?"

"I am bonded to Hunter. I must rescue him, or we will both die," she said, ignoring my question. Long ago, I'd sensed Hunter on Amalthea's aura. Finally I knew why.

"Bonded? Like a Void-spawn?"

"Yes."

"I thought wizards turned into vampires when they formed a dual-soul with a Void-spawn?"

"The word *Void-spawn* is used to describe many different types of beings. I am not like the creatures who make wizards into vampires. Our will, our intentions, define the nature of our bonds.

Those of us who seek to do good form good bonds with wizards; however, those of us who seek to do evil, likewise, form evil bonds. Similarly, our own strength dictates the nature of the bond."

Different types of Void-spawns formed different types of bonds with wizards. Void-spawns existed in a hierarchy, some more powerful and more complex than others; some cruel and malicious, others kind and benevolent. Surely, the more powerful Void-spawns made more powerful bonds, but in the case of vampires, that bond came at a cost. "Hunter never told me he was . . . *bonded* to you."

"I came to him in a dream and asked him to form the dual-soul with me. I'm certain he never quite understood the implications of that dream."

"So, you . . . possessed him?"

"No. Taking control of a wizard's body is not the same as forming a dual-soul. Hunter and I exist in synchrony. He is not subjugated by my will. Furthermore, if the host of a possession dies, there is no threat to the existence of the occupying entity. If one part of a dual-soul dies, so does the other."

That was the difference between the Mara that had taken over Mikey's body and Amalthea. If they were powerful enough, Void-spawns could crudely take over someone's body, residing inside the host like a parasite, but a dual-soul was a special bond, usually mutual.

"You tricked Hunter into forming a dual-soul with you. Why?"

"Because I needed him."

"For what?"

"To fight against the Void's servants."

"So, you formed a dual-soul with Hunter to spy on the Institute?"

"Yes."

"Do you even care about what happens to him, or are you only using him as a tool?"

"We are a dual-soul. If the Void claims him, it claims me as well."

"What happens if you leave Hunter and form a dual-soul with another wizard?"

"A futile gesture: I would carry the Void-touch with me."

"So, you're only here because you're scared of dying?"

She gave me a passionless look. Void-spawns didn't think like humans. To Amalthea, Hunter served only as means to an end—she needed him alive to accomplish that end. Her selfish reasoning angered me, her tricking Hunter into forming a dual-soul, but telling her no wouldn't dissuade her.

"I need to hurry," I said. "Let's go."

Rain slickened the desolate streets outside, making for dangerous, uneven footing. The never-ending rain eroded the skeletal buildings around us. Humanity's fears about Death had created this place, the final gateway to the Void. Its quietly pattering rain—lonely and cold—was a solemn reminder of Death's constant presence.

Amalthea moved swiftly through the streets, never making a sound. That she moved with such alacrity in all that armor impressed me. One couldn't discern that she had ever been anything but human. A dilapidated building spilled rubble into the road, and I tripped and fell while trying to maneuver around it. Amalthea caught me before a piece of exposed rebar could impale me. She kept walking ahead. I took a moment to recover from my near-death experience and made sure to travel more warily after that.

Hunter's aura called out indistinctly. Empowered by Amalthea's bond, the horn perched on her tiara oscillated with a golden light—the same color as the orb I'd followed to the magic pond in the

Dreamhaven. It responded to Hunter's aura, growing brighter the closer we came. Amalthea pointed to a plaza with less debris scattered about. Hunter's aura emanated somewhere north beyond the plaza, but I didn't know where. We traveled until the horn stopped fluctuating and shined brightly, coming to a tall building with blown-out windows. I took a wide step through a window and entered the building, and Amalthea followed. Our investigation led us several stories up, until the deteriorating structure was too damaged to navigate safely, then we turned back and plunged into its depths. We didn't find Hunter anywhere. Amalthea's horn kept shining, though, and my wizard senses still tingled wildly. This had to be the right spot.

We headed outside to investigate the building's exterior, to get a better sense of things, but the ground trembled when our feet touched it. My wizard senses picked up a familiar aura. A second tremor came about, originating in the east. We turned and looked. The hideous pale giant that had chased me earlier lumbered through the city, coming toward us. It could've easily reached us in a few steps, but it stopped moving. Eyes of all sizes sprouted all over its body, and six enormous wings—also covered in eyes—extended from its back. A golden halo formed over its head and started spinning.

"What the hell is that thing?" I asked.

"Death," Amalthea said. She unsheathed her longsword and pointed the blade at the monster. "Run, Johnny! Now!"

"No! If you die it'll kill Hunter."

"Hurry. Find him. Form a dual-soul with him."

"What? How?"

"All humans are descendants of the Void-spawns. I will try to distract the monster so that you can pull off the spell. Look deep within yourself, Johnny. You have all the power you need."

"But what about the Void-touch?"

She changed her stance to a right-hanging guard, eyes still fixed on Death. "I will take the Void-touch onto myself."

A shadowy pool formed under us and widened into a large circle. Several oily, humanoid shapes emerged from it. Their dull fingers grew long and thin, becoming spikes. Big crooked mouths formed on their faces and curved into smiles. The creatures lowered their backs, ready to attack. One took a swing at me. Amalthea pushed me aside, unsheathed her sword, and sliced the monster in half.

"Go!" she said, and I ran.

Hunter's aura continued to emanate from somewhere around the building. I made my way toward an alley on the side, away from Amalthea and the shadows. A power pole-sized tentacle sprang from the vortex on Death's chest and struck the building. It dragged itself across the surface and collapsed part of the building into the street. Concrete clumps crashed in front of me, kicking up a dust cloud. The tentacle swept down again—I leaped out of the way before it could crush me, but it wasn't done. It lashed out once more and smashed behind me with such force that it sent me sprawling. Before it could finish me off, Amalthea jumped in from behind and cleaved it in half. The wriggling tentacle hit the ground and melted into a black slime that scurried away like a rat. I got up and continued into the alley, maneuvering around the debris left by the tentacles attack. Amalthea stayed behind.

I prodded the walls, searching for another way into the building. A black pool formed under my feet and grew until it covered the alley floor. I lifted a leg, and sticky black strands stretched from the slime like glue. The muck burdened my movements, but I managed to make my way to the alley's far end, and to the building's rear. Six blobs rose from the ooze and surrounded me. They took humanoid shape, their hands turning into claws. They hunched down, ready to charge.

I held out a hand and squeezed my fingers around the hilt of a newly manifested light sword, then widened my stance and readied myself for their attack. One creature charged and leaped at me, claws raised. I thrust upward and skewered the monster mid-flight, and it melted back into the pool. Another glob rose from the slime a few feet away and took shape, replacing the one I'd just slain. The other five rushed me, two jumping in from my left while the others flanked my right. I shaped the sword into a lance and threw it at one in the air, but the remaining four swarmed me. They didn't rend me with their claws, though; they grappled me and turned back into blobs, covering me in a heavy tar coat and dragging me down into the sludge. The last one that took shape threw itself on top of me too. Magic surging in my muscles, I swept my arms from side to side, hurling off clunky glops, but the goo under my feet had climbed up my legs and further weighed me down. I screamed and dropped to the muck on my hands and knees.

Amalthea entered the alley, yelling my name, but before she could reach me a spear-like tentacle plunged through her back. The bloody tentacle lifted her into the air. She struggled to pull herself off, but another tentacle came down from above and speared her again. Her tiara's horn broke off and sank into the inky pool. Amalthea reached for me with one desperate, trembling hand. Blood trickled out the corner of her mouth. Several more tentacles erupted from the black slime and stabbed through her all at once.

Her body went limp and the sludge swallowed me.

Chapter 20

Darkness all around me. I raised my hand and formed a light ball, which skittered away the shadows. The pool had dropped me into an underground tunnel, with old rusty train tracks partially covered in dirt running through the floor. Hunter's aura felt stronger than ever, but it was fading, making it difficult for me to track with my wizard senses.

"Hunter!" I called but heard nothing back. Nearby, something shimmered brightly enough to chase away the encroaching darkness—Amalthea's horn. Even when my wizard senses failed, the horn's magic had stayed connected to him. I took it with me.

I started into the tunnel, one hand holding a ball of light and the other raising the horn. Whispers echoed in the passage—vague at first, but the deeper I plunged into the crumbling heart of the Night City the sharper the voices became, their words faint pleas for me to run back to the world of the living and tell everyone of the Void's indomitable power.

Amalthea's horn was like a flashlight helping me find my way through enormous cracks in rubble, under cement clumps with black water running down them in rivulets as I traveled deeper into the lightless caverns.

Another whisper, this one clearer, snake-like: "He is the lonely heart beating in the darkness." I stopped moving and listened closely. "He is the rain's sweet petals tasting somber lips." The eerie voice taunted me, dared me to find Hunter. I sped up, rushing down the tunnel, halting only long enough to listen to the strange voice again: "He is a dream set sail on a cyanic sky, stilled only by your voice." The voice wasn't coming from anywhere in the tunnel; it was coming from inside my head.

"Who are you?" I said out loud.

I am your voice.

"Liar! Stop messing with me!"

Search your heart: in the darkness of night, when you are all alone, I am what speaks to you.

"You're the Void! The endless nothing that eats all life!"

I am the fear of loneliness dwelling deep within your soul.

"No! You're the absence of love and light!"

I am the truth you fear most of all: that there is no love; no light.

"I'll never accept you! I'll fight you until my dying breath!"

Even if that fight proves futile? Even if death swallows everything in the end?

"Even if death swallows everything in the end. Death can never swallow love."

And when humanity dies?

"Love can never die. Love will always exist. Because we experience it. We give it life with words and song and art. We fight wars over it. We build entire nations for it. Because love is the only true thing in this whole, fucked-up, miserable world."

So is death.

Here, on the boundary between life and death, the Void played tricks from the shadows, whispering uncertainties into your ears. Just like Hunter had warned me it would. But it had no teeth here, so I refused to listen. With the horn's brilliance guiding my way, I felt for Hunter's aura, and when I sensed it, I followed it until I found him lying on the floor, unconscious in his letterman jacket. I defused the light ball, fell to my knees beside him, and dropped the horn. It clinked on the ground and slid a few feet away. I cradled him in my arms.

"Hunter! Wake up! Wake up!" He couldn't hear my pleas, though. His life force had dimmed to a weak spark, and the horn's light was dying too.

I pressed my forehead to his and thought back to Amalthea's words. *Form a dual-soul with Hunter?* How was I supposed to do that? A black splotch formed on Hunter's cheek, the skin becoming like ceramic—it cracked then turned to ash and slowly flaked away. I lowered him to the ground and pressed my hands against the black spot, fighting to keep it from spreading, to keep Hunter from crumbling away. How was I supposed to bond our souls as one? I didn't have that kind of power. No one had ever taught me that spell.

"Please, don't leave me, Hunter. Dad always said that a family isn't something you make with a piece of paper. It isn't something you're born into, either. A family is something that can endure anything. You, me, Alison, and Blake—we're a family. And I'm not letting this family fall apart. I need everyone there when we beat the Institute . . . I need you all there . . . I need *you* . . ."

But the blackness spread until his whole body turned to ash and sifted through my fingers. He was gone. And when the light from Amalthea's horn finally died out, darkness engulfed me and I followed . . .

A light beam broke the endless darkness, forcing me to open my eyes. I rose in a golden meadow, like the one near Alwina's farm. Bugs chirped loudly in the midsummer heat. A gentle breeze carried the warm scent of grain.

Hunter's voice called to me from afar: "Johnny!"

He was running toward me, waving a hand in the air, his face glowing with life. I ran to him, yellow tall grass swishing under me. I moved faster than I ever had in my life. We were like two speeding trains on a collision course, and nothing could keep us apart. Not even death. Hunter tackled me to the ground, and we fell laughing amidst aurulent leaves. We looked high into the shining blue sky and screamed with laughter.

I squeezed his cute, soft cheeks, turned them red beneath my fingertips. He gave me the biggest, cheesiest grin, then brought his face down until our noses were only a hair's breadth apart.

And he kissed me.

Our lips pressed, I closed my eyes and the nightmare ended.

Chapter 21

Alison and Blake hovered in my field of vision as I opened my eyes. Alison's face went bright when she saw me wake up. "Oh my God, Johnny!" Linh and Maleeka popped up behind Alison and Blake. They looked shocked that I was awake.

My head still felt fuzzy, but I threw myself upright. "Where's Hunter?"

Alison stepped aside and let me see him lying on the other bed. He rose weakly, balanced on trembling elbows, and everyone gasped. He sucked me into a curious gaze. I felt everything he felt, and his awestruck look told me he felt everything I felt too. The barriers between our souls no longer separated us. We'd become one—a dual-soul. His bare feet hit the cold floor, then he ran over and threw himself on top of me. Overjoyed, I held him close and ran my fingers through his feathery hair. Everyone looked on in disbelief.

Maleeka said, "You . . . saved him . . . from the Void."

Hunter kissed me several times, trying to see if I was real, before settling next to me on the bed. "How long have we been out?" I asked.

"Not long," Blake said, "Linh and Maleeka said we were out for a few hours, and we only woke up ten minutes before you."

"How did you save him?" Linh asked.

Hunter shrugged.

"I don't know," I said, not sure how to explain. "Where're Nephelie and Aquila?"

Hunter's Lazarus-like resurrection had left Maleeka fumbling for words. "They—they went to meet with a local Defector cell."

"Did you tell them it's a trap?"

"Yeah, but we got the information to them too late. Nephelie told us about an hour ago that they were pinned down in some ghost town northwest of Blythe called Midland."

"Where's Luther?"

"He went into that cabinet before they left. He hasn't gotten back yet."

"We have to help them."

"That ghost town is about twenty or thirty miles away from here. How are we supposed to get there?"

Traversing the desert on foot didn't seem like a good idea. Then it dawned on me. "Follow me," I said, getting off the bed.

I led everyone to the green pickup truck parked in the garage. We searched the inside for keys but didn't find any, so I ran back inside and flung open all the cabinets in the laundry room and kitchen until a found them. I came back and handed them to Blake. He hopped in the driver's seat and Alison slid in next to him. Linh looked ready to join, but Maleeka stopped her.

"Someone needs to watch the kids."

"Then leave one of the boys. I'm not babysitting," Linh said.

I looked at Hunter. "Sorry, Hunt. There's no way for us to know if you're fully healed yet."

"I can't let you go without me, Johnny. We just got back."

"Don't worry. I literally saved you from Death, remember?"

Hunter didn't look satisfied by my reassurance, but he stayed behind anyway. Linh jumped in front with Alison and Blake. Maleeka and I kicked all the junk off the truck bed and climbed in the back.

We drove through the oppressive heat until reaching an overlook near Midland. Blake parked the truck there, got out, and walked to the lookout. The desert sands had long ago covered Midland's remnants. Now only a few squat buildings remained, all eviscerated by the elements. A few old vehicles lay scattered about, each partially buried in dirt.

Blake pointed to a black Institute truck parked at an angle amid a cluster of buildings. The vehicle faced the structures on one side and its back doors were open. A Smith wearing what resembled a black, plated bomb suit tromped away from the vehicle, toward the buildings. The armored Smith carried a long rod connected to a fuel tank on their back. A Smith without any armor accompanied them. My standpoint didn't afford me a strong enough view to make out any significant details about either.

"What're those things they're carrying?" I asked.

"Gas guns, it looks like," Maleeka said, walking up next to us. "I've seen them before. They fill them up with eirineftis so they can gas multiple wizards at once. I'm guessing that one's wearing anti-magic armor too."

"Anti-magic armor?"

"It's covered in glyphs and symbols that ward off magical attacks. Those're the Institute's heavy-duty guys."

"How do you deal with them?"

Maleeka pressed her lips together uncomfortably. "Don't get caught, I guess."

We left the truck behind and made our way down the rocky cliff until we found a hiding spot behind a rusted car. The long-rusted vehicle's back end lay submerged in the dirt, the front half tilted at a sixty-degree angle. Not prime hiding-place real estate, but good enough. Another Smith wearing anti-magic armor emerged from around the van, Aquila's limp body slung over their shoulder. Her aura pulsed vibrantly, telling me she was still alive.

"Another one. And that one has Aquila," I whispered.

"Nephelie told me she's hiding in one of the buildings, playing cat and mouse with the other agents," Maleeka said.

Blake maneuvered around the sunken car and crept toward the armored Smith. Alison reached out to stop him, but he moved too quickly. She shot me a nervous glance, and I chased after him. I kept my back low and caught up to him. He directed my attention to the fuel canister on the Smith's back.

There's a line running directly from the tank to the spray rod, Blake said. *And look there.* He pointed to the tubes around the helmet. *It must be a cooling system. They're pumping air into the suit through those tubes. If we switch the tubes on the gas tank with the ones feeding air into the suit, when he hits the spray valve again, it should redirect the eirineftis into his helmet and knock him out.*

Taking on that walking tank was a little intimidating, but

we didn't have many options, and we needed to hurry and find Nephelie. The van's side that wasn't facing the buildings provided cover from the Smith's view. They dropped Aquila into the van, and when they turned around Blake snatched the spray rod and smacked them in the face with it. The blow staggered them, but they swiftly set about struggling with Blake for control over the rod. I jumped on their back while they fought with Blake and started unscrewing a tube on the canister.

Blake tightened his grip on the rod. The Smith jerked to the right and pressed the firing valve, blasting the ground with eirineftis. They pulled left, but Blake kept the nozzle pointed down. The Smith clocked Blake in the nose with the handle, but Blake still refused to let go. I undid the tube on the tank and detached one from the Smith's gas mask as they thrashed around. The Smith knocked Blake down with a kick then swung side to side, trying to shake me off. Blake was getting back up when the Smith gassed him. I finished rerouting the oxygen and the eirineftis before the Smith hip-tossed me to the ground. They pointed the rod at me and fired, but the gas redirected into their helmet. They clawed at their neck and face, hurriedly unlatching the front of the mask and popping it open. Gas hissed and poured out, and the man inside let out one long, exaggerated wheeze before his eyes rolled into the back of his head and he fell over.

Blake got knocked out during the fight. Not wanting the other Smiths to catch us, I motioned for Alison, Maleeka, and Linh to help hide the bodies.

Alison lifted Blake's arms and groaned. "It's too hot for this, Blake." I secured his legs, and we carted him behind the sunken vehicle. Maleeka and Linh did the same for Aquila, setting her down next to him.

Although the armor made the Smith incredibly heavy, Maleeka, Linh, and I managed to drag his body to the van's blind side. Once safely hidden behind the van, Maleeka took off the Smith's helmet. He looked to be in his twenties, with brown hair and freckles. She handed me his helmet. I looked back at her, confused.

"Put it on," she said.

"What? Are you serious? What if he told them with his mind that we were here?"

"Then they would've come a lot faster. My guess is all those wards and stuff"—she pointed at the weird symbols etched into the armor—"don't let them send out psychic messages."

"Fred! Fred!" a fuzzy voice came from inside the helmet. They'd wired a communication system into it. Maleeka was right—the wards kept them from sending messages with their minds.

I snatched the helmet. "This is, uh, Fred."

"Fred?"

"Uhhhhh, yes? Y-yes."

"You all right. I thought I heard a commotion."

"No, I, uhhhhh, don't see any commotion. Do you see any commotion? Because I don't see any commotion, and if there was a commotion, I would definitely see a commotion, but I'm not seeing any commotion."

Maleeka facepalmed. "*Ay dios mio.*"

"Are you all right, Fred?"

"Totally," I said, nodding as if they could see it. "This heat is getting to me."

"The obmagikos is climate controlled . . ."

If I kept talking, I was going to blow my cover. "I'll meet up with you in a minute." I slammed on the helmet. The inside stunk like rotten raspberries, that familiar eirineftis stench. Not enough to knock me out, but it still made me dizzy. We undid the rest of the Smith's armor until he was in his skivvies. The heavy armor posed a challenge. Maleeka told me to lay on the ground, then she and Linh put it on me. After they finished, I lay on my back, motionless because the armor weighed a ton, making it hard to stand. Linh grabbed one arm and Maleeka the other, and they helped me up. A few burdened steps later, I'd gotten used to moving in the obmagikos, as the Smith on the headset had called it, but it was too cumbersome to run in and didn't lend itself to precise movements.

Alison, can you hear me? I said. She didn't respond, proving Maleeka's theory: the armor prevented psychic communication. "I can't talk to you with my mind."

"Let's hope you won't need to," Maleeka said, "Go find those other Smiths. I'll tell Nephelie you have on one of the suits."

Maleeka, Linh, and Alison hurried back behind the sunken vehicle. Certain they were carefully tucked away, I walked over to where I'd seen the other Smiths heading earlier. I passed through an alley between two buildings and found Žižek standing next to an armored Smith, both at least twenty feet away from a hollowed-out cement structure. Of all the Smiths the Institute could've deployed, it had to be Žižek. The armored Smith kept his gas gun trained on the empty building. No doubt Nephelie was hiding inside.

"You can't stay in there all day," Žižek said in his usual, semicomical tone. He noticed me and nodded to the building. "Fred, gas her out." My legs shut down. I told them to move, but they refused—fear weighed them down more than the armor. Žižek looked at me again. "Fred, will you please go and fill that building with eirineftis?"

"There's movement," the armored Smith said.

Nephelie emerged from the shadowy doorway, one hand resting on her hip.

Žižek stepped forward, a gleeful smile on his face. "I'm glad you've chosen to join us. We already have your friend. Why don't you just throw up your hands and give up?"

Nephelie walked until she was a safe distance from the building, then aimed her eyes to the sky. "Sorry, boy. Not today." The clouds turned black and started swirling. They picked up speed and became a stormy vortex. A lightning bolt crashed down, striking the ground between Nephelie and the two Smiths.

Žižek took cover behind the armored Smith and stayed close. A second bolt streaked down from the sky, but before it could vaporize the two Smiths, a green dome of light appeared around the top half of the armored Smith's body. The lightning zapped it to no effect.

"Whoo-hoo, girlie," Žižek jeered. "Looks like you want to party."

Nephelie took a step back and held out her hand, palm up. Golden energy coalesced into a glowing ball above her hand. The ball started expanding, and it kept growing until it was twice the size of her head. The ball exploded into a hundred bolts that flew at the Smiths and futilely bombarded the forcefield, every hit rippling the shield like raindrops on a lake. Nephelie dropped her hand but kept an impassive, focused expression.

Žižek stepped out from behind the armored Smith and chortled. "You really are something else, lady. But I don't know what you think that little light show is going to do." Nephelie held her intense gaze on Žižek. "Gas her."

Intervening would only expose me. The armored Smith clunked forward, raised his gas gun, and sprayed a massive cloud of eirineftis. Nephelie covered her mouth in the bend of her elbow before the fog swallowed her. A few coughs and wheezes sounded from within the cloud, then stopped. The armored Smith released the firing valve and stood at ease. I watched, hoping Nephelie would emerge undaunted, but the mist cleared and she was on the ground, unconscious. They'd toppled her with piddling effort.

"I was hoping she'd lead us to those little runts. I had some unfinished business with two of them. Pick her up and let's head back to the truck. Those kids will die without the adults." Žižek laughed, like the thought of wizard children dying amused him.

"You were slow on the uptake, Fred," Žižek said, studying me. "Did you get . . . taller?"

The armored Smith picked up Nephelie and slung her over his shoulder, then started back to the van.

"No?" I said, not sure how to respond. Žižek analyzed me a second or two longer. His unreadable expression made my heart sink. Even knowing that the armor guarded my thoughts offered little comfort. Žižek soon lost interest and followed the armored Smith. Relieved, I hurried after them.

"So, Fred," Žižek said while we were walking, "how's the wife?"

Fred had a wife? Of course Fred had a wife. Smiths weren't priests. "She's great."

Žižek flashed a sadistic grin. Did he trick me? Did Fred even have a wife?

"Stay here and keep watch," he said when we reached the van. He walked to the van's blind side with the other Smith. Not wanting to tip them off, I turned my back and stood guard.

My helmet risked filling like a water pale if I didn't stop sweating. A tear on the driver's side tire caught my attention. Someone had sliced it open. Probably Alison, knowing her. Now the Smiths couldn't escape. That'd either prove a blessing or a curse. Something tickled my nape. I reached back and discovered an undone oxygen tube—I'd forgotten to fully seal the helmet.

The armored Smith came from around the van. I spotted him approaching with his gun raised, ready to spray, so I grabbed the rod and raised it over our heads. He fired a blast into the air before I forced down his hands and bend the rod. He depressed the valve again, but the gun didn't work anymore, so he unlatched the canister and let it roll under the van, where it clinked against the gas tank and stopped moving. He kicked me in the abdomen and knocked me to the ground.

"Oh boy," Žižek said, coming around from the other side.

Inside the heavy armor, I tossed side to side, trying to fling myself over, but I was like a flailing turtle. Žižek put his foot down on my helmet and pressed. The pressure made it hard to move without straining my neck.

"Fred doesn't have a wife. Also, you didn't screw on your gas mask right." Žižek kicked my ribs, but his toe took the brunt. He yelped and hopped away holding his foot. The armored Smith kicked me, too, but the padding inside my suit didn't dull the impact this time. It winded me. He kicked again, then started stomping on me, denting the plating. Every blow felt like a sledgehammer, and my armor kept me from curling into a ball to protect myself. Suddenly, he stopped kicking, and I felt someone push me over. With momentum finally on my side, I rolled onto my stomach and got to my feet. Alison had snatched the other Smith's helmet and was taunting him from a few feet away. He snarled and swiped at it, but his bulky armor waylaid his movements. Alison tossed it behind him, then Linh caught it and threw it to Maleeka. They tossed it back and forth, further infuriating him.

Žižek stopped tending to his foot. He wriggled his fingers at his side, fidgeting with the vivit apparatus—constructing a fireball.

"Get out of the way," I screamed.

Žižek looked at me as I swung my fist into his mouth. The fireball leaped out of his hands, spinning out of control and striking the eirineftis canister under the van. Alison, Linh, and Maleeka jumped out of the way, but the heavily armored Smith wasn't quick enough—the canister and gas tank exploded and he was engulfed by the ensuing blaze. The blast sent Žižek flying several feet away and knocked me back down.

Instead of struggling against the armor this time, I unlatched the moorings holding me in place and threw off the chest plate and helmet. I sloughed off the armor around my feet too. Luckily, the obmagikos had eaten the impact, so I got away only mildly disoriented and bruise-free. A plume of green smoke hovered over the flaming vehicle, and the lingering stench of eirineftis burned my nose. Maleeka and Linh lay on the ground nearby, knocked out from either the gas or the explosion. At least they were alive.

Someone cleared their throat behind me. A few feet away, Žižek stood with his pristine suit covered in dirt, and a bloody gash stretching from chin to cheek. He gripped Alison's shirt with one hand and held a light sword to her throat with the other. A few scrapes and bruises marked Alison's skin, but she looked more inconvenienced than afraid.

"I can't believe you're damseling me in the year of our lord 2020," she said.

"Keep quiet, funny girl," Žižek said. "The two of you have been giving me headaches for a while." Still clenching Alison shirt, Žižek slowly backed away. He was stalling, with Institute backup probably en route. I kept my hands at my sides, motionless, hoping not to elicit any unwarranted, deadly actions.

Johnny, do something?

What, Ali?

I don't know. Talk to him. Buy some time while I think.

"What're you going to do with her?" I asked.

"Melchior wants you all back pretty bad. I have some buddies coming . . ."

Look down, Johnny, Alison said as Žižek rambled. *The chest plate, Maleeka said it blocks magic. Throw to it to me and I'll use it to block his sword. Then I'll grab that eirineftis tank off that armor, and you'll hit him with that light sword spell—*

No way, Ali, I can't pull that spell off that fast. I'll kill us.

". . . they've never been here, but I'm sure it won't take them long to find it," Žižek finished. He grinned maliciously and changed his face to my father's. "Whatcha thinking about, son?"

I'd had enough of this guy's shit.

I kicked Alison the breastplate. She grabbed it, swung up, and caused his light sword to dissipate. She swiftly spun around, out of his grip, and bashed Žižek in the face with the armor, throwing him off balance. She extended her arm then and the eirineftis canister flew into her hand. I formed a light sword and chucked it at the canister as she shoved it into his hands. The spell pierced the tank as he vanished in a cloud of smoke. He popped back up immediately, about fifty feet in the air, and came crashing down with a crunch. I'd only intended to puncture the canister and incapacitate him, but the gas had knocked him out midteleport.

Alison came up beside me as I stared down at Žižek's body. "I think we won."

"Let's get everyone in that truck and leave before his backup arrives."

We tossed everyone onto the cargo bed and sped back to Sanctuary.

★ ★ ★

Hunter took one look at the truck bed and made a morbid face. "Please don't tell me they're all dead?"

"Nope," Alison said, shouldering one of Blake's arms while I handled the other. "Could you get the door? I really don't want my boyfriend to end up with a concussion."

Luther walked into the kitchen as we lugged Blake in. "Goodness," he said.

We set Blake down in a chair and he almost slumped to the floor. Alison grabbed him and held him steady.

"Luther," I said, "the Institute set a trap for Nephelie and Aquila. We had to go help them."

"Yes. Hunter told me everything. I decided to stay behind should I need to ferry the children away to safety."

"More agents are coming. We've got to get out of here," Alison said.

"I'll activate the moving spell. You bring everyone else inside."

Hunter and I walked back into the garage and picked up Aquila. The children eventually caught wind of what was happening and gathered in the kitchen to watch us drag everyone inside. Luther had moved Sanctuary while we weren't paying attention. I only noticed because, after Hunter and I set Nephelie on the floor next to Aquila, I looked out of the window above the sink and saw the treetops of a misty pine forest.

Alison, Hunter, and I rushed outside to see where Luther had taken us. We sat at the base of a gently sloping mountain covered in pine trees, in the middle of a lake surrounded by much taller, snow-capped mountains. The gray dirt underfoot was slick and muddy, like it had recently rained, and the air carried a light chill. The coolness wasn't much for Midwesterners like Alison and me, but it had a Southerner like Hunter trembling.

Back inside, we caught Luther as he left Nephelie's study. "Where are we?" Alison asked.

Luther walked into the dining room headed to the kitchen. "Wizard Island, Oregon."

"That's a little on the nose, don't you think?"

"It was the first thing that came to mind."

"Is there any guarantee the Institute won't know we're here?" I asked as we came into the kitchen.

Luther looked at everyone lying on the floor like he wondered what to do with them. "No, but it should buy us some time. Let's bring them into Nephelie's office."

We did as requested, setting them on tufted leather sofas in the study. While we waited for them to wake up, we told Luther everything: about the room where the Institute kept the Dreamhaven prisoners, the vampire Alichino and the admins, the quelling being a sacrifice to a Void-spawn called Mammon, the somnambulists the Institute used to find wizards, the Nightmare King and how—through some miraculous means—Hunter and I had formed a dual-soul that had saved him from the Void. The whole time, Hunter and I shared our thoughts effortlessly. It wasn't like reading someone's mind—we were inextricably linked, the fabric of our beings woven together.

Luther scanned me, searching. "It is true," he muttered, "neither of you is Void-touched."

"Has this ever happened before?" Hunter asked. "Have two wizards ever formed a dual-soul together?"

"Not that I'm aware of. As far as I know, wizards can only form dual-souls with Void-spawns. Though this does lend some credence to the myth that we're all descended from Void-spawns."

"What about the vampire? That Alichino guy? Or that Ma-Mammon thing?"

"Vampires are a myth among wizards. Supposedly they were destroyed long ago. An immeasurable panic would clutch wizard society if anyone knew that a vampire had infiltrated the High Council, but if Melchior knew Alichino was a vampire, then it's possible the entire High Council has been compromised. As for the creature they called Mammon, I know nothing about it. The Institute has destroyed much of wizard history and left us in the dark about a great many things."

We pressed Luther for more, but he didn't know anything and didn't care to speculate. I, however, had pieced together a great many facts based on what I'd learned and the book I found in the Night City: During the Third Magus War, wizardkind combatted a mysterious entity known as the Malebranche. Hanno Scherrer defeated the Malebranche by sacrificing his daughter to make a cintamani, which he used to wish the Malebranche away. After the Third Magus War, wizardkind formed a great assembly to protect the world from the Malebranche. Vampires had infiltrated this assembly's High Council and now controlled the Institute, and they used it to kidnap wizards and feed them to a monster they kept in the Dreamhaven. The feeding ritual occurred every thirty years. Gaspar had witnessed a previous feeding, and that galvanized him to form the Defectors to stop the Institute. Gaspar had used us the same way Scherrer did his daughter, but he didn't get to banish the Institute because Hunter used the cintamani to save me.

What common thread ran between the three Magus Wars? What was the Malebranche and how was it connected to the vampires in the High Council or Mammon? Furthermore, what ultimate plan did these vampires have that required them to keep Mammon trapped in the Dreamhaven? I wanted everything to fit together neatly, but we still lacked pieces to the puzzle.

Chapter 22

Everyone woke up an hour after we'd brought them back to Sanctuary. Luther sequestered Nephelie and Aquila in the office, and they discussed the situation in secret. We gathered in the reading room.

"This pisses me off," Alison said. "We saved their asses and they're in there keeping secrets?"

"Maybe we should find a way to eavesdrop?" Linh said.

"We could turn into flies."

"And get squished," Maleeka said.

"What do you suggest we do?" Alison said.

"They can't stay in there all night. We'll ask them when they come out."

"They won't tell us anything," Blake said, resigned. "Y'all already know that."

It was almost an hour before we heard the door to Nephelie's office open. We filed out and surrounded her like an inquisition.

"We want answers," Alison said. "We told you about the Dreamhaven, about Alichino and the admins, that Mammon thing, the eirineftis being pumped into the water supply—we told you everything. It's time you stop keeping secrets."

Nephelie scanned us. "I don't have the strength to talk anymore."

"That's a bad excuse," Blake said.

"It's no excuse at all. Besides, you're all too young to concern yourselves with our next move. You've done enough already. It's time we all rest. The coming days and months may be the hardest of our lives. Now, follow me." We didn't know what to expect, but she led us into the garage, set a few boxes on the floor, and opened them. They were packed with fireworks.

"It's getting pretty dark outside," Aquila said. "Why don't we celebrate you saving our asses."

Nephelie smiled and nudged the boxes toward us with her foot. They said they wanted to celebrate us saving their lives, but really they sought to rest our minds. A great many doubts about our futures still hung in the air, but a festive respite was a welcome thing.

We took the boxes into the foyer and showed the children. Their faces lit up with joy. They gathered sparklers and fireworks and hurried outside. The sun was mostly behind the mountains, giving the sky a purplish hue. The children readied bottle rockets with bouquet patterns, and when they were done, they ran off with lit sparklers, laughing and playing like will-o-the-wisps on the pebbly shore.

We joined them outside. While the others were off making sure the kids had properly set up the fireworks, Hunter took off his shoes and walked to the water's edge with me. I slipped off my shoes, too, rolled up my jeans, and let the minnows tickle my feet with each wave. He slid his fingers between mine. It was a small comfort. Nonetheless, it was a comfort I relished.

Hunter kept his eyes quietly trained on the foamy waves gathering around his feet. The water sparkled under the clear night sky.

He glanced at me with a playful smirk tugging the corners of his lips. "How bad did you miss me while I was gone?"

"Pretty bad."

He went quiet again, like something was bugging him, but he didn't know how to put it. I picked his hand up and kissed it. The rippling water danced in Hunter's pensive eyes.

"It was really dark, Johnny. It was really dark and I was really scared, and you saved me . . . again." Hunter swept up my other hand and cradled them both, like he was clutching diamonds. His somber expression faded, revealing his usual playful smirk. "What'd you miss most about me?" he asked, studying my fingertips.

"Your cute smile."

"Liar. What'd you really miss?" A rosy blush framed the perfect symmetry of his smile. "You missed the D, huh?"

I shook my head. "Shut up, Hunt." Then I leaned forward and kissed him.

The first blaze of pink and purple lit up the sky. Hunter put an arm around me and the fiery green and neon-pink explosions bloomed in his eyes.

Alison came up and nudged me. "It's kind of wild you actually saved him. I can't believe we're still alive after all that."

"We saved him, Ali. All of us."

She rested her head on my shoulder. Blake came over and threw his arms around us. Dad's words returned to me, about families being more than just papers or blood. It was Alison's love and Blake's love and Hunter's love that had given me the courage to stand on my own two feet. But I'd given them courage too. Because we were a family, and a family drinks from the same reservoir of strength.

The End

Glossary

Aura: The mystical energy around wizards, magical creatures, places, and other living things. A wizard's aura always reflects their life and personality, whether it smells like their favorite cologne or sounds like athletes playing sports. When an aura belongs to a magical creature, it usually reflects the creature's nature, whether it's base, atavistic hunger or Machiavellian power designs. Ordinary humans do not have auras. To detect an aura, wizards can use their wizard sight like a sixth sense. The aura then manifests as an emotional reverberation felt psychically. They can also physically see auras using the *hard-reading* aspect of their wizard sight. Visually, auras manifest as a golden envelope around the subject. Although wizards can mask their auras, only very intelligent, advanced Void-spawns and Maras can do the same.

Coins, the Legacy of: A Legacy dedicated to advancing the children of Western banking elites.

Creators, the: A mythical race of Void-spawns who escaped the Void, supposedly to build a paradise where they could experience love. According to wizard lore, and the stories Maras tell, they were wiped out in an eons-long war with the evil Void-spawns.

Crowns, the Legacy of: A Legacy dedicated to advancing the children of Western political elites.

Defectors, the: A rebel group of formerly extracted wizards, and some Lineage and Legacy sympathizers, who are fighting to bring down the Institute and its administrators. They informally refer to themselves as the Legacy of Freedom.

Dual-soul: A permanent union between a wizard and a Void-spawn that confers great power to the wizard.

***Eirineftis* (ειρηνευτής):** A Greek word that means *pacifier*. It is bottled in metal canisters. Per standard regulations, Institute agents are required to carry them. Eirineftis is used to suppress magical abilities, and in higher doses can cause wizards to lose consciousness. It's preferred that agents use little magic during extractions, so eirineftis is deployed to subdue noncompliant wizards. The Institute can also pump eirineftis into its extraction vehicles.

Glossing: When wizards interact with the magical world, whether by manipulating the vivit apparatus or by casting a spell off the top of their head, it leaves behind an ambient signature, usually based on the wizard's aura. This signature can be used to track down wizards. Wizards who want to prevent themselves from being tracked this way can "gloss their auras," or, essentially, use magic to undo the presence of magic. However, this technique isn't perfect, and doesn't work against very powerful wizards.

Guardians: Large robots whose sole purpose it is to protect the City at the End of the World.

Hard-reading: Wizards can psychically sense the magical world around them (soft-reading), but hard-reading describes when they use their powers to physically see the vivit apparatus or the auras around certain things.

Haywire: A state in which a spell loses control and becomes unpredictable. Haywire spells are often extremely dangerous.

Hobs: Small robots whose sole purpose it is to maintain the City at the End of the World.

Keep, the: The Legacy of the Crowns' dorm.

Legacy: One of five fraternal orders within the Institute. Each order corresponds to a sphere of power in the Western world. Although members of a Lineage are always Legacies, Legacies are not always part of a Lineage. The most powerful Legacy is thought to be the Legacy of the Crowns, with the children of old European wizard aristocracy holding the greatest influence in the magical world.

Lineage: A bloodline that claims to have descended from a mythical figure, usually a wizard or God.

Mara: An Institute term used to describe a Void-spawn with high intelligence that resides almost exclusively in Everywhen. Because Maras tend to make even less sense than other Void-spawns, they are stereotyped as being mad.

Night City, the: The border between Everywhen and the Void, life and death.

Night Market, the: A place in Everywhen where Maras gather to trade secrets and memories.

Obmagikos: A heavy armor that is highly resistant to magic.

Somnambulist: *Sleepwalker*. A wizard whose mind is trapped between the material world and Everywhen. These wizards are often incredibly powerful. Being trapped in Everywhen is physically traumatic for wizards, so those who return as somnambulists always have white hair.

Spires, the Legacy of: A Legacy dedicated to advancing the children of Western academic elites.

Thorns, the Legacy of: A Legacy dedicated to advancing the children of Western military elites.

Union, Dream-rave: When two or more wizards enter Everywhen together. To enter a union, or a dream rave, the two wizards must be touching in some way. The most common method of conducting a dream rave is for all participants to lie down in a formation that allows their heads to touch. During a union, all participants can fully view the contents of one another's minds, without restriction.

This can feel emotionally invasive and is one reason why unions are greatly discouraged.

Vampire: A wizard who has become a dual-soul with a powerful Void-spawn. This union causes the wizard to grow fangs and develop an animalistic hunger for blood, which lend to historical stereotypes.

Vivit Apparatus: The magical clockwork the Creators built to govern the physical laws of the material world. When viewed using the hard-reading aspect of the *wizard sight*, the cogs and wheels of the vivit apparatus shine a translucent gold-orange color. Wizards can manipulate the machinery and change the laws of the physical world (i.e., *magic*). While low magic has wizards memorizing sequences to manipulate the machinery with their hands, more advanced techniques allow wizards to control the clockwork with their minds. If a wizard does not know the sequences to control a particular machinery (like a fireball), a spell may either fail, or go *haywire*.

Void, the: A sentient nothingness that predates the universe. Wizard myths tell that all things return to the Void in death and are reborn when they crawl back out. The Creators sought to break this cycle by creating a paradise for the souls of the dead.

Void-spawn: Any entity originating from the Void. Void-spawns exist on a hierarchy, with the most powerful usually taking on human form and having high intelligence, and the weakest being akin to earthly microorganisms. Ordinary humans can't perceive them, but wizards can use the *hard-reading* aspect of their *wizard sight* to see them.

Witch-hunter: A non-Lineage wizard who sells their services as a bounty hunter to the Institute.

Wizard Sight: The wizard's magical senses of the world around them. This is a passive ability that allows wizards to tune in to the emotional frequencies of everything around them, including things humans often claim don't experience emotions (like rocks). Wizards can also use an aspect of their wizard sight called *hard-reading* to physically see the magical clockwork governing the laws of the universe, and to detect *auras* and see *Void-spawns*.

Acknowledgments

First and foremzzzzzzzzzzzost, I want to thank Allen Lau and Ivan Yuen for bringing Wattpad into the world and opening the doors for QBIPOC writers like myself. Publishing can be a merciless landscape for minority writers, but Wattpad has always been committed to giving marginalized voices a (large) platform on which to speak.

A big thanks to my two lovely editors, Deanna McFadden and Andrew Wilmot. As someone who has never gone to school for writing, these two handled me with kindness, patience, and care, and they guided me and helped me grow as a writer in more ways than I can easily express. I may have written this book, but it was 100 percent a collaborative project between us three. As an aside, the three of us worked on this book during a pandemic, so yes, these two are beyond golden, and I could probably gush for another few paragraphs about them alone.

I would like to thank Aron Levitz, the head of Wattpad Studios, for believing in my story and working tirelessly to build a platform for marginalized voices to be heard. My talent manager Monica Pacheco, and Rebecca Sands, Paisley McNab, Sarah Salomon, and Allison Dick. Also the marketing team helping me get my name and book out there so marginalized readers can find it: Tina McIntyre, Holley Corfield, Cait Stewart, and Jananie Kulandaivelu, and the amazing cover designer, Laura Mensinga! Too often all the credit goes to the writer, but this story wouldn't be anywhere without all these amazing people lifting it up and carrying it to the finish line. I am endlessly grateful for the time and love they've shown me and my project.

Working on this during a pandemic wouldn't have been possible without my wonderfully gentle and patient partner, who provides me with the material and emotional support I need to pursue this career. They are the biggest reason I am able to write, and even when it looked like our investment wouldn't pay off, they have always encouraged me to keep pushing, keep writing, because they knew it was my greatest passion. Without them, I would be completely lost.

Also, I want to thank my gay wizards. You're the reason I do this, and every day I work harder at sharpening my writing skills and storytelling abilities, not because I want to be famous—y'all already know how shy I am—but because I want to entertain you, and I want you to feel proud that believing in me was worth your time. My gay wizards have reached out to me, asked me how I was doing during this pandemic; they've been my friends and talked to me online and promoted me tirelessly, and I love all of them for believing in me and believing in *I'm a Gay Wizard*. You've all changed my world, and I don't think a paragraph in an acknowledgments section will ever be enough to convey how grateful I am. But the same as before, I didn't write this book alone, we all did, together.

About the Author

V.S. Santoni is the author of *I'm A Gay Wizard*. He's a Latinx non-binary guy who spends way too much time daydreaming, scouring YouTube for retro-anime movies, and sobbing to sad, old punk songs with his best friend, a Chihuahua named Darla. He lives in Nashville with his husband.

wattpad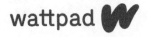

Where stories live.

Discover millions of stories created by diverse writers from around the globe.

Download the app or visit www.wattpad.com today.

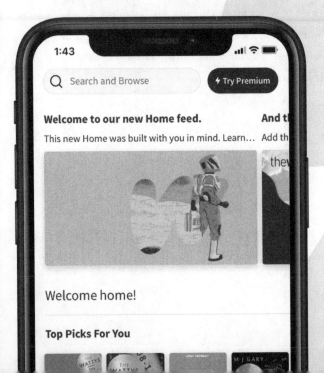

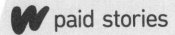

wattpad books

Check out the latest titles from Wattpad Books!

Available wherever books are sold.

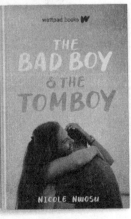